GODFOOL

PÁDRAIG STANDÚN

To order additional copies of this book, contact:
Bookwhip
1-855-339-3589
https://www.bookwhip.com

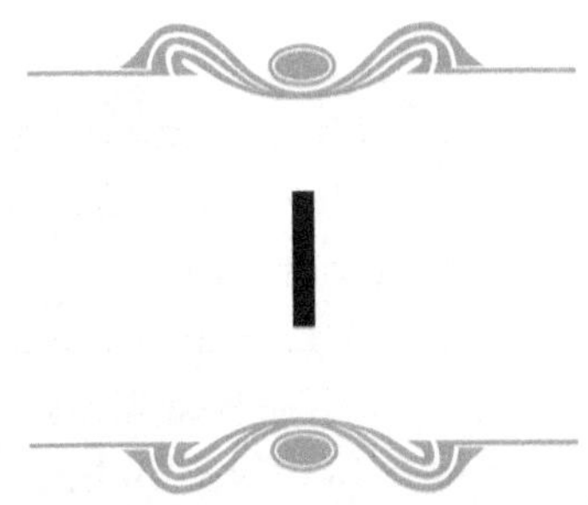

A reading from the new version of The Book of Genesis:

"After thousands of years the man and the woman succeeded in creating a garden that was as good or better than the Garden of Eden from which they were once evicted. When they saw God walk there in the cool of the evening, they asked him to leave immediately. He was neither welcome nor needed.

"Keano! Keano!" shouted Abigail Adams to her brother Cian as she raced goalwards. He kept the ball at his feet as he dribbled past a defender before placing the ball neatly in the corner of the net.

"Good man yourself," his father Adam shouted from the sideline as he gave a high-five hand-slap to his friend, Bill Brown. "Keano by name and Keano by nature. He will be as good as him yet."

"Which of the Keanes do you mean?" Bill asked, "Roy or Robbie?"

"Both of them."

"I thought he held on to the ball too long," Brown said. "Only for your man who tried to block him slipped…"

"Didn't he score?" Adam answered. "That's what is important."

"He should have passed to Abby. She was free in front of goal. She would only have needed a touch."

"Would you have passed the ball to your sister when you were that age? Abby has two left feet," her father said. "Don't get me wrong. I'm not knocking her. She puts her heart and soul into it but she hasn't the skill Keano has."

"Is it Keano or Keanu you call him at home?" Bill asked. "I thought it was after Keannu Reeves that Eve had him christened."

"She might have thought that, but it was of the Keanes I was thinking. Officially his real name is Cian." Adam spelt it out "C-I-A-N."

"Which of the Keanes does he like best himself?"

Adam did not reply. He was shouting "Bollix" at the referee.

"Ease up," Bill said. "It's just a game between kids."

"There are rules, and they shouldn't be let break them. Abby was ready to score there until that little runt tripped her."

Bill laughed: "When I think of all you got away with yourself on the field of play, because you looked so innocent."

You were the opposite, as awkward as hell. All you had to do to give away a free kick was to shake yourself."

"My young fellow is just the same."

"Liam is steady enough, but he will never be Damien Duff or Liam Brady. But who will?"

"Look at him now," Bill said, trying to take the ball out of defence instead of belting it up the field." He put his hands around the sides of his mouth and shouted: "Let it go Liam. Give it the boot."

"Take it easy," Adam teased. "It's only a game between kids."

"*Touché.*" Bill shook his head. "It's so easy to let yourself get worked up about it."

"Bollix," Adam shouted when the referee who was the local priest, Paul Godfool waved a yellow card at Cian who had tripped an opponent.

"Language," Bill said quietly. "Kids."

"They hear the same or worse from all of us at home, and we don't even notice it," Adam answered.

"The priest doesn't like it."

"Pity about him. Should the likes of him be allowed near children at all?"

"As far as I know, he has never been accused of anything," was Bill's reply.

"Can any of them be trusted?"

"There was nobody else willing to referee on a Saturday morning." Bill shrugged: "What can he do out of the way when we are here watching him?"

Adam was not so trusting: "Isn't that how they start, being nice to kids, buttering them up, preening them, preparing them…"

Bill saw things differently: "Father Paul is here long enough, dealing with mass servers and schools, and I haven't heard a word of complaint from anyone. Have you?"

Adam answered his question with another: "Does Liam serve?"

"He's doing it now for a couple of years. Your man is very careful, too careful if you ask me. He never waits in the sacristy with one server, and he leaves the door open at all times so people down the church can see what is going on."

Adam shook his head: "That would make you wonder."

"I can't see why."

"Has he something to hide if he is that careful?" Adam asked. "It seems to me as if the man can't trust himself."

"Fear of the law, I'd say. Litigation." Bill spat that word out as if he had taken a bite of something sour. "Is there an easier way to make money in this day and age than to make a few accusations?"

"To tell you the truth," Adam said, "it doesn't bother me one way or another. Apart from the children's safety, of course. That side of life, priests, church, religion doesn't bother Eve or myself. We live in the real world and that kind of mumbo jumbo is well behind us at this stage."

"Sharon and myself prefer to keep a foot in each camp," Bill said, half-jokingly. "Just in case…"

"Anyone with a smidgen of logic has to reject all that crap," was his friend's considered view.

"If life was only about logic…" Bill didn't finish his statement, as he seemed to look off into the far distance. "I'd give anything to just go down the logical road, accept that there is nothing out there but dust and ashes, but my instinct doesn't just let me go that far. I don't know why, but that's the way I am." He shrugged. "Life would be a lot easier the logical way, but I just don't know."

Adam was convinced: "What can we expect after years, after centuries of brainwashing? It's not easy to escape from that or leave it after you." He told Bill of a recent television programme he had seen which rejected all faiths, and blamed most of the world's problems on religion.

"You're talking about your man Richard Dawkins?" Bill asked. It must be the same programme I saw myself."

"It's a pity there are not a lot more like him," said Adam. "Our own TV channels don't have the guts to show us that stuff."

"I can't see what difference that makes," Bill replied, "when most people have every channel under the sun anyway."

Adam didn't agree: "It would surprise you how many people only have our own conservative channels that aren't going to disturb anyone."

"Thousands think that even those are away over the top," Bill said. "Some people are continually complaining about them. You should hear the mother-in-law." He tried to imitate her: "Filth, muck. Switch it off."

"It's amazing how stupid some people are," was Adam's opinion. "Nothing can change the opinions they grew up with."

Bill tried to lighten matters: "Who would ever expect two men to spend their Saturday morning discussing philosophy and religion?"

"At least the kids are enjoying themselves," Adam said. "Despite what people say about the youth of today, this lot is fit. I couldn't imagine myself running for so long when I was that age."

Bill agreed with him: "It's a lot healthier for them to be active like this than to spend the morning watching television or playing computer games."

"It gives the wives a chance to have a sleep-in on a Saturday morning," Adam remarked. "Sunday is my day for the long lie-in."

"Just like God himself," Bill joked. "Resting on the seventh day. Saturday night must be the night so?"

"You're not suggesting Bill, that we only do it once a week? We're not gone past it yet. I can tell you. Whatever about yourself and Sharon?"

"As the politicians say," Bill smiled: "I'm neither confirming nor denying anything."

"It sounds to me like an admission."

Bill looked across the park as the youngsters gathered together around their referee after the final whistle was blown: "You haven't a clue just how far you are from the mark, Adam."

"Are you trying to tell me something? You're not having an affair?"

"Don't be daft," was Bill's reply.

"The way I look at it is to take your pleasure when it's available, because it might be the only chance you get."

"That's giving me *carte blanche* so," Bill said lightly.

Their children crossed the pitch towards them as if all their energy had drained away with the final whistle of the match. Abigail suddenly leaped for her father to catch her in his arms, Cian and Liam looked on shamefacedly as if to say: "Girls."

Paul asked us to go into the clubhouse for oranges and sweets," Abigail said. "Can we, Dad?"

"What Paul?" her father asked.

"The priest," Bill answered. "Go on," he said to Liam, "but be back here in ten minutes."

"I'm in a hurry," Adam said to Cian and Abigail.

"Ah, Dad," Abigail said, slipping out of her father's grasp.

Cian tried to persuade his father: "He has real orange juice, freshly squeezed. Not like the fizzy stuff from the bottle that's full of "E's"

Adam took his car keys from his pocket: "Didn't I tell you I haven't time. Your Mam is going shopping soon."

Abigail tried another tack: "She doesn't need your car. Hasn't she the Punto at home?"

Her father played his trump card: "I think she wants to bring you with her to the shops and leave the men at home."

Excited, Abigail asked: "Is she going to buy me something?"

"You will find out later." Adam handed her his keys: "Off to the car with you now and I'll be with you in a few minutes."

"I thought you were in a hurry?"

His father grabbed Cian's shoulder: "Back-answers, Keano. What is the rule?"

"You're the boss," he answered sullenly, heading towards the car. Abigail followed him, trailing her sports-bag after her along the grass.

"I don't like this crack at all," Adam said to Bill.

"I haven't a clue what you are talking about."

"Your man, the priest, with his oranges and sweets. For his own sake even. You would think that he would have more sense."

"I think the kids appreciate it. It's thirsty out there," said Bill.

"He could be just trying to win them over. Before he takes advantage…"

"I think you are reading far too much into a bit of kindness."

Adam spoke his mind: "There isn't one grown-up in there with him."

"Go on with yourself if you want," Bill said. "See what he's up to."

"I've looked after my own so no harm will come to them."

Bill said: "There's up to a dozen kids in there. Safety in numbers."

"They're vulnerable kids," commented Adam.

"I see Liam coming now and he looks alright," Bill said. "A person can get paranoid about all this stuff."

"It's a pity a lot more people were not paranoid in days gone by," Adam remarked as he set out to walk to his car. He stopped then and called back to Bill: "I intend to raise this matter at the next club meeting.

His friend didn't answer as he set off in the opposite direction, his hand on Liam's shoulder: "How were things in there?" He pointed to the clubhouse.

"Father Paul is great fun," Liam answered.

"What kind of fun do you mean?"

"Making jokes and messing around."

Bill frowned: "What do you mean by messing around?"

"Putting on silly faces and stuff."

"Does he ever touch anyone?"

"What's with all the questions, Dad?"

"That's just what Dad's do," Bill answered. He decided not to make a big issue of it but to get Sharon to probe a bit deeper. Adam's comments had made him think more of the implications of letting his son anywhere without supervision.

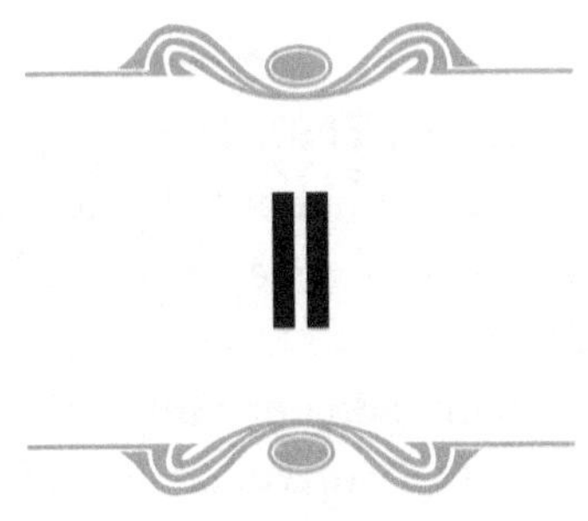

My real name is not Godfool, but you have probably guessed that already. You really don't need to know what my name is. That is just what I call myself. I am in the Pauline 'fool for Christ' tradition. Father Paul Godfool. That's me, Paul in honour of the man who put Damascus on the religious map. I am a kind of rogue priest in that I do not accept fully the rules of Rome or the directives of the Irish Bishops. I refused to become a Parish Priest in the year of the millennium because I felt to do so would seem like a full acceptance of the Church as constituted at present, something I am not prepared to do. That is not to say that I do not accept Jesus Christ and his teaching.

I sometimes feel like running away from the same Christ, hiding from him, resisting him, even rejecting him, but so far, I have failed to escape the hound of heaven. I am a follower of Jesus the storyteller, Jesus the radical, Jesus the questioner, the Christ of grace, the Christ of the cross, the Christ of freedom, Jesus who didn't judge, Jesus who didn't accept all aspects of the faith he inherited, Jesus who wanted to remove rather than impose burdens on people's backs, Jesus who wanted us to be great with God, and God to be great with us in the Gaelic sense.

In this book I intend to give an account of my life behind the altar, the typewriter, the word processor, the computer, the picket line, as well as my personal viewpoint on religion and politics, in Church and State, island and mainland, inside and outside the Gaelic speaking areas (*Gaeltacht*) during a historic period in which the Roman Catholic church was in meltdown in the so-called western world. It is the story of someone who has served at the edges of that church, geographically, spiritually and psychologically, in parishes never honoured by the perceived cream of the clergy as evidenced by the lack of ecclesiastical titles, such as Monsignor, Dean, Archdeacon or Canon.

Although I call this a book, I do not really expect it to ever see the light of day. It is not chick-lit. It is not sensational news. Religion and everything to do with it is not popular in the Irish media scene, or anywhere else for that matter. Priests are pariahs, but much of that is our own fault. We have earned that title. Child sexual abuse is the main reason for that, and even though a relatively small percentage of priests were involved we all carry a collective guilt and deserve to. The official church closed its eyes, looked the other way, changed offenders to other parishes where they continued to abuse. Like the Calvary scarecrow, we have to collectively carry the cross.

Before I thought of the name "Godfool", I had intended to call this book "The Catacomb Church" because I feel that I and many others live underground in so far as the official church is concerned. I feel that I am part of the church's loyal opposition. I am outside it and inside it at the same time, on the edge politically, and in the middle in so far as I ply my trade at the coalface of church life. I can say my church's creed without blushing while disagreeing with many of its political, social, and moral stances. I refuse to fully serve, even though my church is part of my life, part of my very heart. I hang in there in the faint hope that I will live to see it bloom and blossom, that it may yet become what I and disgruntled fellow members of the Catacomb Church would like it to be.

It's waiting I'll be, I'm sure, but I am not without hope. I saw great changes in Mother Church in my youth – in the sixties of the century gone by. Pope John XXIII brought it to the attention, to the centre of the world. People of my age can remember a church that buzzed with excitement. We remember a time when it was challenging and joyful to be a Roman Catholic Christian. Days that could come again, given similar injections of flair and imagination.

"The Catacomb Church" has another meaning in that there are churches within and without the official church. Christians believe that God works through people of all faiths and none, even those who are anti-church and anti-religion. When we look at Jesus at work in the gospels, we see him go outside the borders of the faith of his own people, a kicking over the traces which drew the ire of Scribes and Pharisees. Even his own followers were shocked to find him in conversation with a Samaritan woman or a Roman Centurion.

Jesus was also given a hard time for "eating and drinking with publicans and sinners," for being friendly with personae non grata in the eyes of the orthodox, people such as Mary Magdalen. He was pilloried for breaking the Sabbath, even if that was done to help or to cure. He shocked and surprised people because he refused to harshly judge the woman "taken in adultery." What should stop followers of Jesus from following such example even if it is not popular or acceptable with the righteous, the respectable or the civil service of the church?

Institutions and organisations tend to have more interest in protecting the institution than in anything else, and the church is often more self-defensive than most. This is natural and to be expected. I know I will find myself defending many aspects of the church, but I will also find fault in areas in which the organisation seems to care more for itself than for the teachings of Jesus Christ, areas in which I think church bureaucracy seems more interested in itself than in the grace of God or the love of Christ.

Mr {Dave}Fanning's continued invective subjected his listeners to a description of the Church as "an evil institution."

Broadcasting Complaints Commission, Reported in The Irish Times, 23rd June 2007

"I don't know why I buy a newspaper anymore." Marcas McCabe removed his spectacles and shook his head. "They have no shame."

"I'm sorry you have it delivered every morning," his wife Nora, who lay beside him on the bed, said: "There isn't a day that it doesn't make you contrary."

"Angry. That's what it makes me," Marcas said through his teeth. "There doesn't a day pass without them having a go at religion and the church."

"Nobody takes a blind bit of notice," Nora said lightly, "and you shouldn't either."

"That's what you think. They are the cause of turning the young people away from the church."

Nora gave a little laugh: "The church does enough of that with its stupid rules and regulations."

Her husband looked at her as if he barely recognised his wife of more than forty years: "You should start writing for the papers yourself. Your opinions would fit in well with those biased journalists."

"If the church went back to the basics of the faith, love God and your neighbour, instead of interfering with human nature…"

"There's no limit on what human nature is allowed to get away with in this day and age," Marcas said angrily.

"The nature I'm talking about is allowing priests to marry and allowing women to be priests. The church is destroying itself with those stupid rules."

"There will be no stopping ye at all when ye get on the altar," her husband said, his anger dissolving into humour: "But would I want to go to mass to see some old hag giving out on the pulpit?"

"If it was some good-looking young one it would be a different story, and it's not on what she was saying but on how she was looking your mind would be."

Marcas shook his head slowly: "Will it ever happen?"

"It has to happen or there will be no priests and no mass. That's the day people will be sorry."

"Most people won't care one way or another."

"I never saw people as angry," Nora answered, "as they were over in the half parish when they lost their priest. And it wasn't just the people our age, but young and old. They would have no problem welcoming a married priest or a woman priest or any other kind of a priest."

"Where were they when they had a priest?" Marcas asked, "with only four or five of them going to morning mass on weekdays."

"It's not the numbers that are important," Nora said, "but the blessing on the place and the people and keeping harm and evil away from them. I'm telling you there will be a lot more evil about when people lose the mass."

"You're getting carried away with all this stuff," her husband said, "since you started going to night-classes in the old tech."

"You were the school-teacher. You should know a lot more about Christian doctrine than I do."

Marcas decided to go back to his newspaper, bad and all as it was: "Once we start talking religion or politics, there's no rest."

"It was yourself that started it because of some stupid article in the newspaper. You'll give yourself another heart attack if you back to reading it again."

"I just want to read the sports pages."

"Thanks be to the Lord," Nora said with a kind of a sigh as she turned in the bed. "We will have a bit of peace."

"It's a pity you don't take a bit of an interest in sport yourself," Marcas remarked. "It's a good pastime."

"I can see the sense of playing games," Nora replied, "but I don't see much sense in sitting on your backside watching other people kicking a bag of wind around a field."

"It's a healthy interest all the same compared with moping around worrying and wondering."

"The only worrying I do is about my children and grandchildren, and I think that is normal. And as you know, I often have good reason to worry."

"You would think the worrying would stop when they are reared," Marcas remarked.

"Parents are parents as long as they live."

Her husband looked down at the back of Nora's head as it lay on the pillow next to his. "If there was something wrong with one of them, you'd tell me?"

"I just feel that something is going to happen," she answered. "Call it women's instinct. Call it what you like."

"Worrying about nothing," Marcas snorted. "That's what I call it."

"Just like you and your newspaper, making mountains out of molehills, and not one damn thing any of us can do about it."

"I suppose you are right. Neither you nor I is likely to set the world alight at this stage in our lives. Why should we worry about any of it, now that we have lived our lives and have gone past it?"

"Nora raised herself on her elbow and said forcefully: "you might think you're gone past it, but I'm not."

Marcas laughed: "You must have plans that I know nothing about."

Nora sat up in the bed and looked at him: "I don't just now, but who knows what I may do with myself yet? I hope we will be thinking about new things as long as we live. Maybe all you want to do is wait for death, but there is life in this old dog yet." She kicked up her feet playfully beneath the bedcover.

"I hadn't a fresh thought for twenty years," Marcas said, as if it was a cause for celebration. "Maybe that's why everything I read in the paper is a threat to me and my faith."

"We belong to our time," Nora said, "and there is no harm in that. "We had the same right to live life in our way as the youngsters of today have to live it their way. This is their time. They have the right to say what they like and write what they like, and we have to just grin and bear it."

Marcas mused aloud: "I spent forty years teaching and every year of those I was ready to stand over what I thought in Christian doctrine class. Every time I read a paper now, there are people telling me there is no sense or reason in it."

"Who is saying that?" Nora asked, as if she didn't believe a word of it.

Marcas tossed the news section of the paper in the air: "That crowd that want to denigrate and destroy religion."

"Don't ruin the paper whatever you do," Nora said, "because I'm dying to read it later."

Marcas made little effort to tidy the scattered pages as he pushed them to her side of the bed: "I hope you get more satisfaction from that rotten rag than I did."

"Go back to your sport," his wife replied, and I'll doze for another while." She lay back on her pillow and there was nothing to be heard for some time except the tick-tock of the old clock on top of the mahogany wardrobe and the rustle of newspaper as Marcas turned the pages.

Nora was nearly asleep when she was roused by her husband's shout: "I don't believe this. Look, Nora!"

Sitting up quickly she asked: "What is it? Have you a pain?"

"This rotten journalism is giving me a pain in the arse. Look at this." He showed her the offending article.

"I can't read it without my spectacles," Nora replied.

Marcas read out part of an article about Gaelic games. The main theme was that Sunday mass was being replaced by championship encounters, that Croke Park was the new Irish cathedral and that the footballers and hurlers were the priests of that faith and their managers were the new bishops.

"What is wrong with that?" Nora asked.

"In the name of God, woman! Are you blind or what? They cannot write about sport now without taking the opportunity to attack and insult religion."

"I don't see any insult in that. It's a bit of fun."

Marcas shook his head: "I can't make you out at all."

"I think it is a good comparison, and near enough to the truth when certain teams are playing anyway."

Her husband was still livid: "Can't you see that those journalists only bring religion into the story to mock and belittle it?"

"Even if that was true, it means religion must be still alive or they wouldn't bother with it at all."

"They are just a crowd of bigots out to destroy it," Marcas said sadly and resignedly.

Nora looked him straight in the eyes: "You've had trouble with your heart in the past, and if you let this kind of stuff get to you, it will drive your blood pressure sky-high. If you want to become a martyr for the faith, there are other ways to do it than allowing a few journalists come between you and your night's sleep."

"I have no problem sleeping," he replied, "because I have a clear conscience."

"A paper never refused ink, and that rag will be lighting the fire this evening."

"Somebody must be buying and reading them," Marcas said, "or they wouldn't be selling so many of them every day."

"They are a bit of a pastime, and they are full of advertising, of course. They're read today and forgotten tomorrow."

Marcas spoke like a man depressed: "I'm too long in this world to learn new ways of living. I just can't give a damn about anything and everything like the young people of today."

Nora touched his arm tenderly: "I remember when you were one of the young people, when you were independent and revolutionary and radical, not to speak of being handsome, with all the young ladies running after you."

"That wasn't today or yesterday."

"You are still that young fellow I fell in love with. As I said all the young ones were chasing after you, but I was the one that caught up with you, and I never regretted a day of it."

"Even when I was drinking?" Marcas asked.

"I can't say that I liked it, especially those last years before you got out of it, but you haven't tasted a drop for more than twenty years."

"Marcas pointed at the newspaper: "There are days when I read stuff like that when I feel like going out and having a good blast of whiskey."

Nora looked at him as if shocked: "I thought drinking never crossed your mind anymore."

"It wouldn't be for the sake of the drink," Marcas tried to explain, "but to do something different, to live a bit as they say."

Nora seemed offended: "You are not happy with our life as it is?"

"I'm not finding fault with you or with our lives together. I think I just miss the teaching, the job, to have something to get up for day after day other than reading the paper, walking the dog, eating meals and going to bed."

"You wouldn't be teaching on a Saturday anyway," Nora said. "You would be having a rest until this time at least."

"I'd have the satisfaction of a good week's work behind me. I would deserve a sleep-in, rather than lazing on because I have nothing to do."

"You deserve the break after working all your life," his wife assured him.

"I'm not complaining, just trying to tell you how I feel. Isn't that what women want according to the experts? They want to express their own feelings and hear the feelings of those close to them."

"Would you like to work part-time?" Nora asked. "It would pass a bit of the day for you."

"I would not," Marcas answered definitively. "I hated work those final years, and the best day of my life was the day I finished."

"What is it you are trying to say so?"

Marcas' hackles were beginning to rise: "I am not trying to say anything. I am actually saying that I have rested long enough, that I need to find a hobby or a pass-time to give myself more of a reason to live."

"You could start writing. Or painting."

"You can't teach an old dog new tricks."

"Since you are so into religion," Nora said, "you could become a eucharistic minister, give out holy communion or bring it to the sick and housebound."

"Leave that to someone younger. I would be afraid I would fall down those marble steps. Anyway, they would be asking who brought the drunkard on to the altar."

"It's an awful long time since you were drunk."

"People's memories are even longer," Marcas said. He was quiet for a while before remarking: "I often thought of going into politics."

"You are too old to distribute communion, according to yourself, and now you are talking about going into politics, the man who refused point blank to run in a council election when you were asked thirty years ago. Wait until the family hear about this."

I am not talking about party politics, but to stand up for our senior citizens, or if it goes to that, to stand up for my faith. It is one thing to be giving out about journalists and bigots. It's another thing to take a stand, face them down, show them that they are doing people a disservice by attacking all that they hold dear."

"Are you going to shame us before the world?" Nora asked, looking at him as if he had completely lost his mind.

"How in the name of God am I going to do that?"

"Campaigning, picketing, taking to the streets. Think of your son and daughter before you start any of that. And think of me as well."

"It would be very difficult not to think of you, because you would not be long reminding me," Marcas answered. "As for the children as we still call them in their forties, did they think of us when they were blackening the family name, Jimmy with his debts that we had to clear, Sheila pregnant and unmarried?"

"They were young, without much sense. What is that Irish phrase? Sense comes with age."

"I'm still waiting for it to arrive," Marcas said. "Good sense."

"It's about your own children you are talking here, the people you are most expected to love."

"Loving is the easy bit. Agreeing with everything they do and say is not. Before you say it, I agree that I gave them bad example with my drinking. But I don't see that I need their permission to take a stand on a matter of principle."

"Don't do anything too stupid at this stage of your life," Nora said. "In the name of God…"

Marcas frowned as if in deep thought: "I am only thinking out loud. It would surprise myself more than anyone else if anything was to come from it."

Nora sighed: "I think you are depressed. I didn't realise you were that low in yourself."

"Don't take too much notice. I am just expressing my feelings. Like a woman."

"Well," Nora replied, "if you are that much like a woman you will have no problem with bringing me my breakfast in bed."

IV

Extract from Paul Godfool's Diary

In so far as I know, I'm not responsible for where I came from. Better than me was born in a stable. Was it Irish man and English Lord, Wellington pointed out, being born in a stable doesn't mean you are a horse? Either way I remember my childhood as being happy. If an unhappy childhood is an advantage for a writer, it is an advantage I have had to do without as I write this. My memories of growing up with father, mother, brother's John and Eddie, and my sister, Margaret are good. Our grandmother lived in the house, too, but I remember her better in death than in life.

I can barely see her now, in memories' eye, a kindly old woman in a black shawl coming from the henhouse with eggs in her apron.

I see my grandmother more clearly falling into the large open fireplace and the pandemonium that ensued. She seems to have been in bed in the back room from then until she died. I know from the dates of my birth and of her death that I was not yet three, but a few aspects of her wake are clear in my memory. There was the 'smasher,' the new bicycle my father had bought after the war to bring him to work as a plasterer in Castlebar, now standing idle against the wall. Even more intriguing was my grandmother's coffin on the roof-rack of a neighbour's Model T Ford, the only car in the village. I can still see us children standing by the smasher, twisting the pedal and playing about it as people paused to talk or pat us on the heads as they passed in and out of the house to pay their respects. As for the coffin, I was never allowed to forget my question: "What is the lovely box for?" It was my first dice with death, and I found it generally exciting.

I had in fact diced with death some time earlier but didn't realise the danger at the time. My sister Margaret, a year younger, had thrown her bottle out of the cot, and it had shattered spectacularly on the concrete floor. I had been loitering without much intent when one of the shiny pieces of glass shot towards me. Before anyone had time to react, I had grabbed it and my thumb was split open with blood spraying towards the heavens. My mother held me in her arms and kept a tight grip on my thumb while my father went to the barn for a cobweb. That dirty cobweb clotted the blood and saved my life. I have loved spiders ever since. I sometimes claimed that my decision not to get into a life of crime had to do with the fact that my split thumb would be too easily recognisable in fingerprints. Scarfinger might have joined scarface in the annals of crime.

I mention these aspects of youth to try and show what life was like in rural Mayo in the late forties of the last century. We had no electricity, radio, indoor toilet, or cooking facilities other than the open fire on which great pots of potatoes were boiled for pigs and hens as well as people. Bread was made in a metal oven with burning coals placed on the lid as well as beneath the pot. Strips of bacon were grilled on a tongs over the fire. I can still smell them in memories' nose. I can also taste raw onion dripping in butter and squeezed between the tongues of a red-hot tongs.

The same tongs had a different use on the Eve of Christmas. My father would rise from the table and symbolically break the devil's back – a sod of turf in the fire. After prayers for the living and the dead, the big red candle of Christmas was lit and we would tuck into giblets of goose or chicken. The turkey came a number of years later with American fashions. I remember one Christmas in particular in which my father brought us out to the barn to give hay to the cattle. It was a nightly chore in which straw and manure would be drawn back from the animals, to be thrown out on the dung-heap the following day. Following the lanthern on the return journey to the house, we saw Santa's chariot flash across the sky like a falling star. It must have been him. The presents were in the kitchen when we got back, to prove it.

My first day at primary school is still etched in my memory. It's not so much the school I remember, but getting splashed by the master's car along the way. I could still show you the spot. It was past the big tree that still reaches out across the road, the tree we used to run past in case it would fall on us. It is still there after half a century. There were very few cars on the roads then, and the only one that passed by was the teacher's. My brother John, two years older, was leading me by the hand in the great adventure. I can still see our little gaberdine coats in my mind's eye. The splash from the puddle, as the car passed, probably didn't even soil them, but I felt it wasn't a great start to my public life. In other words, it was a less auspicious baptism than that in the Jordan.

Another early memory is of a group of us gathered around Mrs Galvin's desk as she read us Bible stories. I was particularly fascinated by the story of the raising of the widow's son of Naim from the dead. The miracle itself was great, I thought, but what was this about Jesus touching the "bier?" The only beer I knew was the half barrel of porter tapped with great squirts of foam in a bedroom when my aunt got married and the wedding was in our house. I had a mental picture of the dead man popping up like a jack-in the-box from a porter barrel, but I was hooked on Jesus from then on. I thought he was great. I still do.

Religion was part of life and never seemed an oppression or obsession, as many observers of the forties and fifties remember it. If anything, it added colour to life. Bright vestments reminded me of daffodils, and an upturned daffodil head beside a matchbox became a priest saying Mass. My rosary beads had a crucifix with a white figure of Christ which immediately became a black horse with a white face which jumped over and back across the seat at Mass. I am also credited with the loud whisper; "He likes wine," when the priest went back to the cruet the second time for the ablutions at the end of Mass.

Another storyteller that impressed me was local curate, Tommy Gibbons, a regular visitor to the school. I could stand on snow listening to him telling Bible stories, or Grimm's fairy tales, or sometimes, I think, a mixture of the two. I felt that if I ever met Jesus, he would speak with the voice of Tommy Gibbons. In an age in which priest's had a reputation for harshness and authoritarianism, he was gentle and kind. The word 'laidback' might have been invented for him. I had heard somewhere that a priest's hands are anointed at ordination, and I assumed that was why our priest had yellow fingers. I never associated the colour with the Sweet Aftons he smoked almost incessantly at the time.

When a child cried in church, he told people not to try and silence them. The cry of the child was closer to God than any prayer, he told us. I cried myself at twelve years old when he was changed to Annaghdown. He never became a parish priest and legend has it that he told a fellow priest he met in Galway one day that he was celebrating the Passover. He had just been passed over in the promotion stakes. The big jobs were for those less eccentric and more acceptable to bishops. The fact that many of his parishioners could see him as an alter Christus, another Christ would not weigh very heavily in such calculation.

I have never forgotten the advice he gave me in a letter from Annaghdown when I was sent as a young priest, under somewhat of a cloud, to the Aran Islands, because of an article I had written in a provincial paper. "Don't take yourself or life too seriously," was his wise counsel, something I recall and take heed of when the weight of the world hangs like a black cloud above me.

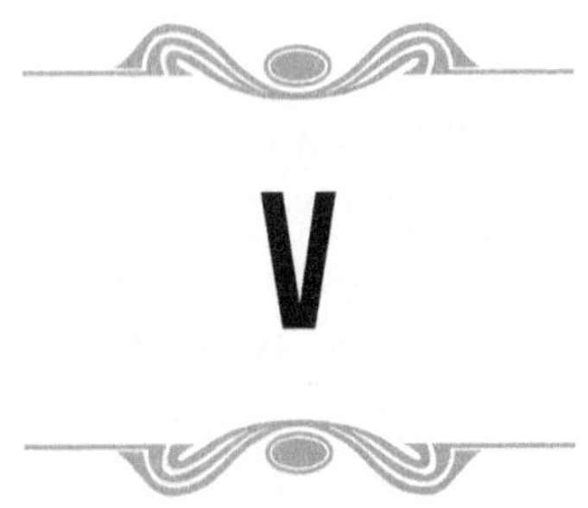

V

*"Lord, listen to my prayer; And let my cry
for help reach you" (Ps: 102)*

Father Paul Godfool trudged back to the parochial house after he had finished refereeing the children's soccer match. He had no time to change his clothes or have a cup of tea before going out to hear Saturday confessions. He slipped a soutane over his tracksuit, adjusted his collar and headed for the church. Not for the first time he told himself he was getting too old for running around a football pitch, but it gave him some satisfaction to think that parents were still willing to allow their children into his care.

"If only the youngsters were as interested in going to the church as they were in going to the football pitch," he said to himself in some amusement, well aware that neither young nor old was likely to be waiting for him outside the confession box. He was right, but at least anyone who was interested would have the opportunity in the hour that followed. The time on his own would allow him to read at his office, the daily prayer of the church, another duty done for the day.

The priest laughed to himself at how often people told him that they were looking for him at that time of day around his house and couldn't find him. "Are you trying to tell me," he would ask, "that the church is the last place you would think to look for me? My reputation as a man of God mustn't be so high." People had only to check his appointments in the weekly newsletter to find where he was, but many didn't even think of that.

Others used the little guilt-trip involved in giving him the impression that they were looking for him all over the place. "You're a hard man to find, Father," was often the opening ploy in trying to skip the queue for masses for the dead. The modern phone had for the most part put an end to that, as he rang back any numbers that appeared on his phone while he was out. The mobile was another great boon to his work as calls to his house were diverted on to that.

Very few people sought confession apart from Christmas and Easter, and few enough went at those times any more. Although it was not officially sanctioned, he gave general absolution at those times of grace. Canon Law, the law of the church, allowed this only at times of war or great danger. "Are we not at war with evil day and night," was his answer to anyone who questioned his right to apply the sacrament in that way.

He had once heard a wise bishop tell a scrupulous priest who raised such a question at a conference: "There are some questions. It is better not to ask a bishop." In other words, "get on with it and don't be bothering me." Paul had no doubt his own bishop was aware that he went beyond the law in those matters. There were plenty of gossip mongers ready to keep him informed, but it would be seen as the kind of instance in which Jesus of Nazareth defied the rules of his own religion when he found them too restrictive or positively damaging.

Children seldom attended for confession except when brought by parents at times of major feasts. It was a big contrast to his own youth when people were expected to attend monthly or even weekly confessions. This usually led to the repetition of empty formulae, which many people carried with them into adulthood. What amazed him most was the fact that Roman Catholics all over the world dropped confession like a hot potato at the same time. It was as if a tidal wave had washed it away, here today, gone tomorrow. Similar waves rejected Papal strictures on the use of contraceptives, the sheep leading the shepherds.

It is not the Pope who is infallible, Paul Godfool thought, but the people of God. Rules can be made, but if people do not accept them, they are useless. The people themselves had more sense than all the theologians in the Vatican put together. They accepted the essentials of the faith, belief in God, Jesus, the Holy Spirit, Mary, the angels and saints. After that the peripherals did not matter too much. It was a matter of take them or leave them after that.

Fewer people practised their faith than in previous generations, but the church itself had eased many of its own rules and attitudes in that regard. People are left to make their choices rather than being railroaded into acceptance. It amazed Paul that so many still chose the road of belief and practice when there were so many distractions. Country churches like his own were still largely well attended on Saturday nights and Sunday mornings. It often made him wonder when he returned from mass and switched on some Sunday show to hear commentators dismiss church and religion as being irrelevant. "Who was living in the real world?" he wondered.

Reading the psalm as part of the divine office, Paul Godfool had a particular fondness for lines like: "I lift up my eyes to the mountains…" He lived among the hills and they helped lift his mind and soul as well as his eyes. The same hills were full of little streams which ran down to the great lake. The echoes of running water, streams in arid lands and the notion of water as life were also constant themes in the same psalms.

A visiting Tanzanian priest had recently told his congregation that one of the best presents you could bring a neighbour in his country was a bucket of water. He contrasted the great expanses of Lough Mask with the arid land in which his own Masai people lived. Both parishes were now partners in a scheme in which almost every town-land in County Mayo had an adopted area in Africa, a scheme beneficial to both sides, and like so many other good news stories, largely ignored by the Irish media.

Paul Godfool thought of many things as he read his breviary, but he admitted to himself at last that he was trying to avoid dealing with the issue that weighed heaviest on his mind. His bishop had asked him the previous night to do one of the most difficult things he could have asked him to do. This was to allow an old college friend to stay with him for an indeterminate time while the bishop decided the man's future. It was a bolt from the blue and one of the biggest crosses he felt he could be asked to bear.

Richard Scapegoat had been convicted five years earlier in a sample case of the abuse of a boy who had been one of his mass servers. He was now to be released because of exemplary behaviour due to the fact that the prison was overcrowded. This had put the bishop in a quandary as he was not expecting such an early release and had made no provision for such an eventuality. "I know you were friends," the bishop had said on the phone, and there are empty rooms in the house, so I thought I'd ask you this big favour."

"Do you realise the kind of difficulty this might cause me?" Paul Godfool had asked his superior.

"Of course, I know. Am I not crucified with it myself every day since I was appointed? But I'm the one with the responsibility. The buck stops with me. As a bishop I can't turn a priest of the diocese out on the street much as I might like to. As a Christian, you know yourself…"

"What is wrong with him staying in your own house?" Paul had asked. "Surely the palace is big enough, and you could get him to do some secretarial work or something. Anywhere he would not mix with children."

That is exactly the offer I made him," the bishop replied, "to organise the diocesan archive, and God knows it needs doing badly. It was himself that asked to be sent to your place. He needs the fresh air and the freedom of the mountains, he said, after being banged up for so long in that place."

"I haven't seen him for six years," Paul said. "I'm ashamed to say it but I never went to see him in jail. I couldn't after I read the transcripts of the trial. After what he did…"

His bishop corrected him: "After what he is alleged to have done. He never admitted it. He pleaded not guilty and he hasn't changed his story since."

"A jury found him guilty and didn't you make a statement yourself apologising to the young fellow on behalf of the diocese."

"Standard practice," the bishop said. "I had no choice but to accept the verdict even though it was only the child's word against his."

"According to the papers the evidence was so harrowing; they had to accept it," Paul replied.

"Guilty or innocent, the ball is now in my court," the bishop said, practical as usual. "I have to deal with the present reality."

Paul tried to postpone any decision: "I don't think we should be discussing such a sensitive matter on the phone."

"I agree," the bishop said, "but I tried to get you earlier and there was no reply. I was hoping you could come in for dinner and maybe stay the night and we could discuss things over a steak and a bottle of wine."

"I had mass at seven and there was adoration of the blessed sacrament before that," Paul explained. "Why didn't you leave a message? I noticed the calls from a private number alright."

"I'm not checking up on you, but as you say yourself it is not appropriate to discuss certain matters on the phone, and especially on an answering service. Anyway, with regard to that I have not mentioned any name or surname, and unless we have a very smart phone tapper I doubt if the story can be understood without much difficulty."

"Your reputation for cuteness goes before you," Paul mocked.

"It's no wonder they call me the fox."

"I didn't know you knew."

"It was yourself that said I was cute," the bishop said. They went back to more serious matters, practicalities to do with the visit of Richard Scapegoat before the fox as his priests called him made some excuse about having to make another phone-call.

Why hadn't he the courage to refuse his boss, Paul had asked himself the previous night and again now as he sat in the confession box. How could he even face his former friend after having airbrushed him from his life for six years or more? The words of Christ in the parable about the last judgment ran through his mind: "I was in prison and you did not come to visit me. Depart from me…"

Suppose Richard was innocent, Paul thought, condemned in the wrong like Christ himself, his own Gethsemane suffered, betrayed by his old friend. Guilty or innocent, it would be difficult to look him in the face, shake his hand without feeling a lot of guilt.

"Wasn't it he that asked to come here?" Paul thought. Maybe he was seeking reconciliation, to let bygones be bygones and start afresh. It would be difficult to shake that hand after what he had read of the court transcript. But was he a Christian or not? Was he a follower of the man from Gallilee who asked people to forgive, to forgive enemies even? Whatever else he could call Richard Scapegoat; it certainly was not an enemy.

Paul's mind wandered back along memories' road. They were in the final of the colleges Gaelic football competition. He was fullback on the team, Richard in goal. The other team were bigger and stronger, close to ordination while they were in the early years. It was like seniors against juniors. The senior team were better all around but their superiority was not reflected on the scoreboard. Richard saw to that, bouncing back and over along the goal-line as if made of rubber, stopping every shot the others tried, while their own team slipped up the field from time to time and took their points. When they were eventually awarded a penalty at the other end, it was their goalkeeper that was called up to take it. Richard made no mistake and was a hero among his colleagues ever after.

Pondering old memories, Paul speculated that their time together might not be that difficult, so long as they stuck to what he called the light stuff, what they had in common, football, drama, college memories. Richard was not just a star on the pitch, but also on stage in the Aula Maxima, where he generally played women's parts as the seminary was an all-male institution until thrown open as a University when they were about half-way through. He wondered if Richard was gay, though he had no reason to think so. Anyway, experts made it clear that there was no link between homosexuality and paedophilia. Questions of that nature had seldom surfaced during their sojourn in Maynooth.

Those were the great days of the sixties, in that life itself as well as their college and even their religion were opening like flowers to the sun. It was freedom time, the time of the Beatles, the Second Vatican Council, Civil Rights activity in the United States, in Northern Ireland, even in the Irish speaking Gaeltachts. Life was exciting, though it had its darknesses, Viet Nam, the assassinations of Bobby Kennedy and Martin Luther King. It was a great time to have lived through, Paul thought. It was a pity that it did not last.

Thirty-three years and more had passed in the meantime, the length of time Jesus spent on earth. "He only did three years of public life," Paul thought, amusedly, "I have done eleven times more. But then he was crucified, I was not. But I might soon, depending on how this is going to turn out."

It was a question he had raised with his bishop towards the end of their conversation the previous night. He had said that he had made the Gardaí aware of Richard's release and that he was already on the sexual offender's list. "They will keep a discreet eye on him."

"So, you are not really asking me to keep him?" Paul replied. "You're telling me, since you have everything arranged already."

"It's easy to change plans if you are not satisfied," the bishop said, "but I was not expecting that you would reject your friend."

"I'll put up with him, but it raises many difficulties for me. If people find out who it is that is staying here…"

"Nobody should recognise him," the bishop replied, "as he did not serve as a priest in that part of the diocese. Anyway, he had a head of hair that time and he is as bald as an egg now."

"It's not your ass that will be on the line," Paul said, "if the tabloids find out where he is staying."

"Don't be always thinking the worst. If anything like that happens, I will take responsibility. I will say that it was on my orders you kept him."

"I would like to see that put on paper," Paul answered. "I am accepting him under protest."

"OK, OK," the bishop said in a throwaway manner. "By the way, Paul, are you still dead against accepting a parish?"

"Whatever reward I am entitled to for doing this favour for you, I'll pass on the parish. That would be like saying I accept everything the church stands for at the moment."

"I respect your point of view," the bishop replied, "though I can't personally see the difficulty."

"I can't see either why we can't try and solve the problem of the declining number of priests by ordaining women or allowing priests to marry."

The bishop assured him that he would have no problem having a parish priest in his diocese that held such a view.

"It's between me and my conscience," was Paul's reply. "I'm happy enough where I am. Well, at least I was until this was landed on me."

They left it like that. Paul did not sleep well, waking again and again, considering every eventuality. He rose early, readied a room for Richard, leaving the electric blanket switched on to air the bed. He always liked practical work which tended to keep away worry.

At last there were footsteps in the church as someone approached the confession box. He never looked at a person as he slid back the little door between priest and penitent. He knew that it was difficult enough to be there without anyone looking at them. The person whose head was within a foot of his did not say anything, but drew a deep breath.

"If you want to confess something…"

"Bless me, Father, for I have sinned." Paul recognised the voice of his old friend, Richard Scapegoat.

VI

Extract from Paul Godfool's journal

My memories of 'home' are those of a child. Everything looks small now, especially the hayfields which were so big when they had to be tackled with rake and fork. Every road, every field, every bush is redolent with memory. I am still the little boy at John Cannon's gate thinking the curlew called my name: "Pa-ul, Pa-ul…" We went to Tuffy's pub for tin-cans of porter on days of the thresher, to Maddens for a loaf of bread and a pot of strawberry jam to go with the bottles of hot tea my mother brought wrapped in thick stockings when we were haymaking. Food never tasted as good.

I remember the day one of our neighbours, Michael Fay, died suddenly while their pig was being killed in the haggard, as small fields near houses into which crops were drawn for the winter were called. Margaret and myself were on our way from school when we came on the commotion. We were less than seven years old. Infant classes were allowed home earlier than the rest of the school.

Michael had died suddenly as the pig squealed after being knifed. He lay on the ground, his feet bare for the anointing. I imagined his soul rising out of him like steam from a kettle as he fell where he stood, just like a cowboy shot in a film. He was a kind man who had often brought us in to his wife as we passed, for something sweet to eat or drink. We had been told never to insult our neighbours by not eating what they gave us. The old woman put nutmeg in stewed rhubarb and caraway seed in bread. There were not many things I did not like to eat, but they were two of them. I still remember allowing that bread to melt on my tongue, before sucking it down my throat so that my teeth would not touch the seeds.

Margaret and myself kept one particular memory of that day to ourselves for over forty years. We remembered a big basin of blood being brought to our house that evening, from which our mother proceeded to make black pudding for the people of the village. Somewhere deep down both of us thought, until we discussed it many years later, that the blood was from the old man. In all the hullabaloo we had forgotten about the pig, stretched, gleaming white on the horse-cart.

I grew up, dressed like a little yank. Apart from a suit bought for First Holy Communion and sweaters and socks my mother knit, the rest of our clothes came from Chicago. We never met the people who sent them, sisters of my grandfather who had emigrated half a century before, and their descendants. Every few months a big square cardboard box arrived, tied in white twine and perched on the front carrier of postman, Tommy Tolster's bike. The box was so heavy sometimes, or he had so many others to deliver that he told us to collect it ourselves in the ass and cart.

There was a ritual to the opening. The white twine was collected, to be tied together until it was long enough for a haystack. The smell of camphor escaped and filled the house as the box was opened. Then shirts, dresses, trousers were taken out and tried on, white trousers we would be ashamed to wear if they hadn't come from the States, so we presumed that they had to be fashionable.

I remember one shirt in particular that I was expected to wear and which I thought looked remarkably like a girl's blouse. There was a kind of flap across the front which buttoned at the shoulder. I didn't like it and wondered how I was going to explain it to the hardy boys in the yard at Clogher school. Then I was told it was an Italian-style shirt and all was forgiven. I had something to show off in rather than be ashamed of. At the bottom of the box, if we were lucky, there were comics in which Mickey Mouse, Superman and a whole range of cowboys and Indians were met for the first time.

For over sixty years, those women sent parcels "home," the home they had left in another age and would never see again. Neither they nor we could afford the crossing. It was not until the early seventies of the last century that a daughter of one of them came "home" for the first time,

Sister Maude, travelling as a retirement treat at sixty-five years of age after teaching all her life. She spent most of the next quarter of a century working with and for the old and poor of Chicago. When she got a special award for her work, the citation said she was one of the few people who would be welcome on every street of the Windy City.

Going to "town" was a big day when I was young. My brother John was often quoted as saying "Tomorrow came at last," when a long-promised visit to town materialised. For the great Irish language novelist, Máirtín Ó Cadhain, Galway was *Gealchathair* or Bright city. We had no city, but we had our own bright town, Castlebar. It was where we went for building materials and for items like shoes or household goods.

Town was Heaven for those reared out the country, high houses, big windows, bright lights, the smell of clothes and leather. I remember seeing 'Turf Accountant' written over more than one door and took it for granted that they sold turf, or peat, though I did wonder where they kept the turf-stacks. One of the Banks carried the legend on its window that it had seven million pounds in assets, a vast fortune for someone very lucky if he carried a shiny half-crown in his pocket.

Then there were the fair days, rising at three in the morning, driving cattle seven miles while trying to keep them on the right road and out of mischief. At Balla fair, the cattle would be made to stand on the footpath outside McEllins, so that they would look bigger. It was somewhat more difficult to do the same in Castlebar, where the fairground was a hilly field. On a good day, jobbers would be out the road to meet you, and cattle could be sold before arriving at the fair. They would still have to be minded until they were paid for and ready to go on lorry or train, but there was a quiet satisfaction if the main work of the day was done early.

Other fair days were slow and boring, jobbers giving the impression they were barely interested, or just wandering around for the good of their health. The worst of all was bringing cattle home unsold, the drovers tired and irritable, the day a failure. Mostly though hands were spat on, palms slapped. Jobbers walked away but returned. Many were from Northern Ireland, well-dressed with high leather boots which never seemed to get dirty among all the manure, men who spoke with strange accents. Protestants, people said, and probably more honest for that. At last the bargain was made, the cattle sold, the money paid.

It was time then hot tea and bacon sandwiches in Carty's Mobile Canteen followed by red lemonade in a pub where jobbers would have one drink maybe and be given their luck money. They never stayed long; they didn't want to lose their sharpness, as they might have many other bargains to close. The cattle sold were often replaced by young calves bought down by the bridge in Castlebar, where bullseyes and *duilisc* were sold from tables on the footpath. We might be lucky enough to get a lift home in a pick-up truck dropping off calves bought by the calf-jobber the day before from milk producers down South in the Golden Vale.

Of all the animals we had over the years, I was fondest of the donkey, or the ass, as he was better known. Words like donkey were considered a bit uppity, and people dressed up in their best Sunday suit, white shirt and tie tended to be told they were "like an ass looking across a whitewashed wall." Another less than flattering description for a person dressed in their finest was: "All out, like an ass's prick." Our ass was not a little black donkey like Padraic Ó Conaire's "*M'asal beag dubh*" but a big black stallion reputed to be father of many little asses in the vicinity.

The same donkey had one big fault; he had no reverse gear. No matter what a person did, he refused to back. This fault was a blessing in disguise when children brought him to the bog to put out turf. There was not the slightest danger of him backing his cart into a bog-hole, though this meant there had to always be enough room left to lead him around in a circle.

Needless to say, I have mixed feelings when I return "home" to the place in which I grew up. I sometimes regret having left the land a generation or two after my people had wrested it from the landlords, the stones and the whins. Like many Irish people, my roots run deep in the soil. My roots are still there but they are torn, ripped, and jagged. I feel like a boat that has lost its anchor. My only consolation is knowing where it was lost.

Perhaps that is why I keep such a tight grip on another anchor, priesthood, even though it would be more popular and profitable to leave it behind me. At this point in my life, it would be much easier to leave than to stay in a calling that has drawn such disrespect and disparagement on itself. But nobody ever said it would be easy, certainly not the one who suggested we take up our crosses and follow him.

VII

"They became prostitutes in Egypt when they were girls. There their nipples were handled and their virgin breasts were first fondled." Ezekiel 23:3

"This is called Bill," Eve Adams said playfully, pointing a finger at Bill Brown's torso as he lay beside her on the bed. She pointed further down: "And this is called Willy. It's nice to find a man with co-ordinated names." They laughed and kissed.

"I didn't believe that happiness really existed until I met you," Bill said earnestly.

"Sure you know me for a long time."

"Not in this sense, I don't. Of course, I know you, to see you for a long time, or to be out with yourself and Adam. But I didn't really know you until we came together."

"That we did alright," Eve said with a smile.

Bill looked her in the face and asked seriously: "What?"

"We came together." Eve kissed him. "More than once."

"Can you be serious for a minute?"

"I'm serious all the time, especially when we are making love."

"You know what I mean?"

"Of course, I do," Eve said. "I feel guilty as well about Sharon and Adam, and then I look at you and I forget all about them. Just for a little while."

"I know it's not right, but I think I could not do without you now. You bring me alive in a way I never thought possible."

Eve moved even closer to Bill: "It all seems right when we are together. I'm glad we managed it this evening or I would be lost without you."

Bill laid his finger on her nose: "Naughty. I heard you were going to bring Abigail to the shops this evening."

"I was to, but I pretended I was punishing them when they came back late from the soccer, and off I went on my own. I wouldn't mind but they blamed you for delaying them. Do you know what I called you?"

"A bold boy," Bill said lightly.

"Worse again."

"A lousy eejit."

"A right prick," Eve laughed. "Little did I know how quickly you were going to prove it."

"Was I really that quick?"

"Don't be so sensitive. That's not what I meant. Anyway, you finished it off in great style. The tongue is mightier than…" Eve laughed: "whatever."

"You will have to teach me how to make it last."

"What makes you think that I'm the expert?"

"You know a lot more about it than I do."

"Are you calling me a slut?" Eve asked.

"I just know there are ways and means to improve things that I would love to learn. There must be books, DVD's, something."

"I'd hate it to get too mechanical," Eve said, "banging away like dogs like you would see them on television."

"I don't watch that kind of programme myself," Bill said in a mock-snobbish accent. "The mother-in-law would hardly approve."

"She must know what it's for or she wouldn't have had Sharon."

"I thought we said we wouldn't talk about them." Bill got up and went into the bathroom. He took his time there. He felt dirty no matter how much he washed himself. "I'm not a good candidate for adultery," he told himself but he was hooked on Eve at this stage. He never had the same level of pleasure and passion with Sharon, even when they first married. In more recent times it was as if she was doing her duty with a sigh, hoping it would soon be over so that she could get to sleep. He had well and truly broken his marriage vows at this stage and he was as well to be hung for a sheep as a lamb. Bill went back to bed and put his arms around Eve.

"I'm sorry I ever mentioned Sharon," Eve said.

"It's OK. We did say we would leave them out of it. No competition. No comparisons."

"I'm sorry," Eve said again and kissed him tenderly. "I suppose I always want to be the best. I was the same with sport. It's just jealousy or something."

"Jealous of Sharon?" Bill looked at her as if that was a contradiction in terms.

Eve shrugged: "Who knows?" as she began to caress him gently with the tips of her fingers.

"We need to be very careful," Bill said.

"Careful that we are not caught?" Eve asked.

"That we are not caught in any way. You didn't even give me a chance to put on a condom last time before..."

"Say it," Eve laughed, "before putting your leg over. Don't worry. I'm on the pill. As well as being on the Bill."

"They say it's safer to use a condom as well."

Eve frowned as if insulted: "I'm disease free if that is what you mean."

"I'm not talking about you."

"Do you think Adam is sleeping about? I don't think so, and even if he was, he is scrupulously clean. You don't think I do this with anyone else?"

"Of course not," Bill assured her with a kiss. "I wouldn't be here with you except it's the most place in the world I want to be."

The time for talking was over as far as Eve was concerned and she did not speak again until they had finished making love. Having held each other for a little while she sat up in bed and said: "One of the great advantages of you being an estate agent is that we have a different pad every time. Do you think I should write a report for your clients about the love-making possibilities of the various beds?"

"That might help get the property market back to where it was a few years ago," Bill laughed.

"Being in different houses and apartments reduces the chances of being seen," Eve said.

Bill looked at the windows: "I would prefer the curtains pulled myself but it might look strange when I am supposed to be showing a house to a customer."

"I much prefer the curtains pulled and the light of day," his lover said. "I love to see you properly, handsome, lean, fit and naked."

"Don't go over the top altogether," Bill smiled. "I'm no male model."

"To me you are."

"It's funny the way you always bring your own sheets," Bill said.

"I have no way of knowing how clean or dirty the people were that were in bed before us."

"I'd hardly be trying to sell a property with dirty sheets on the bed."

"All the more reason to bring our own and clean up after ourselves," Eve explained.

Bill smiled at her: "What will Adam say if he sees you going out the door with a set of sheets under your arm?"

"There could be any amount of reasons. I could be going to the laundry or exchanging sheets that were not large enough. He is well used by now to me coming and going carrying shopping bags."

"You have so many different plans up your sleeve," Bill said half-seriously, half-jokingly, "that I sometimes wonder how experienced you really are at this kind of thing."

"You are the one I always wanted. You must have noticed me looking at you. Especially that time we were all on that sun holiday together. When I saw you in your wet swimming trunks… Wow."

Bill ran his fingers down Eve's jaw-line: "I was looking at your lovely face for years, and little did I think we would ever be together. I would have thought you to be away beyond me. In a different league."

Eve put her arms around him and tickled his sides: "Are you saying that I am not in a different league?"

"You certainly are. In more ways than one."

Eve sat up in bed and spread her hands across Bill's hairy chest. "Just lie back," she said, "and forget all the difficulties of life. Think only of our love, our being together this evening. Forget about tomorrow or any other day."

"Is this some kind of yoga?" bill asked.

"Just listen and think of nothing." Eve closed her eyes and when she opened them again, she noticed Bill checking his watch. "Are you in a hurry?"

"Not really, but I have to pick up Liam and Sharon and bring them to the Saturday evening mass."

Eve gave a sarcastic laugh: "Are you telling me that you are going to get out of my bed after an evening of love making to bring your wife to the church? And I suppose you will be traipsing up to communion with them."

Bill was shamefaced: "The least attention we draw on ourselves, the better," he said. "We just have to carry on with the ordinary things of life, doing what we always do, even if it's thinking of you, I am, every minute we are not together."

Eve laughed: "God will be very amused. You in the church, your wife and son beside you and your mind on what we spent the evening doing."

"Ah, Eve, don't make it any more difficult than it is."

"Does it not make you feel like a hypocrite?"

"Of course, it does," Bill said, "but that is something I have to put up with so that we can be together. I have to deal with that in my own way. If I don't turn up at home at the time arranged, there will be questions."

"Where are you supposed to be?" Eve asked.

"Meeting a client, selling a house. The usual. I'm supposed to have a meeting with a couple who are only free on a Saturday. They are the Joneses, as in keeping up with, if you want to know the extent of my lies."

Eve was amused: "Is this the house in question?"

"Are you stupid? I hardly want Sharon to arrive outside with a message while we are having fun inside."

"So that's what it is? Having fun. And incidentally I am not stupid," Eve said tetchily. "Anyway, if she wants to contact you haven't you a mobile?"

"I knock it off when we're together."

There was mischief in Eve's eyes: "I knock it off when we're knocking it up. Are you afraid I'll hear her on the phone to you?"

"I don't want her to hear background noises," Bill explained. "Anything likely to give the game away. I heard about a colleague recently who didn't realise every sound was going out on air while he was in the toilet."

"Can't you give Sharon a ring now," Eve suggested. "Say that you are delayed. Let them go to mass together. Give us a bit of extra time."

Bill was shamefaced: "I promised Paul Godfool, the priest that I would read one of the readings. He put pressure on me after football this morning. What could I say?"

Eve laughed: "you could have said that you were planning to give your lover a right good rollicking for the evening."

"I thought you were going to the shops with Abigail at the time."

"Isn't it a funny thing," Eve mused, "that Adam has is in no way religious but he is less of a hypocrite than either of us."

Bill was not sure how to reply: "Everyone has his own way, I suppose. I thought both of you were of like mind about those issues."

"What makes you think that?"

"Something he said," Bill replied.

"So, the two of you discuss religion in the early morning mist while you are watching the kids play soccer?"

"You know the way things come up."

"Men never cease to amaze me," Eve said.

Bill tried to explain: "It came up this morning because the priest was the referee, and Adam was wondering was that appropriate because of all that has happened in recent years."

"And my husband said I had no religion?" Eve asked.

Bill answered as carefully as he could: "He gave the impression you were both of like mind about bringing the children to mass and stuff like that."

"It just shows you how little he knows about me. Lack of communication. That's his problem. Lack of real communication. No wonder I'm here with you this evening."

"I thought we were supposed to leave Adam and Sharon out of the equation when we are together," Bill said.

"It was you brought it up. It's a pity the two of them wouldn't get together and shag the holes out of each other," Eve said angrily.

"You mean Sharon and Adam?"

"Who else?" That is my prayer, night and day, that those two would have the imagination to get together. That would free up the two of us to spend the rest of our lives together."

Bill was wondering was that what he wanted as he showered and dressed before kissing Eve goodbye as she curled up in the bed-clothes.

VIII

Extract from Paul Godfool's Journal

Boarding school brought an end to a relatively happy childhood. In my mind's eye, I still see two of the senior boys, seventeen or eighteen-year olds, but big men to me, standing inside the door of the main toilets, giving communal kicks in the backside to all first years that passed them by. Some of the same seniors were at the head of the table at mealtimes, doling out as much or as little food as they wished, according to whether they liked people or not. They sometimes kept the choicest bits to be passed on to their own mates, leaving the rest of us hungry. I am not saying they were all cruel and merciless, but favour and favouritism played a big part in the life of that college.

Much of that favouritism had to do with Gaelic football and a person's ability on the pitch. The same sport was a little God, if not the big God even in some cases among students and most of the staff. I have no argument with the players or football stars who gave us many moments pleasure on fields as far away as Tullamore or Limerick, with the resultant day out and opportunity to sample other than college fare. My argument is with the ethos of a college in which those without silken playing skills were second class citizens. The skills with which many of the students there grew up had to do with farming, but they were disparaged and laughed at, while those reared in towns with little to do except kick a ball against a wall or around a field were kings of that college.

Apart from one layman, it was priests who taught there, and the iron fist, the cane and the strap were the principal teaching methods, the educational tools in use. There were exceptions among the staff, who showed that kindness and praise could be more effective than the heavy hand, but most of the teachers there at the time took the easy way out.

Still, life was changing in the early sixties, and the influence of the Beatles and the Rolling Stones reached even the staid confines of a boarding schools. Radios or record players were not officially available, but there were always ways around even the most stringent rules. Transistor radios had just reached the town, and one electrical shop was even renting them out for something like a shilling a night. A few pence each from everyone in the dormitory meant we could have the latest pop songs available after lights out.

The dean came around one night, cane in hand, ready to stamp out whatever subversion was afoot. The young man in charge of the radio that night was unable to find the on/off button in the dark beneath the bedclothes at such short notice, so he squeezed the radio between his knees until the music died. The dean snapped on all the lights and walked menacingly from bed to bed, each of us pretending to be asleep until he had passed by. Snores and farts broke through the silence and the tension, but while the dean knew there was something up, he did not have enough evidence to start caning.

One time a couple of us stole tomatoes from the Christian Brother's greenhouse which was just across the college wall. It was not a difficult operation, and we only had a couple of tomatoes each for our trouble. The trick was to climb up on top of the wall and reach in the windows where they were open or cracked. Reports came back to our college and the student body were assembled in the chapel. The dean threatened to "put blisters as big as the tomatoes they stole on the arses of those involved." Two of us owned up, but there were no blisters. The matter was allowed to drop, that particular bark worse than the bite.

Although I disliked boarding school, we did have plenty of fun and enjoyment there. People always find a way to beat the system. We worked on the farm any chance they got, spreading seed potatoes in the Spring or harvesting them in Autumn. The reward was permission to go to the pictures. Ryan's in Shop Street was a more attractive proposition than any film. There was a fire there, a jukebox, chips, coke, girls, not necessarily in that order. We were big men there.

Another organisation that gave us a break from boring college life was the FCA, the local defence force, or Free Clothes Army, as we used to call it, as we were provided with uniforms and army boots. There was a kind of fashionability about these big red boots that Doc Martens had about thirty years later. We strutted around the college walks after tea at night before second study, boots open, hobnails knocking noise and sparks off the tarmac, real hard men in our own minds. It was not just the clothes that were free, we got free meals after army training on college half-days. We thought those meals a cut above college fare, although in fairness meat, potato and vegetable were surely far healthier than burgers and chips.

American President, John F Kennedy, didn't manage to meet me when he was in Galway the Summer before my Leaving Cert. I didn't manage to meet him, neither, though we were in the same town that day. We FCA men were confined to barracks in Renmore. Our authorities were probably afraid the President would be in more danger from amateur defenders like us than the kind of sniper attack that left him dead in Dallas before that year was out. Renmore barracks was not all a holiday. Training was tough enough, marching around the square shouldering a Lee Enfield 303 rifle of First World War vintage, a Sergeant barking: "Hey you, you're walking like a pregnant duck."

I think of those as historic days, not because I was in the army but because John F Kennedy was in Ireland and there was a new Pope in Rome shortly afterwards. What looked like a small, pale, slightly frightened man called Montini was elected to replace big hearty John XXIII, the grandfather of the church, if not of the world in many eyes. Many thought of John's short reign as being challenging and uplifting, when the Spirit was temporarily unleashed and allowed dance like a lamb in the garden of life. It was under his inspiration that I was drawn towards priesthood. I know now that it did not take the Roman Curia very long to put a halter the Spirit once more.

Even as a teenager on temporary army training, I had an interest in the papal election and I remember watching the news those days on television in the army canteen. That in itself was a novelty as we had not yet TV at home and only occasional access, mainly for big sporting events, while in college. My attention was not all on the Pope, however, with the city of Galway like a jewel at my feet after training every evening.

After Renmore we went for further army exercises in Finner Camp, outside Bundoran, Co. Donegal. I recall a glorious fortnight, weather-wise and socially, on artillery exercises among the sand dunes by day, walking into Bundoran or Ballyshannon by night, chatting up girls with the lilting unfamiliar accents of the North. Little things stand out in the memory, like seeing Elvis Presley on screen for the first time in Ballyshannon, little thinking the same Elvis would be wooing another young generation almost forty years later.

We were at evening tea in the refectory of Saint Jarlath's College when they announced that President Kennedy had been shot in Dallas, Texas. We were told shortly afterwards that he had died. Our big red military boots knocked no sparks from the stones that night. A pall of sadness hung over us as we walked the pathway around the college's football pitches, each lost in his own thoughts. It was like a death in the family. It felt like the end of an era, a golden era, the death of Camelot as that period had come to be called. It was like as if we were grieving hope itself. Life had turned as dark as the night.

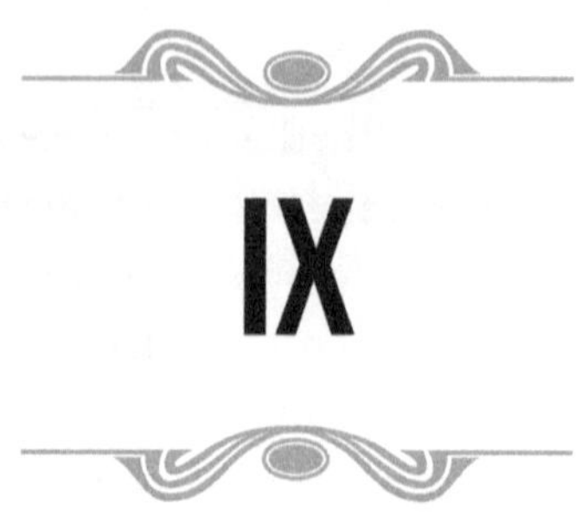

IX

"I tell you solemnly, whatever you bind on earth shall be considered bound in Heaven; whatever you loose on earth shall be considered loosed in Heaven." (Mt: 18:18)

When Father Godfool left the confession box, Richard Scapegoat was on his knees in the nearest pew, his head between his hands obviously saying his penance. Richard then stood, blessed himself and kissed the cross of the rosary beads in his right hand. He looked Paul in the face, stretched out his arms to hug his old friend. Godfool was reluctant to respond after what he had heard in the confession box, but what could he do? The seal of the sacrament meant that he could not repeat what he had heard.

"It's been a long time." Paul Godfool pulled away quickly from the embrace.

"It's great to clean the slate. I couldn't confess to any priest but yourself, Paul. I've been carrying around that burden for years."

"I'm sure you are dying for a cup of tea." Godfool tried to be normal even though he seethed with anger at the trick played on him in the confession box which meant that that subject at least would be off the agenda when they sat around the dinner table. He decided to be as impersonal as possible. He had intended to apologise for never visiting Scapegoat in prison, but felt his old friend had already taken his revenge for that.

"How have you been keeping?"

Godfool ignored the question in order to ask an inane one that would keep the other man at his distance: "I'm sure you don't miss the boring old

Saturdays in this business? The long evening with the Saturday night and Sunday sermons hanging over you like the sword of Damocles."

"I used to kill the afternoon watching soccer matches on the telly, and Gaelic ones in the summertime. It eased the nerves," Richard said. "Anyway, they saw that even the greatest actors are nervous before a performance."

"I don't look on the mass as theatre," Paul replied bluntly as they walked one after the other on the narrow path between the church and the presbytery.

"It was always difficult to keep up with those long footsteps," Richard tried to ease the tension between them. "It's no wonder that you were such a good full-back."

Paul was more comfortable with that kind of conversation: "Anything that went past me I knew that you were there to stop it. You had the flexibility of a snake between the goalposts."

"We could have made the county team except that they wouldn't even let us out to play a match in the early years, and we were gone past it when the college opened up. By that time, I was hooked on the acting."

"Just like I was on the picket lines," Paul Godfool said. "They used to joke about 'rent a crowd,' but we picketed everything from the visit of the Springboks to President Nixon, not to speak of the Dublin housing action movement."

Paul was switching on the kettle in the kitchen when Richard asked: "Did they ever manage to preserve those Georgian houses that were in the news at the time?"

"I wasn't involved in those," Godfool answered. "I felt I was too much of a socialist for that elitist stuff. I was caught up in that famous photo on the front page of one of the newspapers under the banner – 'Victory to the Vietcong.' The President was livid when he called us to his office. But he did eventually make a joke of it: 'There's always some section of the church on the side of the winners.' That's how it has survived for so long."

"You were far more radical than I was," Richard said. "I was back in the college studying."

"Just like the boys who went on to be bishops. They kept their heads down and their powder dry. Sure, we all dried up in the end, I suppose."

"How do you mean?" Scapegoat asked.

"It's a long time that I did anything more radical than giving a yellow card to a ten-year-old in a soccer match, something I was berated for by an angry parent this morning. I haven't opened my mouth on any serious issue for many a day."

"Sense comes with age, they say."

"I doubt it," Godfool said, "but what does come with age is tiredness and cynicism." He put up his hands beside his greying hair and beard: "How would Santa Claus look on a picket line?"

"You would be like Abraham or Moses in some old painting, the hair of your head like a halo." Richard rubbed his hand on his own head: "At least you're not as bald as a baby's arse."

Paul didn't comment on that. He didn't know if it was a figure of speech or some kind of loaded sick joke. He changed the subject: "How has your health been? Most people have some difficulties as they get older."

"I had some chest pains a while back, but they found nothing wrong after an angiogram. I think it might have contributed to me getting out early. They didn't want the publicity of a coffin coming out the gate."

"It must be a relief to be out," Paul said gingerly. The more they steered away from that subject the better he liked it.

"I don't know to tell you the truth. It was a bit like the college long ago, everything organised, everything arranged, everything done by the clock. Leaving was much different, of course. Leaving college, we had the big world out there ahead of us, waiting to be saved. In our innocence and stupid idealism."

Paul said wistfully: "Those weeks after ordination were a kind of honeymoon, bonfires, welcoming committees, people lining up for your blessing."

"A dry ride of a honeymoon," Scapegoat commented.

"You used not be so cynical."

"How would you be if you had my future to look forward to? No welcome anywhere. A non-person, a ghost made flesh."

Godfool did not know what to say: "Your family…?"

"What can they do?" They don't want a crowd of heavies at the door threatening to burn me out and them with me. To give them their due they were good to me when I was inside, but I could not lay that burden on them. The only home I have now is wherever I'm lucky enough to lay down my head for the night." After a pause he quoted Jesus with a deep sarcasm: "The son of man has nowhere to lay his head."

"You will be alright here for a while," Paul said matter of factly, but I need to lay down some ground rules."

"You are the boss. It's not as if I am not used to rules."

Paul spoke quickly as if rushing to finish an unpleasant task: "You are not to leave the house without you with me. I walk a lot and you are welcome to join me, no for mass, or to town or anywhere else I go. You are not to go anywhere on your own, and it goes without saying that you are to have nothing to do with children. I think that is reasonable enough in the circumstances."

"Don't worry. The fox has already laid down the same set of regulations. The last thing I want to do is draw trouble on you, Paul. I'll be a saint."

Paul Godfool asked about their bishop: "How was he with you?"

"Sound enough, but what choice had he?"

"You drew a lot of trouble down on him."

"We are big boys now," Scapegoat replied. "When he took the job, he accepted the consequences. And he knows that I know a few things about himself that he would not like revealed."

"Did you threaten him with that?"

"There was no need to. He knows what I know. We were in the same town parish early on. Let's say he was a big hit with the girls."

Paul raised his hands: "I don't want to know. It has nothing to do with me. I don't want to hear of any scandal."

"There are skeletons in every cupboard." Richard smiled: "Except in your own, of course."

Paul leant over and opened a kitchen cupboard: "There is nothing in this one except mouse droppings."

"I don't know how you managed to keep your slate clean this long," Richard said. "You would think you would have put some young one up the pole or something. It happens to bishops."

"Is there anything wrong with living according to your conscience, keeping the rules, keeping your pants on if it comes to that?" Paul asked, but he winked at his visitor at the same time.

"There must be some gap in your armoury, some Achilles heel in which to put an arrow. Do you remember the day you said after Greek class that it was between his legs that Achilles had his heel, but that the historians were too timid to say so?"

"I never said such a thing," Paul insisted. "I wouldn't have had the imagination to think of it."

"I remember you saying it as if it was yesterday. We were coming up the Long Corridor, and you had the rest of the class in stitches. It's amazing how many things people said that they can't remember. Because it doesn't suit their image in this day and age."

"It's not easy remember every detail of what happened forty years ago," Paul said. "Some people seem to live those days for ever. I try to live in the here and now."

"It's not half an hour since we were discussing football matches from those days," Richard reminded him.

"That is natural enough, because that is really all the two of us have in common. Our lives have gone in different directions since then."

Richard Scapegoat mused: "Seven years is a long time together. Seven years at a time our minds were developing, nowhere else to go most of the time. Those kinds of memories last."

"I understand, but it is easy to make too much of them. I'm not the person I was then, ready to go on a picket line at the drop of a hat. It would take a lot to move me in that way now."

"You still look the same to me," his old friend said, "apart from the hair, of course and the few extra pounds."

"You were a wizard on the stage," Paul recalled. "You could have left and gone the way the likes of Ray McAnally did in a previous generation. On to the stage of the Abbey."

"I had a go at writing a drama myself when I was inside," Richard revealed.

"Great stuff. What is it about?"

"It's about those daft television shows, reality TV as they call them. There wasn't much else to watch while I was there. 'Celebrity Big Bollix,' I called it. It's about all that crowd, too big for their boots on the television."

"Have you a script?" Paul asked. "I'd love to read it."

"It's in the bottom of my bag somewhere. By the way I left my bag behind the door of the church. Is it safe there?"

"It should be. We will get it now if you have finished your tea. I wouldn't like to see some old dear getting a heart attack if she came across 'Celebrity Big Bollix.'" As they walked towards the church, Godfool asked: "Have you sent the script to any of the theatre companies?"

"I intend to, but I will have to use a pen-name, for obvious reasons. Would you mind if replies were care of your address?"

Paul was hesitant but agreed: "We need to be careful. For both of our sakes."

"If the play was to succeed," Scapegoat said, "it would be like a new beginning. Life after prison. Life after priesthood."

"Are you thinking of leaving?"

"Have I any choice?" Richard answered, before adding sarcastically: "A priest forever," they used to say. "A priest forever until you become an embarrassment, until they want to get rid of you."

"You were convicted," Paul Godfool said quietly.

"I never admitted anything."

"You never admitted anything in court." Godfool stopped when he remembered the seal of confession.

Scapegoat gave him a sly smile: "Do you believe everything you hear in the box? I thought you were one of those who thought outside the box."

Paul Godfool stopped, confused in the middle of the footpath. His mind was in complete confusion. He didn't want a row with this man he was going to live in his house for the foreseeable future: "Look, you go on and collect your bag. I'll wait here. I just need to sit down."

"Are you alright?"

"I'm tired. I didn't sleep much since the fox called last night, and I spent the morning refereeing ten-year-olds. I'll be alright when you come back from the church. Don't be long."

"OK, boss." Scapegoat saluted, dramatically, sarcastically before walking away. He stopped after a few steps, turned around and said: "Thank you, my old friend."

Paul didn't reply. It was as if he couldn't stand the sight of Richard. He couldn't wait to get back to his room, pour himself a stiff whiskey and lie down on the bed with the clock set to awaken him for evening mass.

X

Extract from Paul Godfool's journal

remember the Summer of 1964, the three-month break between secondary school and seminary as being a very special time in my life. I got to know my father in ways I never had before as I worked with him for Mayo County Council during the last Summer of his life. Although his trade was plastering, he was working then mainly as a general handyman for the Council. I was taken on as a labourer, and we worked mainly on health centres, which were then part of the care of County Councils before the establishment of Health Boards.

There was a new health centre being built in Westport. It was there I met a carpenter called Mike O'Meara whose advice included one-liners like "One man watching is better than ten men working." It was not that he was not a good neat worker himself, but he believed that under the law of averages County Council engineers and overseers tended to arrive at those moments a man might draw breath, take a few moments break or have a cigarette. An eye on the road prevented people being caught unawares.

My father and the ganger who was in charge of the job decided one day to play a trick on the talkative carpenter. Mike O'Meara had been given a large pike by a local fisherman, which he had stored in a cool place at the North side of the building. The tricksters slipped a number of nails and pennies down the throat of the fish, and asked a reporter from the Mayo News who often stopped to talk while he was passing to give a mention to their prank. The next edition told of how Mr. Michael O'Meara, the well-known dryland fisherman had caught a specimen pike, inside of which he found some rusty nails and old Roman coins.

I worked for the Council and loved doing so, until the very last day before going to college. We finished on a small stone building beside the ruin of Ballinrobe poorhouse. I still remember attending the dance in the Royal Ballroom of the Traveller's Friend Hotel in Castlebar the Sunday night before going away. The band sang *"Those wedding bells will never ring for me,"* as if they knew I was in the audience. In Biblical terms I felt I was "putting my hand to the plough." There was no turning back now.

XI

Sharon Brown brought her son, Liam to see her mother, Ann McDonagh while her husband Bill was meeting clients on Saturday evening. She visited almost every day since her father had died about six months earlier. She had often heard of someone dying with a broken heart soon after the death of a partner. As she watched her mother lose weight at an alarming rate, Sharon wondered would this be true in her case. All the advice and cajoling in the world had failed to get Mrs McDonagh go to see a doctor.

"She's a lovely doctor," Sharon said, "a woman doctor. She wouldn't keep you ten minutes."

"There is nothing wrong with me," her mother insisted.

"Why are you going to the toilet so often so?"

Ann rubbed her hand on her stomach area and spoke to her grandson as if his mother was not in the room: "The old plumbing isn't as good as it used to be. An old person has to go often."

Sharon looked her mother straight in the eye: "From the coughing and the spitting I hear, I'd say you are vomiting every time you go to the bathroom."

"Aren't you the right Miss Marple? You should have joined the Guards and became a detective. But of course, you weren't tall enough, even though you were wide enough. Maybe I ate something that didn't agree with me."

Sharon persisted with her questioning: "What was it that you ate? If you have food poisoning, we have to get the cause of it. It could be salmonella or something like that."

"I didn't have any fish. You know I never liked salmon."

"What had you for your breakfast?" her daughter asked.

Ann addressed her grandson again: "When you grow up, Liam I hope you are not deafening your mother with daft questions."

Liam raised his eyes from his book, smiled at his grandmother and went back to his reading. Sharon went over and opened the fridge.

"Good girl," her mother said. "Wet a drop of tea."

Sharon moved smelt a few things she took from her mother's fridge: "In a minute. From what I can see you didn't eat anything since yesterday."

"Do you know what curiosity did to the cat?" Ann asked Liam.

"Did it give him a sick stomach?" Liam asked to the great amusement of his grandmother.

"Nobody can survive on an empty stomach," Sharon said.

"I couldn't keep anything down," her mother replied.

"And you're still retching even though there is nothing in your stomach?"

"Don't worry," her daughter said. "There is no danger it's morning sickness. You are not likely to have a little sister or brother anytime soon. Even though that would mean that Liam would have an uncle younger than himself." Liam looked up from his book with great interest,

"What uncle, Grandma?"

"Go back to your book," his mother ordered before chiding her mother: "Such talk in front of a child."

"Wasn't there some old lady in the Bible had a son in her old age," Ann said. "Wasn't it Elizabeth with John the Baptist? I'm sure they learned about that at school."

"Long enough he will be listening to that kind of talk," Sharon said.

"He will be a young man soon. He will have to learn about life," the child's grandmother insisted.

Her daughter disagreed: "A lot of children are growing up too fast and their parents are encouraging it, buying miniskirts for little slips of girls, doing them up like little tarts. I'm glad I don't have a girl."

"I'd hate to have a sister," Liam stated, his eyes still firmly on his book.

"Your mother was very fond of the style in her young days," his grandmother said to him, "squeezing herself into jeans it would take a shoehorn to put on her."

"What's a shoehorn?" Liam asked.

"I suppose they don't have them any more either," Ann said. "Just as you wouldn't know what to do with a harrow or a hames or a hoe or any of the things we used to have once. The old life is gone forever."

"Was Mammy bold when she was young?" Liam loved trying to find out what his parents got up to in their youth.

"She was a right little devil, in and out of every press. As for climbing. Every tree was a challenge to her."

Sharon sounded as if she felt a need to defend herself: "Every child is pulling out presses when they are two years old."

"Tell me again about the tree." Liam loved to hear the same stories over and over again. "And about the ladder."

"Your mother went up to the top of that sycamore that is hanging over the old barn. Your grandfather, God be good to him, had to get the ladder and climb up and carry her down."

"Were you scared, Mammy?"

"I was sure I would fall because the branches at the top were light and swaying. I was up there a good while before anyone knew where I was because the big summer leaves were hiding me. I was shouting at the top of my voice and nobody took a blind bit of notice."

His grandmother winked at Liam: "We thought it was an old cat screeching or an ass braying."

"Don't be telling lies to the child," Sharon chided her.

"Were you afraid the next time you climbed it?" Liam asked.

"I never climbed anything after that, and I hope you never do. I learned my lesson. I could have been killed if I fell down on that galvanize roof."

"You would have gone straight down through it," her mother said, "the weight of you."

"I hadn't a pick on me that time, I was only ten."

"Did Grandad bring his walking stick up the ladder?" Liam asked.

His grandmother's eyes took on a faraway look: "I suppose you never saw him without his stick, but he was a fine fit and agile man at the time. He was the dead split of yourself but a bit older."

"Used he play soccer like I do on Saturday mornings?"

"There was no talk of football that time," Ann answered, "apart from kicking a pig's bladder around the garden."

"Yuck," said Liam. "Was it full of blood?"

"It would be washed and cleaned when a pig was killed," his grandmother said. "There would be wind put into it with a bicycle pump."

"I like blood," Liam told her. "In computer games."

"It's far too many of those things you are watching," Sharon said. "Your Dad and myself will have to have a look at them some night to see if they are suitable for a boy your age."

"He's a fine boy." Ann had time to say no more as she rushed to the bathroom door, her handkerchief to her mouth.

"I'm not hanging around any longer," Sharon said, as she searched for the emergency phone numbers. By the time her mother returned from the bathroom her daughter was able to tell her that the doctor would visit in half an hour.

"God help me, and the house like a pigsty," was Ann's first reaction.

"The house is fine," Sharon assured her but she started to sweep and clean immediately. Liam was pressed into action, to take out ashes, set the fire, bring rubbish to the bin. He was told then to bring his book to the back kitchen while his grandmother was being examined.

The doctor quickly decided to send Mrs McDonagh to hospital for tests and she sent for an ambulance to take her to hospital.

"Is Grandma going to die like Grandad?" Liam asked from the back seat of the car as his mother followed the ambulance towards the town.

Sharon was concentrating on the road and on other arrangements she needed to make: "I have to call Bill," she said aloud, more to herself than to Liam. "He was supposed to bring us to mass, but we won't be there now."

"That is against the law," Liam said when he saw his mother trying to call his father on the mobile phone as she drove along. "Dad doesn't break the law because he has a right mobile for his work in the good car."

"It's a pity he doesn't answer it," Sharon said, frustrated. "He's engaged or switched off. I don't know why he has to work on a Saturday." She thought then of her son's question that she had not answered: "I don't know what is wrong with your grandmother, Liam. I hope she will be alright.

Let's not worry until we find out exactly what is wrong. It may not be much. Say a prayer she will get better."

"Prayers don't do any good," Liam answered definitely.

"Who told you that?"

"Cian said it and Abigail and himself don't go to mass or anything, because their parents are not old-fashioned."

"Don't take any notice of talk like that," Sharon said. "Maybe it's they that are wrong." After a while she asked: "Do you think your Dad and I are old-fashioned?"

Liam tried to be diplomatic: "Kind of, now and again. Grandma is very old-fashioned altogether, but I wouldn't mind about that because she is so old."

"I thought you were very fond of serving mass and everything, and you couldn't wait for your first holy communion."

"God let me down when Grandad died. I prayed for him to get better and he didn't," Liam answered.

"You loved old Grandad very much," his mother said sympathetically.

"He died and I don't have a Grandad any more, and I mightn't have a Grandma either soon."

"Your Grandad was a great age, and it's natural that a person dies after a long life, and in his case a good life. God called him to his reward."

"Maybe he has a reward from Grandma too."

"I don't know what is going to happen but your Grandma was ten years younger than your Grandad, so she has a better chance of living another while. We will have to see what the doctors say."

They were at the outskirts of the town and Sharon was watching the traffic carefully. She tended to drive mostly around the local village and was not sure about roundabouts and one-way traffic. She felt her best bet was to follow the ambulance closely as cars tended to get out of the way when they heard the siren and allow it a free run.

Traffic lights changed to red and Sharon's car almost crashed into the back of the ambulance when it stopped suddenly. Despite her anxiety, she burst out laughing. The headline: "Daughter kills mother by crashing into ambulance" crossed her mind.

"Are you alright Mammy?" Liam asked anxiously.

"I'm just relieved that the brakes of this old banger stopped us in time."

"There are great brakes on Daddy's beamer."

"It's a pity we couldn't get him on the phone or we would have come in the good car," Sharon said.

"Try him on the mobile again before the lights change," Liam suggested. "He should be home now to bring us to mass."

"He knows my mobile number if he wants to ring," his mother replied. "I need to concentrate on the traffic until we get to the hospital."

"I can ring him on your mobile," the boy suggested.

"Good lad. It's great to have the brains. In fact, we will have to get you a mobile of your own for your birthday."

"Cool," Liam cooed. "Can I have a yellow one like Cian's?"

"You can choose the colour, but don't imitate everything Cian has. Be your own man." Sharon passed the phone to Liam in the rear seat.

There was no reply then either but he left a message and texted as well, which explained where they were. They did not have to wait long for attention in the casualty department as the letter from Ann's doctor suggested urgent attention. There was no bed available so she was placed on a trolley in one of the corridors. Sharon was raging but kept that from her mother. She told Liam to stay with his grandmother while she went outside to ring his father.

Bill answered his phone with the question: "How is your mother? I've just got Liam's text. He spelt it h-o-p-s-i-t-l-e."

"Where were you all evening?"

"Didn't I tell you I had to meet clients."

"It's strange that you had your phone switched off for so long."

"It's hardly appropriate to be on the phone to someone else while showing people a property."

"You could lose a lot of business with that attitude," was Sharon's reply.

Bill reminded her she hadn't answered his question when he asked again: "How is your mother. Is she being kept in?"

"She is in the corridor on an old trolley you wouldn't put a dead pig on."

"That mightn't be a bad sign. If she was really serious, they would deal with her immediately," Bill said.

"No doctor looked at her properly yet so they have no way of knowing how good or bad she is." Sharon quoted one of the nurses who had said they had to make her mother comfortable first: "She would be more comfortable on a supermarket trolley than on the old thing she's on. It's like a galvanize gate on its side."

"You will be there another while so?" Bill asked.

"What choice have I? Would you mind collecting Liam, and I will stay with her until they do something?"

"Of course, I will," her husband said, "and I will leave you the BMW so that you will be safe coming home later."

"You be careful in the other old bucket. Liam and myself might have been killed when we almost skidded into the back of the ambulance."

There was a young Asian doctor who looked no more than twenty examining her mother when Sharon returned to the line of trolleys in the corridor. He was kind and friendly and said she would have a scan the following day, so she should not eat anything in the meantime.

"If I was to eat it itself it would be up again in a shot," she said. "You wouldn't want to be standing in front of me or you could get a right mouthful." The doctor laughed and said that she reminded him of his grandmother.

Ann slept soon afterwards as the doctor had given her something to help her to do so. Sharon sat awkwardly on a chair by the trolley, moving frequently and excusing herself as people passed by and the work of the staff progressed. She felt tired and was afraid she would doze on the chair and fall down on the terrazzo floor. She had begun to go jogging in an effort to lose weight. She felt that was the reason she was no longer attractive to her husband. The running seemed to have little effect so far so she was very disappointed with that.

XII

Extract from Paul Godfool's Journal

The room I shared with a friend in the seminary was next to what is known as the ghost-room. A couple of tragic suicides took place about twenty years apart in and from the window of that room in the first half of the nineteenth century, not very long after the college was founded in 1795. The front wall of the room was removed and an altar erected and that is the way it has been left to this day.

Rumour has it that a bloodstain on the floorboards could never be removed. Another legend has it that a priest volunteered to sleep there and came out the next morning with his hair turned completely white. Needless to say, these and other bloodcurdling stories were relayed to first years foolhardy enough to study and sleep next door.

Neither of us ever heard anything other than each other's snores. That is not to say that I was ever comfortable walking from the toilets to the room in the middle of the night, the black space of what was once a wall reminding me of why it was no longer there. We had the advantage of knowing each other before going to Maynooth. The two in the room at the other side had never met until they got there, and one neglected to tell the other he was a sleepwalker. When the other student woke during the night to see his companion moving around, he began to shout at him not to jump. The matter was quickly sorted out by the college authorities by giving them separate rooms in another part of the building.

The Tower of Babel has always come to mind when I have thought back to those first days in Maynooth College. Although all ninety-three of us were supposed to be speaking the same language – English – we had great difficulty in understanding each other's dialects. The variations from Cork to Derry, Galway to Kildare were so pronounced that it seemed we were all speaking different tongues. We went onto silent retreat before we had time to adapt to our differences in accent and dialect.

The thing I remember most from that first retreat was an overwhelming desire to sleep during lectures and sermons. I would wake up with a start and think of Christ's reprimand to his apostles in the Garden of Gethsemane: "Could you not watch one hour with me?" Here I was after giving myself to Jesus and I couldn't stay awake for ten minutes, never mind an hour.

At first, I blamed the hard physical work I had done all Summer for my tiredness, and the fact that I had worked right up to the very last day. Then there was the heat in the chapel, from the Indian Summer sun on the copper roof and through the stained-glass windows. A look around told me that I was not the only one heavy with sleep, and I began to realise the preacher was not exactly taking the roof off the church with powerful speech. I came to realise with some regret that the physical act of going to Maynooth had not turned me into an instant saint. I was still all too human.

The Spiritual Directors were Vincentian fathers, kind and good confessors, which, as their title implied, was probably their main purpose. Most of them did not set the world alight as preachers, though I do remember one statement that helped wake me up. It was a late evening lecture and I suspect the preacher had at least one glass of wine with dinner. After reading the scriptural passage about Abraham being called on to sacrifice his son, Isaac, he announced: "Before very long all of you will be asked to sacrifice your little Isaacs." It didn't take much to work out what exactly he meant.

I hadn't known what to expect from seminary life but soon found out the main thrust of the day had more to do with study that could be described as secular rather than with spirituality or prayer. Apart from morning meditation and mass and evening prayers, most of the day was, from an academic point of view, little different than that of any degree student, or even from life in secondary school. Lectures and study were still the main focus of the day. The main difference was that we were free to study or not in the evenings. Although expected to be in our rooms or the library, there was nobody to check were we working or not.

I soon found out that it had been a mistake to cremate my Greek grammar, the Diegma on the college refuse incinerator on the way out from my last Leaving Cert examination about three months previously. I was back to the old subjects at a slightly more intense level. The response to the first exercise I sent to the Professor for correction caused me more than a little surprise. The male horse I had sent across a river in one of the sentences for translation was female when she arrived at the other side. This drew the sarcastic remark from the Reverend Professor William Meaney: "What happened in midstream? Did a shark bite it off?" It was easier shock me then than now.

I think there was more intended than giving my classmates a laugh at my expense. I feel the Professor set out to shock, to open our eyes, to show us there was more to literature, Greek, English and otherwise than the fairly innocent reading allowed by Irish censors and available to us in either spiritual or recreational reading. He tried to open our eyes with Lucien's "*Vera Historia*," or the Greek playwrights, from whom he generally appeared to select the most – to my then eyes - outrageous pieces.

Around the same time Father Peter Connolly, Professor of English in Maynooth, gained national prominence, if not notoriety, by publicly praising the novels of Edna O'Brien, which, as far as I know, had been banned at the time. Although few might care to acknowledge that now, I think such a courageous stand – in the climate of the early sixties – led to the repeal of the censorship laws during the Justice Ministry of Brian Lenihan.

One of the funnier episodes of the time was the night that famous Cork-born short-story writer, Frank O'Connor was invited to address the students in what was to be his last public appearance before his death. He would not naturally have been on the top of Maynooth's wanted list of famous speakers, as he had not spared church or clergy his acerbic tongue, though some of his stories show a great understanding of the humanity of priests.

The literary society which invited Frank O'Connor to speak pulled a little wool over the eyes of the authorities in the process. They sought permission to have Michael O'Donovan address the students, and as there was nobody with that name or surname on any blacklist, permission was duly granted. It was reported that people in high places were fit to be tied when word emerged that Frank O'Connor had addressed the student body, though they were too embarrassed to admit they didn't know Frank O'Connor was the pen-name of one Michael O'Donovan. The blow was softened by the kudos gained when it emerged a few weeks later that the Cork-man's last stand was inside the very walls of Troy.

XIII

"Never set your foot on the path of the wicked.
Do not walk the way the evil go." [Proverbs 4:14]

Eve Adams sat up in bed with a start. She was delighted to be awake and well after her nightmare, but scared and frightened at the same time. She had dreamt that Abigail was under water. She was covered with flowers and petals in a way that reminded her mother of a picture of Ophelia in a book of Shakespeare's plays, except that Ophelia was dead above the surface. When Eve had tried to wade into the water to reach her daughter, her legs were heavy and slow, dead weight beneath her. It was then that she woke up with a start: "Oh, Sweet Jesus…"

She was about to say "Save her," but didn't need to as it was only a dream. She was still in the bed she had shared with Bill Brown for the afternoon. This must be divine retribution, Eve thought, after her afternoon of illicit passion and pleasure. Abigail must be in some kind of trouble or danger.

Eve had lain back in the bed after Bill left, still angry with him for putting his wife and son's churchgoing before her. All she had to do was gather up her sheets, tidy up the apartment and pull the door closed after her. She had obviously fallen asleep and slept much longer than she might have expected. Night was falling and she was cold and naked in the bed.

Eve searched in her bag for her mobile phone, then remembered that she had left it in the car. She tried the phone in the apartment and felt lucky that it was working. She was even more delighted when Abigail answered their home phone, alive and well. That got rid of the daft thought that her daughter had gone in the water as revenge for not being brought to the shops.

"What is it Mom?" Abigail asked when she thought her mother was going over the top asking was she alright and telling her she loved her and always would. "Are you drunk or what?"

"Such a thing to say to your mother."

"Sometimes you drink gin with your friends and get a bit tiddly." Abigail giggled. "I hope that you are not driving."

"I had absolutely no drink," her mother assured her. "I am sorry I didn't take you with me to the shops, though. Next time?"

"I don't mind." Eve could see Abigail shrug in her mind's eye the way she always did when saying she didn't mind something or other. "Did you get me anything?" her daughter asked.

"How could I forget my little darling?"

"Are you sure you are alright, Mom?"

"Why are you asking that again?" Eve asked crossly.

"You are talking a bit strange. What did you get me?"

"You'll see soon enough. A surprise."

"A big one or a small one?" Abigail asked.

"That's for me to know and you to find out." Eve was wondering where would she find a shop open at that time on a Saturday night.

"Dad wants to talk to you," Abigail said.

Adam's first question was: "Where are you ringing from?"

Eve realised the number would have appeared on their home phone so she did some quick thinking: "I ran into a friend from school and came back for a cup of coffee to a flat she has rented."

"Which friend?" His question sounded almost too casual.

Eve was surprised at how quickly she was able to snatch a name out of the air: "Amanda. She was one of the boarders. You wouldn't know her. We hadn't met for ages. She is something in IT. You know the way. We started yapping about this and that, kids, school, teachers. The evening drifted away and I didn't get to do any shopping. Don't tell the kids. I'll pick up something for them on the way home. I'll be delayed a bit doing that. Is everything alright there?"

"Fine, but don't be too long, because we have a lovely dinner prepared. The kids were great doing the vegetables," Adam said. "Maybe you could pick up a bottle of wine with the other things on the way home."

Eve felt that she had enough to do getting presents for the children: "There are four bottles there on the rack. That is unless you went on the tear for the evening."

"This is a special occasion," her husband responded, "and it deserves a special bottle of wine."

"What occasion?" Eve began to rack her brain. Had she missed a birthday or an anniversary?

"You will find out when you get here. Hurry. We need you, we want you, we love you," Adam said airily before hanging up.

The only shop Eve found open was the local petrol station. The older shops still clung to the old tradition of closing at the time mass was held on a Saturday night or Sunday morning. Her choices were greatly reduced, so she bought two colourful footballs for her soccer-crazy children and the dearest bottle of wine in the shop. She did not recognise the label but hoped that expensive meant good.

Eve still felt she was in a state of considerable shock following her dream about Abigail, so she resolved never to see Bill again, difficult and all as that was going to be. He had brought excitement to her life, not to speak of pleasure and passion. He was a fast learner. It was not that Adam was poor in that department but their lives together had become boring and repetitive. It was as if the grind of daily life had worn away the excitement with which they had started out together in married life, and the even more exciting period that they had lived together beforehand.

"Is this all that there is to life?" Eve had asked herself one Monday morning after dropping the children off to school. Adam was at work. The day stretched long before her. It wasn't that she could plan a pleasant day, a while in the gym, a while in the swimming pool followed by the Jacuzzi. Legs could be waxed, facials arranged, hair done. There were art exhibitions, films, shops. All enjoyable for a while but ultimately lacking in satisfaction.

Eve had a good job in the Bank before she got married, better than Adam though he was never prepared to admit as much. She gave up work before Cian was born and didn't return because Abigail was on the way soon afterwards. Adam and herself had decided she would stay at home then until the children had started school. When that time came, they were well enough off not to need the extra money. Eve knew she had slipped behind in the promotion stakes, and decided not to return to work in her old position.

Adam had proved in the meantime that he had the Midas touch. His investments in Spanish rental properties had paid off big-time in the glory days of what had become known as the Celtic Tiger. They had retained one beautiful apartment for themselves in the Canary islands with access to a communal swimming pool shared with just three other families. Quite often they had it completely to themselves as the other holidayed at different times. The area was too hot as far as Eve and Adam were concerned in mid-summer, so they avoided those times, charging extra rent of course at the same time to eager holiday makers.

Eve had been thinking for some time of how lovely it would be if she and Bill could spend a fortnight, or even a week together in the apartment. The fact that her husband and her lover co-operated so closely in the development and sale of apartments might make this possible. They even had some kind of partnership agreement with Sharon and herself as shareholders even though neither of them played an active role in the business. The idea of giving a whole new meaning to sleeping partner was an exciting one.

The two families had holidayed together the previous year. It was partly a working holiday for the men, the wives and children around the pool for the most part. They shared some evening meals but more often than not one set of parents babysat while the other went out on the town. Sharon and Eve barely tolerated each other. The word hick was the quickest to Eve's mind when she thought of the other woman, someone that lacked style and breeding as far as she was concerned, good-looking enough in a homely kind of way but a couple of stone overweight. She was obviously a good mother, but they had nothing in common really, apart of course from fancying the same man. Anyway, Eve thought ruefully, that was not going to matter anymore because Bill and herself were no longer an item even though he did not know that yet.

As she drove home, Eve was determined to put every thought and desire she had about Bill from her mind. From now on she would concentrate on her husband and family. What if she had that kind of nightmare about Abigail if she was off in the apartment with Bill? She would be out of her mind with worry. She could call home, of course, like she had done earlier that evening, but would be thinking of danger all the time. She promised herself and God that she would accept her life as it was and be thankful for the comforts she had.

Abigail and Cian seemed less than enthusiastic with the presents she bought them. "Another ball," was her daughter's reaction. Cian looked at his with something approaching disgust: "I would prefer the colours on Abigail's."

"I prefer those colours too," his sister said.

Cian hopped his and allowed it roll into a corner as if he never wanted to see it again. "I hate girly colours."

Their father was getting annoyed: "What are they except something to kick? You should be glad to get anything. Let Abby have the one she wants," he instructed Cian who had picked it up. "She is the youngest."

Cian fired the ball at her forcefully: "She is a pet and she gets everything that she wants."

Abigail dodged and allowed the ball bounce against the flat-screen TV to get her brother into even more trouble. "I'm not a pet and I don't want either of them now."

Adam checked that the television set was not damaged. He was determined not to get angry and said between his teeth: "It's time for dinner. Wash your hands both of you." Cian reached the downstairs toilet first so Abigail ran upstairs.

"The competition never stops between those two," Eve remarked. "Were they like that all evening?"

"They were fine." Eve seemed embarrassed when her husband stood back and looked at her intently. She hoped there was nothing about her that would give away the fact that she had spent the afternoon with Bill. Adam opened his arms: "Come here and give me a kiss, thirteen years to the day since I first set eyes on you."

"What a memory." Eve was glad to know what the special occasion was. It was not something she would have been expected to remember, like a birthday or anniversary.

"Yuck," Abigail said when she came downstairs and saw her father and mother embracing and kissing in the middle of the floor. "Not in front of the children," she said grandly, quoting a phrase she had picked up from a television soap.

"I'm dying with the hunger." Cian acted as if he had not noticed what his parents were doing.

"Sit into the table," Adam announced solemnly, "until I release the duck from the oven." He addressed Eve: "Would you mind releasing the cork from that good bottle?

Eve searched the cutlery drawer: "Where is the opener?"

"That's not the bottle I mean," Adam said, "but the one in the fridge. It's only a half-bottle, but it is Moet and Chandon."

Eve laughed: "Far from champagne we were reared."

"That may well be," her husband said, as he set the duck aside to settle, "but it won't be true of the new generation. What will the two of you have to drink?" he asked the children.

"Champagne," they answered together.

"You are far too young," their mother shook her head.

"We had a little drop in the Canaries last year," Cian said. "It was lovely."

"And it went up my nose like a fizzy drink," Abigail added.

"When was this?" their father asked seriously.

"Both of you were drunk," Abigail said bluntly.

Her mother was not letting her away with that: "We were never drunk, and certainly not when we were minding the two of you."

"You sold a chalet or something," Cian reminded them. "Liam's Mom and Dad and himself were with us too."

Abigail roared with excited laughter: "Mom kissed Liam's Dad on the mouth because you were all drunk."

"Listen young lady," Eve said sternly as she avoided Adam's gaze: "You know as well as I do that it is wrong to tell lies."

"You did kiss him," Cian said, "and Abby kissed Liam."

Abigail kicked him as hard as she could beneath the dinner table. "I did not kiss him. I hate him." She wiped her mouth with the sleeve of her dress as if to remove traces of their non-existent kiss.

Eve attempted to downplay the kissing: "I remember that now. Of course, I do. Because your Dad kissed Sharon as well."

"A little peck on the cheek, maybe," Adam said lightly.

Eve looked crossly at Abigail: "That's the kind of kiss Bill gave me too."

Adam raised his champagne glass: "Well I hope we have nights like that again, apartments sold, money made. By the way," he said directly to Eve, "Bill tells me there is great demand for the units in the new development. They are flying out the door, despite the downturn here. Or because of it, maybe."

They clicked their glasses: "That should keep the wolf from the door for another while," Eve said.

"Bill has to go out there in a couple of weeks to meet planners in the local government," Adam said casually. "He asked me to go with him."

"Oh…" Eve wondered why Bill had not mentioned that to her. "So, the boys are off on holiday together?"

"Business, not holiday," Adam answered.

"Still you will manage a round or two of golf, I'm sure," Eve said lightly. "When the hard days work is done."

"The trouble is I can't go," Adam said. "Work commitments, and I don't want to waste my holiday entitlements on business matters." He looked at Eve directly: "Would you go with him? You are a partner in the business officially, and you could sign anything that has to be signed."

"That's when the neighbours would have something to talk about," Eve answered as if she had never heard such a silly proposal. "Bill and myself away on holiday together."

"As I said it's not a holiday, and we might lose valuable time if one of us is not there to represent our side of things."

Eve was very wary, fearing that Adam knew more than he was letting on. For one awful moment it occurred to her that this dinner might be all a sham, that he had poisoned the champagne, or the duck, or the sauce. She had heard enough stories of that nature about men scorned. But Adam. He wasn't the type. His own children? She put the thought out of her mind thinking she was getting completely paranoid. She still felt a shiver going through herself despite the warmth of the room.

Adam noticed as he stood up and put on an apron: "The champagne is rising in your head. It must be the hunger. I thought you might have had something to eat with … whats-her-name? Amanda?"

"We just had coffee and too much of it. It had me completely spaced. I'm sure the lovely meal will soon sort me out. Thanks very much for preparing it, by the way. All of you."

"You're welcome, Mom" the children said, almost together while Adam shrugged his shoulders and smiled: "Just enjoy."

Adam swung the carving knife exaggeratedly, the head of the household about to feed his family: "There is no way any of you are going to be hungry after this. Eve offered to take the vegetables and roast potatoes from the oven, but her husband told her to sit back and enjoy the meal as it was primarily in her honour.

"Do you think I am not capable of standing up after the champagne?" Eve joked. By now Adam had opened the red wine. He poured some for Eve and himself and about a table-spoon each for Cian and Abigail.

"Ah, Dad," Cian said. "That's nothing."

Abigail tasted hers and declared that she would prefer champagne.

Adam stood to propose a toast: "To the good times we have had together, and to those that are yet to come."

The others echoed his words, but Cian did not stand like the other two. He was already slicing into a piece of duck. Adam remained standing: "We have to do this right."

"Take no notice," Eve said about Cian. "Let him eat his dinner."

Adam remained standing, his glass raised: "Manners and formality re an important part of life. Cian eventually stood up, reluctantly.

"Now," Adam said: "Put your glasses together. "To times to come, health and happiness."

"It's like being in church or something," Cian said with a surly scowl, "standing up and sitting down every second minute."

Adam tried to explain: "We don't go to church regularly, unless there is a funeral or the wedding of someone we know, but there are other occasions just as solemn in life such as an important family meal. Those have their own rituals and traditions that are important to observe."

The meal continued in silence until Abigail asked suddenly: "Will we be doing our confirmation?"

Adam looked at her as if his daughter had just let him down in a serious fashion: "Why do you ask that question at this particular time?"

"No why," Abigail shrugged. "Well just because you said something about church. I got three hundred euro for my first communion but we were not at mass even once since."

Eve tried to ease matters: "Your Dad and myself have not discussed confirmation yet, because you are still too young."

Cian chimed in: "Liam will be doing his. His Mom and Dad bought him this cool suit, a bit like a soldier's uniform."

"The teacher was wondering who would be doing it when we were at school the last day," Abigail said quietly.

"What did he say about it?" her mother asked.

"That we have to make up our minds if we are for Jesus or against him, if we want to be confirmed or not," Cian said.

Abigail announced: "I don't want to do it because the bishop gives you a slap in the face and people are crying and everything."

"He barely touches you," her brother said. "Maybe girls would be crying alright. Cry-babies."

Adam spoke slowly and carefully: "Could we leave this conversation until such time as we are not in the middle of an important meal? I'm easy either way. Your Mom and myself will talk about it at another time."

"This is important for the children," Eve reminded him.

Adam was more cynical: "It's important to them how much money they get out of it. As a businessman, I have no problem with that, but this is not the time or the place to discuss it."

"Eve was not finished yet: "It is more important than that to the kids. Their friends will be doing it, dressing up specially for the occasion, and they could feel isolated if they are the only ones who are left out."

"There are no fancy dresses like first holy communion," Abigail said, "just everyone wearing the same kind of robe so that they won't be comparing, because some families have more money than others. That's what the teacher said anyhow."

Adam stretched out his hands in exasperation: "Can we drop the subject now?"

Eve looked him in the eye: "We can't make little of the children's feelings."

"We will discuss it sensibly and carefully without wine or champagne," her husband answered tetchily. "Now is anyone ready for another roast potato?"

The tension lasted for the rest of the evening despite efforts at polite conversation. At bedtime Eve surprised her husband by initiating the lovemaking in which she gave herself to him more fully than she had for a long time. As far as she was concerned, she was finished with Bill and this was how it was going to be from then on. She wondered at the same time had the passion earlier in the evening awakened that fire in her which surprised even herself. Perhaps it was the champagne, she thought as Adam slept quietly beside her. "I'll have to have more of that," she smiled to herself as she stretched like a cat in the sunshine.

Sleep did not come easily to Eve that night, probably because of her sleep in the apartment earlier. She got up and tackled the dishes which they had left on the dinner table until morning. She filled the dishwasher, cleaned and tidied, thinking through the events of the day. Eve told herself that she would see to it that their children were confirmed. From now on she intended to assert her own beliefs, get God on her side. That nightmare in the apartment had been a warning she intended to heed. And she could have as good a time with her husband as with any man.

Eve looked at the picture taken on a rowing boat on the river on their wedding day. She had been scared if the canoe would capsize but you would not know that from her smile. She had broken her vows. Perhaps Adam had too, but she doubted it. They might never get back the love they once had, she thought, but maybe real love was struggling along, making mistakes, trying to do their best for the kids. They had been resting on their oars, drifting on the stream, but there was nothing to stop them taking control of their lives again, making plans, doing more together.

In fairness to Adam he had made a big effort that evening with the dinner. It hadn't been perfect but how often was life perfect? Maybe that was her problem, expecting too much. Eve remembered the great times Adam and herself had in their young days, travelling around, camping here and there, just enjoying life. "We are well past the tent in the field now," she thought, "but there is no shortage of luxury hotels around the country, with spas and swimming pools and every kind of water treatment." She searched the Internet until she found and booked just such a hotel in Kilkenny. She printed out the information and left it on Adam's bedside locker. "He is not the only one capable of springing a surprise," Eve told herself.

XIV

Extract from Paul Godfool's Journal

Education is not all about school or college. In my second year in the seminary, I accepted an invitation from a classmate to join him in Birmingham where his two brothers and sister lived and worked. I got the train from Castlebar, the cattle boat from the North Wall and another train from Holyhead. I had never been on a boat before, never mind on such a long journey so I arrived fatigued in the Brum, as that great city was and still is known.

I had an address and I arrived at my friends digs while they were at work. I spent most of the day wandering around, carrying my bag and trying to stay awake. Although I knew that I would only be there for the Summer, I felt desperately lonely in this huge city. How would I be, I wondered, if I was emigrating for good? All was well when they returned from work, digs were arranged as well as the "start," a job with a subcontractor from Mayo.

It was the nicest job I had in the college holidays that I spent working in England. I have often felt that I got more education during those visits to Birmingham and London than I ever got in Maynooth. Education about and for life, education about emigration, about work, about people of different races working side by side, although there was a certain amount of racism evident as well. I loved it there and the day came when a bomb in Birmingham affected me more than anything that happened in Northern Ireland. It was home from home.

We worked near the gasworks in Saltley that first year. A gas-pipe a couple of feet in diameter had been put down next to the canal. Our job was to shovel in soft sand from barges to prevent stones and rubble scraping the delicate protective covering that kept the pipe from rusting. We worked hard enough when the shovelling had to be done, but had a good rest as the barge was towed away for another fill of sand.

Water was leaking into a barge in which we worked one day, no threat to anyone as it only reached halfway up our Wellington boots. The ganger, Bert, was a kind Englishman who had served in the army in Burma. To make conversation, he compared our watery boat to the rice-fields he had seen on the other side of the world: "Just like the paddy fields, eh Pat." The Pat in question was a Cavanman and he did not take kindly to any Englishman disparaging the four green fields of Éireann, as he thought.

His shovel was raised angrily, and Bert got a concise, colourful and precise history of Ireland from the Norman invasion until that very day. He was told who built the motorways, the bridges, the tunnels, the houses and the high-rise buildings in England. Paddy had done it all. Paddy didn't want thanks, but he didn't want to be insulted either. The ganger is probably still wondering what he said to deserve such a diatribe, but we heard no more of paddy or any other kind of fields. If he is still alive, I can imagine "The fields of Athenry" as sung at rugby and soccer matches, sending a shiver down his spine.

When I had settled in to job and digs I got a night-job as well, to try and earn as much as possible and be less a burden on my mother and family. I became a barman in the Angel pub in Sparkbrook every night and all-day Sunday. The work I had done in Castlebar the previous year was a big help. The hardest thing to learn was the penny difference in the prices of drinks between the four rooms that opened off the central bar.

The Irish for the most part occupied one of those rooms, Pakistanis another, English a third, with a mixture of races in the fourth. My head was addled at first trying to remember the penny differences and get change right. Soon enough I didn't need to even think, as many people gave the right amount anyway, or I got used to the different prices. I enjoyed the camaraderie and the conversation. It was much better than staying in a little bed-sitter all night, and I was getting paid as well.

I can still see myself and my workmates eating horsemeat steaks in an Italian café on the way home from work, or hear one of the defining songs of the era on the jukebox: *If you're going to San Francisco…*" We were far more likely to have sand in our hair than flowers, but we understood that life was changing, changing for the better as far as I was concerned. I looked forward to getting back to Maynooth and getting my teeth into theology, which I considered was what I was really there for. The BA and the philosophy were the starters. The main course lay ahead.

Although college rules were no longer as strict as they had been, it was difficult to return to a life ruled by bells from a life in which one was master of one's own destiny. Theology on the other hand I found to be a new eye-opener, as I tried to grasp the fundamentals of the faith, the core which had been overlaid with devotion, the politics of control as well as changeable social theories. I wanted to separate basic principle from foggy overgrowth. I felt a buzz of excitement in finding the church didn't need to be as she was, and has become again.

XV

When Father Paul Godfool returned to the presbytery after Saturday evening mass, he found Richard Scapegoat sitting in front of his computer. He wondered for a moment was he downloading child pornography, but a glance at the screen assured him that this was not the case.

I was just trying to access my e-mails," was Scapegoat's explanation.

"I would like to be asked before you use the computer."

"Sorry," Richard said: "I just presumed…"

"You might wipe out something important."

"Like your sermons?" Richard joked.

"Mock all you like, but it can help sometimes to go back over old ideas."

Richard asked: "Will I tell you how I found your pass-word?"

It hardly takes a detective to notice that most people use their surname. "I have nothing to hide," Godfool said bluntly.

"I should have waited until you returned, but I have no other way of keeping in touch with my relatives. They feel that there is a tap on the phone at home."

"Are the Guards that interested or organised?" Paul asked.

"It's not them but the gutter press. They targeted a fellow who was in with me and the family had to move out when he was fingered by one of those lousy tabloids."

Paul Godfool felt he should go easy on his old friend as he realised the implications of how he would have to live the rest of his life. He had put in his time, paid his debt to society. It was better not to push his face any deeper in the gutter. "Had you any tea?" he asked.

"I made a couple of sandwiches and waited for you to come back. As they ate, Richard asked: "How was mass?"

"The usual."

"Boring, you mean, as the kids used to say."

"If it is, it's my fault," Godfool replied, "for not putting enough effort into it."

"Is it true that people are taking more responsibility, playing a bigger part in the ceremonies?" Scapegoat asked.

"It is and it isn't. They are still inclined to leave a lot to the priest if they have one. Strangely enough, it's the places that have lost priests that are beginning to take responsibility, to run their own shows. And do it well."

"You're kept fairly busy so?" Richard asked.

"As busy as I want to be. I need to do something to pass the time," Paul said easily. "There's scarcity and scarcity in it."

"I'm not sure what you mean," Richard said.

"When I think of fellows who did this job a hundred years ago, when there were twice as many people, the roads were bad. He was lucky if he had a horse to get around on. No phone, no mobile, no car. We are spoiled in this day and age. There is no reason why I couldn't cover six parishes to do purely priestly work, so long as people themselves were organising the rest of it."

"But there are no replacements, long-term," Richard said. "Isn't that the real problem?"

"The solution is obvious. Ordain women. Ordain married men. Take back those who have left to marry and would be willing to work part-time or fulltime. There is only one thing stopping it. Misogyny."

"They'll never change," Richard said, "the boss-men in Rome."

Godfool shook his head: "They'll have to." He topped up their tea mugs before asking: "Do you miss it yourself? Priesthood?"

"I suppose I miss the routine. There used to be a little diary called 'The rhythm of the seasons.' I always like the way the church seasons fitted the passage of the year. Easter came with new growth, Whit with a few rattles of thunder and all that. I missed the kind of people you would visit on a First Friday, people who had lived, who were full of humour, and seldom complained even though they had more reason than most to do so. But you grow out of it when you are away in a place like I was."

"What do you intend to do?" Godfool asked. "have you any plan for the longer term?"

The answer was direct: "I could kill myself. Don't get me wrong. I'm not trying to be morbid or to look for self-pity. But it is the first option that stares me in the face when I look at what I have to live for. Nothing."

"It's that bad?" Paul asked.

"It would be easier to do it now than inside. At least I have a belt in my trousers. I'm not ready yet. Don't worry. I won't do it here. I won't let you down. You can see the tabloid headlines: 'Perv has a nerve.'"

Paul said: "You won't do it. You were never a quitter."

"A bloke has to quit when he's beaten," Richard replied.

Godfool tossed out an idea: "Isn't it a pity there is not some monastery that would specialise in taking in people who have nowhere to go."

"There is," Richard answered. "I spent my last five years in one of them, did my penance. It's a pity I had to ever leave it."

"I often wondered was that the reason monks were sent out to the Skeligs and monasteries like that long ago," Paul said. "To do their penance in a place where people they had offended could not take their revenge on them."

"Why don't you dump us out in the sea altogether?" Richard asked: "Get rid of the vermin and what caused the problems in the first place is never dealt with."

I think it's terrible that you have nowhere to go. That's why I suggested to the fox to give you some administrative job."

"I'd prefer the Skeligs to that," Scapegoat answered. "I could never step outside the door without the paparazzi after me. As far as I can see I have no choice but to go to some faraway place where there is not much notice taken of such things."

"Is there any such place?" Godfool asked.

"The law is not put into effect in some places. Any law."

"So, children have no protection?"

"They take their chance like everyone else." Richard stopped to think: "Don't get me wrong. I have no intention of ever ending up in any jail. Or being sentenced by some kangaroo court that might chop off a hand or worse. I'd just like the space to live a very quiet life and not interfere with anyone."

The two men sat in silence for a while, each deep in thought. It was Richard who spoke first: "I think there is some kind of comedy programme on the television. We've had enough of the heavy stuff for one night."

The programme was a competition between stand-up comedians, and the standard was varied, some genuinely funny, most trying to outdo each other in sexual innuendo and bad language. One poor man was so bad he was slow handclapped from the stage by the studio audience.

"I know how it feels," Godfool said.

"The slow handclap?"

"No, dying on stage. Or on the altar in my case. I have tried to tell what seemed like a reasonably good joke and the congregation looked up at me as if I just announced that the Pope had died."

"You mean out here in the church?" Richard asked.

"It's not bad here. People have a sense of humour, but I have been at weddings in town and my jokes went down like lead balloons."

Their attention was suddenly attracted by one of the contestants joking about religion. Some of it was good but he went on to call priests 'shites' and worse. The presenter led the applause and praised him highly.

"A bit over the top, I'd say," Scapegoat remarked.

Paul Godfool shrugged: "It's what we have to expect after all that has happened in recent years. Respect has to be earned, and we have thrown away whatever respect there was for us. He was just putting into words what young people think. Didn't you hear the round of applause he got?"

"I did, but I don't think he should be allowed to get away with it on the public broadcasting service."

"People get away with a lot worse." Paul felt uncomfortable that this might be interpreted as a dig at Richard so he moved on swiftly to say: "It's a free country and people can say what they like. We had censorship for long enough."

"I obviously can't say anything," Richard said, "but if I was in your shoes ..."

"The head would be chopped off the person who raised their head above the parapet about that," Godfool replied. "It would be inviting the whole weight of the media down on top of you."

"Have we completely lost our confidence?" Scapegoat asked.

"As a church we have, and as individuals as well. Most of the hierarchy are keeping a very low profile, and it is usually left to a spokes-person who is not one of themselves to make statements and take the flak."

"What about all these laypeople who are supposed to be the future of the church?" Richard asked. He pointed at the television. "That there was not funny. That was not comedy. That was naked bigotry under the guise of comedy."

Godfool shrugged as if to ask: "What can I do about it?"

Richard Scapegoat continued: "If that was said on TV about Protestant or Jewish or Muslim clergy, our illiberal liberals would be standing up in the Dáil and tearing their hair out because of it."

"Are you suggesting a fatwah?" Paul asked. "Another Salman Rushdie? That would just make a hero of the so-called comedian."

"Who am I to talk?" Richard Scapegoat tossed up his hands: "Let them at it. Let them tear down the oppressor? But what are they going to put in its place?"

"The funny thing I see," Paul remarked, "is that newspaper columnists and commentators have taken on the role they criticised Parish Priests for in the past, and they do not even recognise it. I heard one guy talking about clergymen on their High Nelly bicycles, but you should see himself when he gets up on his high horse."

"Giddy-up Nelly." Richard slapped himself on the thigh. After a little while he asked: "You wouldn't think of coming out of your own shell and giving them a blast?"

"You are more worked up about it than I am," Paul answered. "I suppose I have got used to that – shite, and I don't expect anything else. Do you want cameras at the door? What can we do except put up with it?"

"Spoken like a true martyr. But look at the man you profess to follow. Ok, he put up with insults and gossip, but he stood his ground when the Temple was being misused."

"I'd agree with what you said earlier that it is laymen and women who should take up the cudgels on matters like this," Paul Godfool said tiredly, "but apart from a few right-wing crackpots it seems that Catholics generally, clerical and lay have lost their bottle, lost courage and confidence, and we know why."

"They lack leadership," Richard suggested. "They would rally behind someone who would put into words what they feel."

"Find some fool other than me," Paul smiled.

Richard pointed at the television again: "Why should anyone pay a licence if they are going to be insulted like that?"

"Now, that's the best idea you had all night," Paul said. "That is probably the one thing that would waken them up. When you think of it, those who feel insulted by that could send that station to the wall if they withheld their licenses for a couple of years."

"Sure, the Government would bail them out."

"Would they?" Paul Godfool asked. "I'd say there are a lot of people in government who wouldn't mind teaching them a lesson. They would let them go very near that mythical wall before saving their skins."

"But how would it be read?" Richard wondered. "Perception is everything. It would be seen as just another example of the church trying to censor the media."

"One way to get around that would be to withhold some of the payment," Paul said. "Allow for the fact that most of what they do is good, but punish them financially for insulting what many people still hold dear."

"There you are." Scapegoat said. "Send them a hundred euro or so and let them sing for the rest."

"I'd be tempted, but I don't know if I have the courage to take a public stand about anything anymore. I would just end up drawing the ire of the media on myself. They hunt in packs and they protect each other."

"As far as I can see," Richard said, "the different newspapers hate each other's guts."

"Those in charge maybe, but scratch one journalist and you scratch them all. The conspiracy of the cocktail circuit I call it. They hang out in the same bars, eat in the same restaurants."

Richard interrupted the flow: "They only talk to each other."

"And that explains why they lack all sense of balance and are so out of touch with the people of the country."

"Who lacks balance now?" Richard Scapegoat asked. "I thought you were the most sensible one of us but you are really the most cynical."

"About the media I am," Paul Godfool acknowledged.

"Well why don't you take action so?"

"I just might set the ball rolling. Offer them part of my TY licence and see what they say. I can always pay up if I lose my nerve." Paul looked at his watch: "Time for an old stager to go to bed."

Richard was enjoying the conversation and begged him to stay up another while: "You don't want to turn into an old fogey yet?"

"I have to face a couple of congregations in the morning, unlike you who can sleep until midday."

"I could say the masses for you," Richard suggested. "Give you a break."

"I know…" Paul left the rest of his answer hanging in the air.

"The fox wouldn't like it, of course."

Paul frowned, unsure of himself: "In fairness to him he didn't say what to do apart from not really letting you out of my sight. That means I couldn't sleep in and let you go on the altar on your own. And there is also the question of the mass servers. I better go ahead with it myself and give it a bit more thought during the coming week. This is all new to me."

"I won't put any pressure on you," Richard answered resignedly. "By the way, thanks for tonight. It was almost like the old days."

"You seem much fonder of the old days than I am."

"I see it now as a kind of golden age, the life I had before I messed up. For you the past is just the past."

Paul shrugged his shoulders: "Once around the block is enough for me. It's not that I haven't enjoyed a lot of it, but one spin is enough on this particular marry-go-round."

"Do you still believe in the other life?" Richard asked, or have you grown cynical about that as well?"

"I hope that something good awaits us, and I preach the Christian message at every funeral. If there is nothing there, it wouldn't bother me, because I wouldn't know either way anyway. It would be just another kind of eternal rest."

Richard pondered: "There are days I believe and days I don't. It seems to depend on what mood I awaken in each morning."

"I'm almost too tired to think seriously about anything most of the time," Paul Godfool admitted, "unlike long ago when we sat up half the night mulling over the great questions of theology and philosophy."

"For all the good that it did," Richard remarked.

"I suppose young people have to put the great questions of life because they are new to them, and so exciting."

"And then they find out that the same questions have no answers," was Richard's comment. "And that it doesn't really matter one way or the other anyway."

"I suppose that we are too hung up on logic in this part of the world," Paul replied. "Friends of mine who worked in Africa say most people there could not even imagine there not being a God, whether it's our kind of God or some other."

"Maybe they are right, or on the other hand you might say they are simple and have not begun to ask the big questions yet."

Paul Godfool had his own view on the matter under discussion: "It's as if Adam and Eve have come back to Eden and given God the push."

"But are we likely to send a saviour to rescue God the way he is supposed to have saved us?" Richard asked before answering his own question: "Not bloody likely."

"Perhaps God has enough of us and just wants a bit of peace. He is tired of getting the two fingers from the human race."

"God is not getting the two fingers from most of the world," Richard reminded him, "only from the so-called West. And what are we but a pimple on the backside of the world?"

"Maybe we backed the wrong horse, the wrong God?" Paul suggested.

Richard continued with his own theme: "Look at the influence of religion on Presidential and other elections in the United States. European journalists can't seem to get a handle on that at all, and the influence of Islam is beyond their powers of comprehension altogether."

"It's the 'why can't everyone be like us?' syndrome," Paul said.

"Godless, gutless, dry shites." Scapegoat went on: "That's what I call them, the generation that rejected God, the dry-shite generation, because they lack wit and intelligence, not to speak of imagination."

Godfool smiled: "Now that's what I call a general statement, and like a lot of general statements it tars far too many with the same brush."

"Didn't you hear it yourself tonight in that so-called comedy programme? That was not comedy or wit. That was calling names and throwing dirt."

Godfool laughed: "Ten minutes ago we didn't know how strongly either of us believed in God. Now we are defending him as if our lives depended on it. And we are doing it by the very method our old logic teacher told us to avoid – argumentum ad hominem, arguing against the person."

XVI

Extract From Paul Godfool's Journal

For a church to argue against the availability of condoms, for instance, in the face of an AIDS epidemic, is tantamount to the criminal. Even the church's own argument of double effect, should allow the use of condoms to prevent the spread of disease. The people of God in general made up their own minds and ignored church directives in this area of life. The official church lost much of its credibility, especially among women, because the letter of the law seemed more important than compassion and human understanding.

I was a long way from centres of religious or theological debate the day Pope Paul the Sixth's controversial encyclical was published. I read about it on the *Daily Mirror* in a galvanize hut on the back of a lorry on the way to work in Perry Barr in Birmingham. My Irish workmates had little interest in the big story of the day. It is not that they were not religious, in the sense that caps came off and men blessed themselves when there was thunder and lightning. They were men of the world, who gave the impression that their sex drives and sex lives were in perfect working order, Pope or no Pope, although there was little evidence to support that claim.

The two men who shared a room with me never went anywhere except to the pub in the evenings, but they spent their days boasting about the blondes that had them so worn out they had to walk bandy-legged. There were always two in the big double bed across from me, but it was the two mates sleeping off the night's pints. A Kerry-man was assigned the single bed across from mine one night. When I awoke later on, I wondered was there a leak in the roof, and if there was how come the water I was being sprayed with was hot. Failing to find the toilet, my comrade had decided to relieve himself into the fireplace, and I was the recipient of the spray which ricocheted from the tiles.

I probably learned more about the harshness of emigrant life that year than the previous one. Pay was better but the work was much tougher. I was part of a work-gang that had to dig up a big electric cable and replace it with another. A digger had damaged one of six big cables laid close together. Some kind of oil had escaped from its core so it had to be removed. The cables were about six feet underground, and although a machine went down about five feet, we had to shovel out the rest of the soil with special beaded shovels that would not damage the cables. This was like trying to do a delicate job with a very blunt instrument, so we were often given ordinary shovels to speed up the work when there were no inspectors about.

I was down in that ditch with a number of other Irishmen the day the first man we know about stood on the moon. A big metal bucket we had filled with our diggings hung above us from a crane for a long time, its warning bell ringing because the bucket was overloaded. Nobody seemed to care. We were only paddies, dispensable and re-placeable, without status, union or insurance. The days "big step for humanity" was a world away from us in more senses than one. A job was being done, and if there was an accident, too bad. There would be others to take our places before we were even buried.

There was pity for nobody. The person too old or weak or injured got the road. I saw an Achill man, probably in his sixties, get weak as we pulled in a section of new cable. The ganger gave him a dressing down for wasting his time and sent him to collect whatever pay he was due from the office. We stood there and let it happen. Any step out of line and we would be following the man who had been "lamped off" to the office.

Most were working on the "lump" system, pay into the hand without tax, insurance, stamp or card, above all without question. Pay was "subbed" in advance for that night's drink, no talk of tomorrow. Dreams of going "back yonder," as Ireland was referred to, were just that, dreams. There was talk of "going home for Christmas" one of the years. Most knew them would never go "home," unless there was a whip around to send someone back if a parent died, or to send them home to "back yonder" if they died.

Those of us who were students worked inside the system for the very good reason that we would get our tax back later in the year. Gangers and agents thought us awkward and bothersome because anything other than the lump meant paperwork for them. They couldn't understand why we would want to pay tax to the Queen, as they saw it, but for me that tax was as good as money in the bank, a welcome boost to the finances sometime before the following Christmas.

I made an effort to raise some of these matters at the Union of Students of Ireland Annual General Meeting at Rosses Point in Sligo later that year. If anyone ever cares to read the motions on the agenda, they will find some of the more radical ones came from Maynooth. One was that students working overseas make an effort to unionise their fellow workers, and that attention be focused on the plight of Irish emigrants in Britain. The great student socialists of the day, who went on to careers in politics took no interest. Inter-college rivalries and the election of officers seemed far more important.

As I write this, I am aware that the happenings of different Summers spent in England are running into each other. It was not days spent behind shovel and jackhammer that affected me most, however, but the time I spent with the Simon Community in Kentish Town in London in the Summer of 1969. The founder, Anton Wallich Clifford, had spoken to us in Maynooth during the previous year and I had been greatly impressed by the man and his work.

Named after Simon of Cyrene, who helped Jesus carry his cross to Calvary, the community had been founded a couple of years previously by Wallich Clifford, a former prison and parole officer, who saw that many former prisoners ended up homeless on the streets, before generally finding their way back "inside." He wanted there be places available where those not welcome or wanted in hostels would be able to have something to eat, to wash if they wished, to sleep for the night, and to be treated with basic dignity.

Many town and cities now have branches of the Simon Community, refuges for those who have nowhere else to go. They are not always welcome by residents or business people, which is understandable enough because those availing of the service look rough or dangerous. Without Simon, though, many people would have an even tougher existence. When I reached Kentish Town in the Summer of 1969, I thought I had arrived in what was as near as possible to get to a New Testament Christian community.

I gradually got to know Wallich Clifford, his wife Marie Therese as well as other volunteers and nightly visitors. There was always a huge pot of soup on the range, and we scavenged the local markets for bruised vegetables, fallen tomatoes and leftovers at the end of the day, all of which were washed and added to the pot. Butchers provided cutaway meat and bakers, bread. We took turns on the night-watch so that there was always someone to answer the door.

I wondered at first how Anton, who looked such a thin bearded and wizened man of forty-two could have attracted and wooed such a beautiful twenty-one-year old as Marie Therese. Could I have been a little jealous? I understood as time went on. The thing I came to admire most about Wallich Clifford was his openness. Of all the people I have ever met, he has seemed the most open, the most ready to learn from life. Simon, being a new concept at the time, was a matter of trial and error. If one scheme or manner of operation did not work, another was tried, without any hand-wringing regret for what had gone wrong. This to me, seemed the mark of the true revolutionary.

XVII

Nora McCabe was afraid that her husband, Marcas, would get a heart attack after he had seen the television programme in which Roman Catholic priests were called insulting names. She was sitting beside him on the couch at the time, reading a magazine and not taking any notice of what was on TV.

Marcas was pointing at the television set: "Those crowd will have to be sued. It's worse they are getting by the day. Even Cromwell in his worst days was not as anti-Catholic as that lot."

"What in the name of God is wrong with you?" his wife asked.

"Don't tell me that you didn't hear it and you sitting beside me."

"My mind was so far away that I didn't notice a thing. I was remembering the children when they were young. Do you remember the day…?"

Her husband's mind was elsewhere: "What is the point of sitting in front of the television when you are not watching it?"

"What was said anyhow that was so bad?"

Marcas could not bring himself to repeat the perceived insults. He had in so far as possible never allowed curses of any kind to pass his lips, and still wore a little white star he had got in Training College in his lapel as a sign of this: "I couldn't repeat them," he said. "They were that bad."

"They are inclined to go a bit over the top sometimes," Nora said.

"Over the top?" Marcas was nearly shouting. "They don't know what over the top is. They have gone so far this time the Government should just take them off air and shut down the station. They should be ashamed of themselves, the television authority and the government."

"If you are so upset about it, why don't you bring it up at the next Cumann meeting. You have given your life to that Party."

"But it wasn't for the likes of that." Marcas pointed his index finger at the TV set as if it was a mad dog that had once been tame.

"No more than the morning paper," Nora said, "you shouldn't look at it if it is going to upset you so much."

Marcas was not listening: "I'll bet Padraig Pearse is turning in his grave at this very moment. Was it for this that red blood was spilt in 1916? I never thought I would hear myself saying so, but we were better off under the British. At least they had a bit of courtesy and civilisation about them."

"You mustn't watch too many of their channels," his wife commented. "As for bringing back the British…"

"That's not really what I mean," Marcas answered, "but I don't know why we have to take this from our supposedly national television channel."

"What can I do about it?" Nora asked. "There isn't much point in giving out to me about it. Write to them, or to the newspapers."

"I wouldn't dirty my pen writing to them," Marcas replied angrily.

"Well write to the local TD's so, or take the company to court. Don't be deafening me about it. I have enough to worry about."

Marcas was thinking out loud: "There wouldn't be much point in me taking them to court, but the priest could. It was him and his fellow clergy that were insulted on the programme."

"I don't think that it will bother Father Paul or any other priest. They have been called worse in recent years, and in fairness to those who didn't do anything out of the way, they put up with it with a lot of dignity."

"Well," Marcas said, they were not called the likes of this on national TV."

"I don't know what was so bad because you won't tell me."

Marcas tried to speak diplomatically as he said in a low voice: "Some of the words had to do with women's privates."

Nora began to laugh. She put her hand to her mouth but could not keep the laughter in. She just had to laugh uproariously.

Marcas looked at her angrily: "Are you drunk or something? I am trying to talk about a serious matter, and all you can do is make a mockery of it."

Nora tried to explain when she finished laughing: "I'm sorry, but I just couldn't help laughing when I realised that you are so innocent that you could not mention a part of a woman's body to someone you have been married to for more than forty years."

"It's a word I have never said in front of you and never will because I respect your privacy and dignity."

Nora began to laugh again: "How did you know it was a bad word so?"

Marcas spoke angrily again: "You can't even take the insult to God's representatives on earth seriously. I don't know you have the time. I don't know if you are the woman I married at all."

"Well I know," Nora laughed, "because I have put up with you from every one of those years. As for the priests, the best thing that ever happened to them was to be knocked down from their pedestals. They are as human and as sinful as the rest of us, and thanks be to God for that. I'd prefer a priest who was human any day than some kind of a bloody saint."

"There are sinners and sinners in them," Marcas replied. "There are ordinary sinners like ourselves and there are those devils who abused children."

"Those are fewer than three per cent," Nora said. "You can't tar them all with the same brush."

"Do you think I don't know that? That's why I don't like to see the rest of them insulted like they were on that programme tonight."

Nora was in no way perturbed about that: "That will wash off them like water off a duck's back. Aren't they well used to it at this stage? As long as they know that their own communities are behind them, they can put up with a lot."

"You'd pity them all the same," her husband said.

"Let them look after themselves, and let you say your prayers," Nora suggested. "It's well time for you to be in bed when you have to be up for mass in the morning."

"How can I sleep with all that on my mind?" Marcas asked. "Do that crowd on the television ever think that they will have to face the judgment of God?"

"I wouldn't think God bother them too much either way, and maybe they are better off. I'll make you a drop of cocoa. It always helps you to sleep."

Marcas had thought of a plan when Nora returned with two mugs of hot chocolate: "Do you know what I'll do after mass? I'll go into Father Paul in the sacristy and I'll offer some moral and financial support to fight that television crowd in the courts."

"You will do no such thing," Nora told him. "Anything we have we need ourselves, and we have our children and grandchildren to think of. Have you forgotten your own family? Or is this silly obsession with journalists more important to you?"

"They are big enough now to look after themselves, the children that is. They're big children now."

Nora was going around locking doors and switching off lights at this stage: "Finish up that drink, good man. It's time for bed."

"What's your hurry, woman?"

"If you wait up any longer some other programme will come on the telly and drive your blood pressure even higher. You would be a lot better off to go to bed and read a book if you can't sleep."

"I have nothing to read. I forgot to go to the Library."

"Isn't the house full of books?" Nora said.

"I have read most of them already."

There's the Holy Bible," she joked, but that might drive you mad too with all that wedding and bedding. Was it twelve wives Abraham had?"

"That was then and this is now," Marcas tried to explain. "Morality hadn't been worked out the way it is now."

"But there must have been a lot more fun then?"

Marcas stood in the middle of the floor, one foot in and one foot out of his pyjama bottoms: "Do you know what? You will soon be as bad as that crowd on the television?"

Nora was about to give a sarcastic reply until she noticed the smile on his face.

XVIII

Extract From Paul Godfool's Journal

The day James Callaghan brought the British army into Derry, I was in another derry, as derelict buildings were called, sharing a bottle with Manchester Fred, a tall thin man with a snow-white beard, and a former RAF pilot from West Cork, whose name I will not mention in deference to his relatives. It's not that he had anything to be ashamed of for falling on hard times. He was my guide through the city, teaching me how to go anywhere on the Underground for sixpence.

This Corkman could charm the birds from the trees, and legend had it that one day he actually sold a derelict building to a developer, before informing him it was not his to sell. He would sometimes visit old comrades in an army club and bring back a few pounds or a bottle. Like many others I got to know there, he was basically a happy man, free of the usual burdens of life, not at all the lonely depressed and desperate kind of person I had expected to meet among the homeless.

Because of the existence of the Simon Community, I would not have any great fears about ending homeless on the streets of Galway or some other city. It is not beyond the bounds of possibility if I run into difficulties in the priesthood. As was learned by Pádraic Ó Conaire and others, there is a companionship and freedom about life on the streets, despite the cold and poverty. I think I could feel at home being homeless.

The Troubles, as they are known, had broken out in Northern Ireland for about a year at that stage, though I don't believe anyone could have foreseen the carnage of the next thirty-three years or so. Emphasis was on civil rights at that stage, and it was not just in Ireland that marches were taking place to highlight the grievances of the Nationalist population in Northern Ireland. Hardly a Sunday passed that there was not a march in Birmingham while I was there, or a rally in Hyde Park in London while I was with Simon.

The earlier marches were good-humoured, similar marches for civil rights in the United States, or against the Vietnam War, being imitated. *"We shall overcome"* was sung virtually non-stop. It was like a kind of carnival for young and old which usually ended with a few speeches before people dispersed quietly. There was general anticipation that the authorities would grant the necessary reforms, even if grudgingly and under pressure, that there would be a fair voting system, disbandment of the B special police force, and life would revert to normal. As we well know this did not happen.

Of all those killed in more than thirty years I always looked on the death of an innocent man, Sammy Devanney in Derry as the real start of the Troubles. Word of his death filtered through during a civil rights march from the Bullring in Birmingham to a hall in Sparkbrook. The good humour of previous marches was replaced by tension. The young MP Bernadette Devlin was to address the rally that day, but she had cancelled due to Devanney's death.

There was an anger among the crowd that day that included Irish as well as English, as this man's death was seen as a major turning point. I can still see a wiry man in his fifties stand at that meeting in the hall in Sparkbrook. He was a communist, he said, who had walked up from Stoke, "to see Bernadette." He was like a man who had made a pilgrimage to Lourdes only to find there was no statue in the grotto. Although I didn't speak personally to him, I left there with a high regard for that man's commitment to his cause, and passion for it, as I wondered why had I not the same burning enthusiasm for what I believed in.

I saw communists of a more cynical variety in London. It was clear that they had long experience of marches and of how to rouse a crowd. They would begin with slogans nobody on those particular marches would question, "Brits out, North and South," for instance. As the march progressed and people echoed every slogan, they would change from shouts that had to do with Northern Ireland to anti-police slogans in general.

There would be a rush at the police at the end of the march, as a letter was being handed into Number 10 Downing Street, or wherever. I never quite understood whether they expected the whole crowd to join them in a general riot, or did they themselves just want to be arrested as martyrs for their own cause. The vast majority of those marching left them to it, and dispersed peacefully while the handful of activists were being bundled into police vans.

These methods of street politics had an obvious influence on methods I have used over the years to make political and social points, picketing, protests, forty-eight-hour fasts, etc. In that sense I can still claim to be a child of the sixties, though a fairly hairy child at this stage. My heroes were Mahatma Ghandi in India and Martin Luther King in the United States, the two leaders most effective in the last century in bringing about change by non-violent methods. There obviously had a big influence on John Hume, Austin Currie, Ivan Cooper and many of those involved in civil rights in Northern Ireland. Civil Rights were on everyone's lips at the time, from South Africa to the Gaeltacht areas at home.

I returned to Maynooth more a political animal than I had been. The college was now open and very different from the almost monastic atmosphere of when I had gone there first five years earlier. The number of students who were not for the priesthood had increased dramatically, young men and women in the bright colours, flared trousers and bright dresses of the hippie era flooding the grounds, the new coffee shop and the classrooms. There was a flurry of building activity in what used to be the potato fields across the road, and the word "campus" became part of college vocabulary.

The TV series, "The Forsythe Saga" was popular at the time, and a name not unlike that, the four shite saga was used to describe a particularly excruciating and boring morning's theology that seemed untouched by the changes wrought in the church by the Second Vatican Council. There was an unease and anger among the students at the quality and relevance for the emerging world of the theology being taught.

This unease led to a student strike, which soon led to rumours that the hierarchy were about to expel the ringleaders, or possibly one whole class. The President, Dr. Jeremiah Newman, later bishop of Limerick came to a public meeting of theology students one night, and with tears in his eyes, told us his head was on the block as a result of the strike. The will for further action dissipated, the strike ended, but there was little sign of improvement in the quality of, or the teaching of theology, the staple diet of our training.

Other memories of the time point to a sense of humour as well as a seriousness among the students. The college swimming pool was seen as a potential source of sin and scandal, now that there were women on the campus. A rule was made which left an hour between the time the last male left, and the first female entered the swimming pool. No man's desire was expected to survive an hour in a shower, and this holy hour was quickly dubbed the safe period, a phrase well known in an era in which natural family planning was being strongly encouraged. Dr. Kevin McNamara, as Vice-President signed his name to that particular edict, and it was not long on the noticeboard until a line had been drawn beneath Vice in his title.

I was a class representative on the student's council about that time, and I must say that I found the President, Dr. Newman, both courteous and helpful at all times, and willing to listen to student complaints on practical matters to do with food and facilities. I say this in an attempt to balance his reputation in later years, when things seem to have become too much for him, and he acted aggressively as well as treating some excellent students unjustly and unfairly. When I knew him, he seemed to have a vision for Maynooth, and I still remember that it was from his lips I first heard talk of the need to prepare for the twenty-first century.

One thing that did anger him around that time was a picture of some of his students on the front page of *The Irish Press* under a banner, "Victory to the Vietcong." U.S. President, Richard Nixon was in Dublin at the time, and a number of us were out to express our disapproval of the Vietnam war. Some students inadvertently found themselves beneath that particular banner, though, in fairness to them, I would say they wanted an end to the war, without a victory for anyone. Looking back thirty years later, it could be claimed that we are such a broad church that some branch of it always manages to be on the winning side.

Another movement that took us on to the streets was the anti-apartheid protests against the visit of the South African rugby team, the Springbocks, to play Ireland in Landsdowne Road. It was there I first heard of Nelson Mandela and was privileged to walk the same footpath as Kadar Asmal, now a Minister in the government of a South Africa, he believed he would never see again in his lifetime. Other people I recognised from television were Máirín De Búrca and Tomás MacGiolla, prominent in Sinn Féin at the time. One of the best slogans I ever saw was outside that stadium, "IRFU – FU," the IRFU in question, for the uninitiated, being the Irish Rugby Football Union.

A series of marches were organised that year which were to bring students from all quarters of Ireland to Dublin to take part in a demonstration for all forms of civil rights, from contraception to political and social equality. I waited on after the Easter ceremonies and headed for Dublin on Easter Sunday evening. Students were gathering from Cork, Galway, Belfast and Dublin. Even the more radical were often under pressure from home. I heard of one leader who had a message sent to him from his father by roundabout means not to be publicly associated in any way with the making available of condoms.

In Trinity College that night I heard a passionate speech from a young graduate which had me wondering why, if the revolution was already taking place, I had heard nothing about it. I was told his thesis on Marxist economics was one of the best ever written, and that he would go places. Were we so protected and brainwashed in Maynooth, I wondered, that we had been completely kept in the dark about the realities of political life?

Hitching West the next day, I got a lift from a man who, whatever else, was not a left-wing revolutionary. Joe Foyle was on his way to the Christus Rex congress in Breaffy House in Castlebar and he was kind enough to drive me to my mother's door. Like those on the road to Emauus another Easter, we got to talking on events of the day. I told of my experiences of the previous night, and he told me he was aware from a newspaper article who the fiery young revolutionary who had impressed me so much was. "Watch him," he said, "until you see how quickly he ditches his Marxism and becomes a millionaire." I did, and I know he certainly made his fortune.

Not all, and not by any means a majority of Maynooth students were involved in protest, except perhaps for marches for civil rights in Northern Ireland. The majority kept their heads in their books and their noses clean. That is why they are in positions of authority now and I am at the bottom of the clerical barrel. Would I change places? That is the question, and the answer is no. Well, nearly no. Give me one week in the chair of Saint Peter, and I will return to my humble curacy, my work done, women ordained, priests married, sins forgiven, or at least absolution given more generously than it is now.

Not all of my time during those years was spent in political protest. Apart from attending lectures and doing some theological and in particular, biblical study, I got involved in stage dramatics. I was never an actor, in the stage sense anyway, but I worked backstage, making sets, and lighting scenes. This gave me opportunities to see drama from the back and the side as well as from the front. The words of a drama would be heard fifty times or more by the person working the lights, and especially if different lighting was needed for nearly every scene.

Involvement in drama helped me escape the humdrum life of the college in other ways as well. As a thanks to the Aula Maxima Committee for our voluntary work, we were allowed travel to Dublin to see plays or pantomimes in various city theatres. Among those I remember were a dramatised version of Brendan Behan's *"Borstal Boy,"* John B Keane's *"Big Maggie,"* Tom Murphy's *"The Morning After Optimism,"* and *"The Sanctuary Lamp,"* Tom Kilroys *"The Death and Resurrection of Mr. Roche,"* and *"The King of The Castle"* by Eugene McCabe, as well as seeing Maureen Potter, Rosaleen Linehan and others in revues, pantomimes and other kind of show.

Life was varied and exciting for students for the priesthood both inside and outside the college at that time, a vast improvement, a different world almost to what it had been three or four years previously. Every now and again, an effort would be made to reintroduce some stringency to the rules, but it was generally accepted that there was no going back to the old days.

One new rule introduced without consultation with the students' union was that clerics would have to sign themselves in at the gate-lodge when returning to the college at night. The book would be brought to the President's office for inspection next morning. Four of us were returning late one night and signed ourselves in in the names of our four Archbishops, William Conway. Dermot Ryan, Thomas Morris and Joseph Cunnane. That particular book was quietly withdrawn. Point made.

Maynooth students, as Irish citizens, had always had the right to vote in general elections, but it was only in the late sixties that canvassing or speeches from politicians were allowed. The first example of this, as far as I am aware, was during a by-election in Kildare. Paddy Power TD spoke on behalf of Fianna Fáil, and Senator Jimm Dooge for Fine Gael, both with the blessing of the authorities. That seemed to be that until someone thought to phone the Labour Party office which sent Dr. Noel Browne down to talk to us.

I still remember the hush in Loftus Hall as people strained to hear Dr. Browne, who began to speak in a very low voice. You could hear a pin drop as he talked of his parents and of a childhood in places like Ballinrobe and Athlone. He spoke of the effect tuberculosis had on himself and his family, the lucky break he got which led to him being educated in England. Then of his time in Trinity College, as a young doctor, TD, Minister.

Noel Browne spoke of the first John A. Costello led coalition government, the fight against TB, the mother and child scheme, his resignation, the fall of that government and his subsequent political career. It was like listening to living history. He did not mention the Labour Party, or its candidate, Joe Bermingham, but it is said that seventy-five percent of his listeners that evening voted Labour the next day.

When I look back now at the verses or attempts at poetry I was writing at the time, I see that my Summers in England had a big effect on my consciousness and imagination. I see the pneumatic drill or jackhammer in the image of the cross: *Crucified, throbbing on a jackhammer..."* I was seeing or at least trying to project myself as a member of the proletariat.

I began work officially as a priest a couple of months after ordination. I hated my new job as Prefect of Studies in the local minor seminary. I felt that my time as a student had been wasted. I felt that everything I had learned in order to do God's work, as I saw it, wasted. I was basically a nanny babysitting the children of the middle classes. Boarding schools of this nature had been founded in almost every Roman Catholic diocese in Ireland at the beginning of the nineteenth century, to educate young men, in the hope that some of them at least would go to train for the priesthood in colleges in major seminaries such as the one I had just left, St. Patrick's College, Maynooth. Those who did not become priests were expected to be good Catholic laymen, so the church was in a no-lose situation.

As Prefect of Studies my job was to preside over and keep discipline on about three hundred students in a huge study-hall for three hours or so every evening, six nights a week. I felt that it was a policeman more than a priest that was needed for such a job, but who else would do it? I did have some religion classes, which gave me some semblance of priesthood. At morning Mass in the sacristy of the college chapel, my congregation was two nuns. I had no axe to grind with them, but felt that it was not for this that I had been ordained.

Having been deeply influenced by the worldwide civil rights and anti-war movements, it was against my principles to use corporal punishment, even though that was still the chief method of discipline in the college. Attachment to my principles meant that some students took advantage of the lack of physical punishment, and there was danger of the situation getting out of hand. Some of the older students appreciated what I was trying and they agreed to help keep discipline on the younger ones in the desks nearest them. I was gone, however, before that method was properly tested.

Just before the November break, I had an article published in a weekly newspaper under the title: "The Dog Collar – From The Inside." I gave vent to my frustration with the work I was expected to do as a newly ordained priest. "Supervising the rat-race from the inside of a dog-collar certainly wasn't my idea of priesthood," I wrote, "but here I am, a three-month-old baby priest providing a police service for those parents who can afford to send their children to secondary boarding school…"

I continued, with a kind of mission statement of what brought me to priesthood in the first place: "And yet I was delighted to be ordained priest of this Church, to get a chance of serving God and people, mainly by making the body of Christ present in the form of bread and wine, by absolving sin in his name, and by preaching his gospel – the gospel of Jesus Christ according to me and as understood by me, from a particular background, with my chips on my shoulders and my axes to grind. And God is foolish enough to let me do it, just as he is foolish enough to let the Church I have been criticising speak in his name. He has got his way of doing things."

I made it clear that I had not completely lost confidence, that I still had some idealism mixed with my naivety and not a little innocence: "I still look to the faraway hills, to the excitement of serving God, the elusive God who is just beyond our grasp, who is too big for us to see, who is the great Lord of contradictions… And (I look forward) to serving man, the great searcher of the real God and the great buyer of contradictions."

That said, I made it perfectly clear that I was far from satisfied with my job in in the diocesan college: "Seven years ago I decided to be a priest. I still want to be a priest… but the priesthood at the moment is a struggle with frustration – the frustration of being a non-priest, an ordained policeman, a spoiled layman." Within ten days of that article's publication, I was on the Islands ferry, sailing out the Bay on a frosty morning, the newly appointed curate of the smaller islands, Inis Haon and Inis Dó. Punishment, some said, but as far as I was concerned it was one of the best days of my life. I knew that I had a lot of problems to face, the Irish language, the sea, the loneliness and hardship of island life. I didn't care. This is what I felt I had been ordained for, so no problem was unsurmountable.

My bishop had to spend a few days in hospital for a minor operation at the time, and the question of why he was there was raised in the priest's refectory in the college. My replacement as Prefect of Studies, aware of my newspaper reference to a "three-month-old baby priest," is said to have replied: "He might be gone in to have another baby priest." That was the time bishops and priests were not generally known to have babies.

My exile was not my first visit to the Islands. I had gone to Inis Dó the previous Summer to try and brush up on my Gaelic, or Irish, before it was too late. I wrote an account of that first visit more than twenty years later in a locally produced book; "The Islands; A Personal View." It had such a profound impact on me that I remembered almost every moment of that magical day.

I began like this: "I set foot on the Islands for the first time on an August Sunday in 1970. I was on my way to the well of the Irish language, following in the steps of John Millington Synge, Pádraig Pearse, Douglas Hyde, Eoghan O'Growney and many more. As a student priest, I knew that I was likely to be posted at some stage to a Gaeltacht parish, and was preparing myself rather belatedly at the beginning of my last year for such an eventuality."

I had spent the previous couple of weeks doing voluntary work as a labourer on a building site on the outskirts of the City. Tired from the work and a beery farewell to my mates in the Trapper's Inn the night before, I slept most of the way out through the Bay on that quiet foggy Sunday morning. It was the noise of the boats anchor that woke me as the big ferry lay to about a hundred metres from an Inis Haon still cloaked in fog. I had reached a new world.

Currachs suddenly appeared out of the mist, frail looking basins of laths and canvas bouncing on the sea as men that spoke in an unfamiliar language collected people and cargo from the "Steamer" which then steamed on to my destination, Inis Dó. Here I was disgorged from the bowels of the ferry into a currach which was rowed ashore to a narrow slipway beside a stubby pier.

Although born and reared in the middle of Mayo, no more than sixty miles to the north, I was not ready for the culture shock of traditional homespun trousers and waistcoat type vest worn by the men, not to speak of their footwear of rawhide pampooties. The women were altogether more spectacular in brilliant red petticoats with multicoloured dream-coats of shawls thrown over their shoulders.

And then there was Irish, Gaelic, the language that I, the stranger did not know, even though I had spent the best part of twenty years at school and college. It came as an even bigger surprise later that day to hear the children of the house in which I was staying, speak in this Gaelic tongue that I was unpsychologically prepared to think of as a natural language. The use of patronymics too, I found strange, people being known by the names of their forefathers and mothers rather than by surnames.

Thus, began my romance with the Islands. The sun soon burned off the fog and dried the rocky grey expanse of limestone crag before shining out to reveal a blue sea, with the faraway Twelve Pins mountain range of Connemara and the skies overhead looking as if they had been painted by Paul Henry, on secondment from that great studio in the sky. The local priest had thrown me in at the deep end as regards practising my pidgin Irish. I was to visit every house in the island, doing a kind of census of those who had emigrated. This forced me to meet the people, speak the language as best I could, and above all, realise my inadequacy.

I returned to the Islands under a different kind of fog than that experienced on my first visit. I was introduced to two old men who came on the boat off Inis Dó, on their way to hospital. I found it hard to understand what they were telling me, but knew it was something to do with the evil eye. I think I groaned inwardly with the thought that I would have to face years of this kind of superstition. I was completely wrong, as I never encountered the likes again in all the years I spent on the islands.

As we sat listening to the radio at teatime, I remember the loud "Ssssh" with which my predecessor put an end to my ramblings. The weather forecast was on the radio and he told me: "You better listen to this, as your life could depend on it for the next few years." He was right. The forecast could be a matter of life and death for those having to cross between the islands by currach. Although my life has not depended on the sea for many years, as I write this, I still find myself listening to or watching the forecast on television with great interest.

The most dangerous and exciting aspect of being a priest on the islands at that stage was the Sunday morning crossing by currach between first and second mass. Each house on both islands took it in turn to transport the priest from island to island, a pleasant experience on a summer Sunday, a hair raising drama quite often on a wintry morning. With all due respect to the Gospel story of Jesus calming the waters, there was no way I or anyone else was going to fall asleep on the transom of a currach as he did on Galilee's lake. Waves like rows of two-storey houses thundered through the aptly named Foul Sound between the islands. Currents, tidal changes, and the sudden squall of wind that accompanies a shower caused further complications. The skill and coordination of the men on the oars was a beauty to watch and I always felt safe unless they began to show some sign of panic.

It takes a landlubber like me a long time to understand the sea. On a day I would look out from my window on a seemingly calm surface, men would talk of a *farraige mhór*, a high sea, and sure enough there would be a swell causing treacherous breakers along the shore. Another day the wind would have the sea alive with white horses, but the verdict would be: "Níl farraige ar bith inniu ann". (There is no sea at all today.) The swell is infinitely more harmful than the harmless splashes the wind would cause. I always had a sense of exultation afterwards. Maybe it was the excitement, the danger, or just the freshness caused by the sea splashing the face. When mass was over, the morning adventure on the sea had changed from the frightening to the romantic. The shape of the currach conjured up images of the shoe of Christ walking on the water.

XIX

"They knew nothing of the way of peace, there is no fear of God before their eyes." [Rom 3: 17-18]

Richard Scapegoat was readying a leisurely breakfast for himself in the priest's house when a knock came to the door. "You would think they would know by now what time the priest has mass on Sunday," he said aloud to himself. He hoped that the person knocking would go away, but it continued. Richard pulled a soutane belonging to Paul Godfool on over his pyjamas and answered the door. A well-dressed aging man stood before him.

"I beg your pardon," the old man said. "I was looking for Father Paul."

"Isn't he at mass?" Richard asked.

"He was, but he's not now. Mass is over this twenty minutes."

Scapegoat looked past the visitor in the hope of seeing Paul Godfool: "Do you want to sit in the waiting room?"

"Why not?" The man had slipped past him and entered the priest's sitting room almost unnoticed. He stood in the middle of the room rubbing his hands together. "It's much more pleasant in here than out there."

"You obviously know your way around," Richard said. "I'm readying a drop of coffee. Would you like a cup?"

"I'd like a cup alright, but only if there is something in it." The man laughed nervously at his own joke.

"Maybe you would like something stronger than coffee?"

"I'd prefer a drop of strong tea to anything else. If you don't mind. I haven't drunk anything stronger for more than twenty years. I had a bit of a problem with the hard stuff, but I managed to overcome it with the help of God." He held out a hand: "Marcas McCabe, formerly of the teaching profession."

"Richard, Dickie to my friends." Scapegoat shook his hand. He was wondering what was Paul had said about talking to strangers. So what? This fellow had brushed past him and he couldn't do much about it now. He had no notion of telling him his surname, or his real Christian name for that matter.

Marcas was looking at the loose soutane Richard had pulled around him: "I see you are in the same business as Father Paul."

"This actually belongs to Paul," Richard explained. "I pulled it on in case too much would be exposed. Letting it all hang out as they say."

Marcas half-frowned at that remark. "Are you long here with our priest? If you don't mind me asking?"

"I came yesterday. Just for a few days. We had a late night, as you might expect, since we hadn't seen each other for years."

"I was talking to Father Paul a few days ago and he never mentioned visitors, because if he had, I would have asked you both to the house to visit myself and Nora. That's the wife, the missus as they say. A great cook, the best in the business. The two of you will have to visit." Marcas winked: "Father Paul is a lovely fellow, but I don't think he is tops in the cooking department."

Richard colluded in their private joke. "I'd say he could boil one mean egg. Two maybe, in an emergency."

"I see you are a bit of a joker," Marcas laughed. "The two of you will have to come for your dinner this evening. Nora has taken a fine leg of lamb from the freezer and we'll be eating it for days if we don't get a bit of help with it."

"I suppose you had better discuss that with Nora first," Richard suggested. "And with Father Paul, too, because I don't know what he has planned for the rest of the day."

"I doubt if he has any plan," Marcas remarked. "There are no matches today because the pitch is too wet. What else is there to do around here on a Sunday afternoon?"

Richard tried to deflect a possible visit to Marcas' house, an idea which he thought of as being worse than a nightmare: "I'm sure Father Paul is tired, because we talked late into the night. And the lid came off the bottle – you know how it is yourself when old friends meet?"

"The lid came off and didn't go back. I had many the headache myself on account of it. It's grand when you are drinking it, but it's the devil out of hell in the morning."

Richard Scapegoat took the opportunity to keep the talk away from himself: "How did you manage to give up the jar?"

"Strong will. God's will and my will. It helped of course that the AA, Alcoholics Anonymous was starting in the village at the time. We have a meeting each week in the little room at the back of the hall, oftener if someone feels the need for it."

Richard felt he was playing the conversation like a fisherman with a trout on the end of his line: "There wouldn't be many alcoholics in a small rural community like this one?"

"There are, unfortunately. It is one thing to count those who admit their alcoholism, another to get those above in the pub at this very moment to admit that they have a problem."

"Do you think loneliness is the cause of it?"

Marcas considered before answering: "It's the cause of some of it, but the biggest cause without a doubt is what we might call male bravura, that we might sum up in the Irish word *gaisce*."

"*Gaisce*?" Richard was not sure what he meant.

"Hard men. You know yourself. Hard men in their own minds, brave men when they are at the counter, but they don't have the guts to try and deal with their problems."

"The zeal of the converted," Richard thought, as he kept control of the conversation: "I suppose some people go to the pub who have no problem with addiction?"

Marcas nodded his head slowly: "You could be right, but they are few in number. You have to remember I know those fellows since they were little nippers going to primary school, and I could tell you then which of them would eventually turn out to be alcoholics."

"You never could!" Richard was tempted to say that the example of their teacher might have had an effect on them, but he didn't want to rub the visitor up the wrong way: "Isn't it lucky for them that they have the likes of you to turn to when they are in trouble?"

"I do my best," Marcas said, as humbly as he could. "What can anyone do but his best?"

Richard nodded in agreement, but felt that he had been put on the back foot when Marcas asked: "I suppose it's on the missions you are yourself, Father?"

"I suppose every Christian is a missioner in a sense," he replied.

"True enough," Marcas countered, "but not everyone is called upon to convert the savage foe, as the poets might put it."

"There is more of a mission needed at home in this day and age than to the countries far from home that have more priests than we have."

Marcas winked: "I know what you are getting at now. The ones that need the mission most are that crowd in the radio and the television and the newspapers."

"Now you've said it." Richard sat back aware that he had hit the nail on the head. All he had to do now was sit back and allow Marcas give vent to his anger. It was if he had lit the fuse on a rocket. The old man was gone into orbit. This man might be a dry alcoholic, he thought, but he has found himself a new addiction. Anything to keep the questions away from himself, he asked, when he got a word in edgeways into Marcas' rant: "Well, did you notice that just the same as I did?"

The older man presumed Richard was home from the church's foreign missions: "I'll bet you don't recognise the country you left a number of years ago? It's gone to the dogs altogether. I'd go so far as to say it's gone to the devil."

"It certainly is not like it used to be."

"The upper-hand has been gained by those with no God, no faith, no morals. Island of saints and scholars, how are you. Island of bigots and blasphemers."

"I mightn't go that far." Richard's reply barely interrupted Marcas' flow of speech: "Things were not so bad until the devil went into some of the priests. A minority I must admit. They began to interfere with children – because they had no woman at home, I suppose."

"Do you think that was it?"

"They say there is no link between the two," Marcas said, "paedophilia and celibacy, but I don't agree. If a man and woman had a natural life at home, there would be no need to go messing with children."

"An interesting point of view," Richard remarked, as he tried to avoid any meaningful comment.

Marcas was definite: "I know it for sure. As a good Catholic I used to agree with Rome recently about not allowing priests to marry, but since this work of the devil came to light, I have changed my mind. God forgive me."

"Everybody has to follow their own conscience, right or wrong."

"Conscience my foot," Marcas almost snarled. "The ones who do those things to children have no conscience. Castration wouldn't be good enough for them."

"Some call it an addiction," was Richard Scapegoat's reply, "that those involved can't really help it. It's like kind of a sickness. A bit like alcoholism really."

"Sickness my arse." Marcas was suddenly embarrassed: "I beg your pardon, Father. I get carried away a bit on this subject. It's one thing to get carried away by the drink, but to start messing with little children is another matter altogether. You know as well as I do what Our Lord said about the likes of those. They should have millstones tied about their necks and be drowned in the depths of the sea. And how right he was."

"Some cultures think it's natural," Richard commented.

Marcas looked at him with a frown: "What country are you in yourself?"

"I'm in this country at the moment." Scapegoat hoped his effort at humour would defuse the situation.

His reply did not seem to register with Marcas as he continued: "If the people in the country in which you work think paedophilia is natural, they are certainly a long way from being Christians. There was no talk of that stuff among the pagans in this country before Saint Patrick came among us."

Richard threw another spanner in the works: "Plato and some of the other Greeks recommended it. You can ask Father Paul. He studied the classics as well as myself. In fact, we were the last class in the college to do so."

"I know all about Plato and those other devils. Do you think I never went to college myself? Tell me this. What does platonic mean in this context? The same Plato could have done with a touch of the squeezers.

Do you know what that is?" Marcas answered his own question: "A device by which a bull becomes a bullock. I never pined for the loss of the classics from the secondary school curriculum like others did. I knew the kind of thoughts Plato and the likes of him would put into the minds of the youth if they continued such studies in university."

Richard Scapegoat resorted to some flattery: "I'd say you are a very learned man, educated by schools of philosophy and of life. To my shame I've forgotten much of what I learned in those years. As far as I am concerned much of them were wasted translating dead languages."

Marcas was nodding his head: "I'll bet those languages were not lost on you completely. When you were off in those faraway lands learning new languages, I'll bet Latin and Greek words came to you quicker than the words you were searching your brain for."

"Now you've said it," Richard said, approvingly. "Have you travelled much yourself?"

"Years ago, Nora and myself and the kids, when they were young, went south in search of sun. But the wine was too cheap and too tasty for a man who was fond of a drop. After that we spent our time getting to know our own lovely country, North and South. We were often up in the Glens of Antrim, one of the most beautiful places in the world, when most people south of the border were too scared to go up there."

"Many a one has seen the whole world and hasn't got to know their own backyard," Richard observed.

"I'll bet that is a proverb from a faraway land?" Marcas said.

"A proverb is true wherever you go." Richard was pleased that he had managed to steer their conversation away from child molestation. What would this old codger think, he thought, if he knew where I had spent the last five years and why? It was strange to be talking so naturally to a man who would be happy to have him castrated. He looked at his watch: "I don't know what has happened to Father Paul."

Marcas settled himself in the big soft armchair: "He will be back, sooner or later, and he will have missed a fine piece of conversation. But at least we were not fighting."

"Sure, what would we have to fight about?" Richard asked lightly.

"There is something very healthy about good debate," Marcas said. "You gave as good as you got when you were acting the devil's advocate there on behalf of Plato and that crowd. In the end, I'd say we finished evens. I'm glad we met and I hope to see you at my place before you leave. Nora will enjoy the craic with you."

"Is she as interested in religion as you are?"

"She is especially interested in the missions. Herself and other women in the parish make priest's vestments and embroider them beautifully for what they call the apostolic work. Who knows but you might have worn a set of the same vestments far across the water unbeknownst to yourself?"

"Who knows?" Richard looked at his watch again.

"Don't let me be delaying you," Marcas said. "You might want to read your office, or take a shower or something?"

"Do I smell that bad?"

"You don't smell at all…" Marcas laughed when he realised that Richard was joking. He took a Sunday newspaper from under his arm: "I'll be having a read of this until Father Paul comes back.

XX

Extract From Paul Godfool's Journal

Islands can be places where tension builds because there is no outlet, nowhere else to go most of the time. Having done some three-month stints without setting foot on the mainland, I was well aware of the build-up of tension and isolation that can make small problems big, molehills mountains, that can make one forget that there is a world out there beyond the sea. That is one of the downsides of island life and it can affect the born islander as much or more than someone from outside. People need to get away from time to time.

I experienced some times of great tension while on the islands, all of which were associated with progress and change and how to deal with it. This manifested itself in disputes in particular about where piers should be built. As this was or had the potential to be a matter of life or death, it was only natural that views were deeply held and that people were willing to fight their corners. I tried to avoid taking sides as much as possible, but I tended to have a strong view, too, and never shirked from sharing it. That was a side of island life, and not the sea or the language, that I found most difficult.

This enmity would be quickly forgotten, or at least put on hold if there was someone sick or in trouble, and especially at times of tragedy or drowning. Memories include sitting at wakes while the noise of hammer and saw could be heard outside as the coffin was made in the yard, often by someone who would have made a currach for the man being waked. The coffin would be covered in a white sheet, and the stark simplicity always appealed to me in comparison with many of the ornate or even ostentatious coffins seen on the mainland.

There is a spirituality in the people that one notices in their attendance at mass, at rosary, and particularly at occasions of prayer in the graveyards, especially during the month of the dead, November. There are few other places where you would see young men doing the Stations of the Cross during Lent, or sometimes up to a fifth of the community at mass on days other than Sundays. One reason for this I would venture, is that people of the islands live in proximity to the elements, to the sea, to the danger of being drowned, to the perils of airplanes, to the dangers involved in fishing, to gales, storms, and to the high seas of winter that one would have to see to believe.

"Is mór an spóirt é an tAifreann," an old man said to me one day. This could be translated directly: "The Mass is a great sport," but this would not, of course convey his meaning, something more like: "Isn't the Mass wonderful?" He spoke from a deep faith, but he came from a generation that didn't depend on the Mass alone, as could be said of many Catholics today. He said "Read a gospel for me," (Léigh gospel dom) more often than "Read Mass."

The coming of spring and the return of the tourists always brought a great lift to the islands. One day a tourist wanders up the road. A rare flower blooms. A lark sings. A feed of new spuds, fresh salmon, spinach. There is swimming and sunbathing on big unpolluted beaches. I always thought that tourism was welcome on the islands more for the buzz it brings for a couple of months, than from the commercial point of view. The commercial side of the business is welcome, too, but it is of benefit to a relatively small number of people. Many people would make a sweeping claim that day-trippers with packed lunches leave nothing behind but litter. That is not to say, however that they should be discouraged. Many a day-tripper fell in love with the islands, returning again and again for longer holidays.

One of the things that impressed me most about the islands was the way the new and the old could comfortably co-exist side by side. I remember in my second spell there seeing a man winnowing corn in what is probably the oldest method known, beating a sheaf on a rock. A neighbour up the road worked on a state of the art computer knitting machine. There was no sense of competition, contradiction or comparison between old and new. They would have a pint together in the evening, equals.

This lack of contradiction between new and old can also be true in religious matters. I look on a pagan past more as a source of pride than of shame, and the fact that elements of that pre-Christian past have survived for fifteen centuries shows how deeply rooted it was and is. The very fact that the new religion "christened" holy wells, mountains and other religious sites was in itself a recognition of these as holy places. God was being worshipped on what is now Croagh Patrick long before any Christian set foot there, and I am as proud of one tradition as the other when I climb that mountain.

This approach is in the tradition of Saint Paul when preaching in Athens, drawing attention to the shrine to the "unknown God". He turned it round to say in effect: "Here is the God we know," and even though he did not get much of a hearing, his sermon was preserved as an example of building on foundations of faith already there. My pre-Christian ancestors believed in the transcendent, and worshipped to the best of their knowledge, so theirs is an important part of the tradition to which I and many others belong.

A flash of lightning and a peal of thunder came together one squally night as I was on my way past an island cemetery to say a rosary at the wake of an old man in his thatched cottage. I thought the sand-hill beneath the cemetery had exploded and I fell flat on my face on the ground. I had been unaware of the black thundercloud behind me, and when the lightning and thunder came together, it was like a bolt out of the black in so far as I was concerned. I was apparently so pale when I arrived at the house that I was asked immediately what was wrong. A glass of whiskey helped restore my colour, and probably led to my leading a more impressive than usual five decades of the rosary.

Another fright came with death as well. I had just returned from a priest's retreat on the mainland, where older priests had regaled me with stories that had to do with customs of the past. One of those was that a man would always accompany a priest on a sick call at night, to protect him from the devil who would inevitably be in the vicinity trying to steal the dying person's soul. I was mildly amused by their tales until I was called out to attend a woman who had had a bad turn late on my first night back on the island. The woman in question was too weak to receive holy communion and died shortly after I anointed her. I was invited to stay on for a while, but said I would put the eucharist back in the church which was only a few hundred yards away and return in ten or fifteen minutes. When the woman's son offered to accompany me to the church, I said "Not at all." He was needed where he was more than walking the road with me.

I regretted that decision when I was within an asses's roar of the chapel. I heard a chain rattle behind the high stone wall to my left. I was rooted to the ground with fear, and felt the cold sweat running down my back. Mocking was catching, the devil I had dismissed was right beside me. I prayed harder than I had done for some time. I put my trust in Jesus in the Blessed Sacrament which I was carrying and asked him to protect me. It was then the donkey began to bray and rattled his chain again, and I felt there was an ass outside the wall as well as inside.

I told the story at the wake later to explain another bout of paleness. One story then followed another as is usual on such occasions. A couple of young men told of a strange vision they had seen one moonlit night they were on their way home from the pub. They saw a strange looking beast between themselves and the low moon. It seemed to have a short body on long legs, with a big head and horns. It was as near as could be got to the traditional picture of the devil. They too were stuck to the ground until the donkey before them turned sideways, and no longer looked sinister

XXI

Sharon Brown had spent one of the most difficult nights of her life. She had sat beside the trolley in the hospital corridor on which her sick mother still lay. The nurses and their helpers had done their best but no test or examination had been done apart from the preliminary one when she was first admitted.

"Don't expect anything to be done before Monday," one young girl had said as she tried to settle Ann comfortably. "Most of the doctors are free for the weekend except in cases of extreme emergency."

"She would be a lot better off at home than here," Sharon said.

"You couldn't say a truer word," the young girl had answered, but is it worth while taking her home now and bringing her in again in the morning?"

Sharon was thinking out loud more than anything: "Anyway she might lose whatever place she has in the queue for examination."

"Queue," the girl smiled before moving on to the next patient: "I wish things were that organised here."

The one crumb of comfort Sharon had was that her mother was sleeping most of the time since one of the nurses had given her the tablets recommended by the young doctor. The awful bouts of retching that produced only a green bile had eased. "How could she vomit anything when she had eaten nothing?" Sharon asked herself guiltily, as she wondered how long that had been going on without her noticing it. She had always prided herself on being observant and she wondered vaguely was there anything else she should notice. She checked that her mother was still asleep and went to the coffee machine at the end of the corridor for one more cup of what she considered warmed up urine.

Sharon felt as if her stomach was distended from all the coffee she had drunk all night, but at least it had helped her to stay awake. It wasn't that she hadn't dozed from time to time only to wake with a start as she thought she was falling as her chin hit the top of her chest. She would feel cold then for a while. She had left the house in a rush, never thinking she would have to stay the night in the hospital without cardigan or coat. She walked up and down the corridor in an effort to keep warm.

"What in the name of God is the matter with you?" an old man on a trolley had asked as she walked past him one more time. "You would think they would give you drugs or something to quieten you down."

Sharon had a good laugh at that, but she felt too embarrassed to walk past him again apart from when she went for coffee. At some stage in the early morning the heat came on. The radiators were roasting and the corridor went from being cold and draughty to being unbearably hot and stuffy. Body odours that were not apparent until then pervaded the narrow space, as well as ample evidence that some of those lying on the trolleys were incontinent.

Sharon thought of her son, Liam and how difficult it would be for him to accept the death of both his grandfather and grandmother in the same year. He had never known his other grandparents. Bill's father and mother had died even before she had got to know him. "But Liam is young," Sharon told herself. "He will adapt. He will realise that an old person's death is natural. With the help of God, he will not have to deal with death again for a long time after that."

She thought of ringing home but it was far too early. Liam needed his sleep and tended to get contrary without it. Bill too, seemed to be very tired lately. Sharon smiled to herself when she thought that what she really wanted was something to pass the time. Why hadn't she thought to bring a magazine or newspaper even? She had seen a tabloid paper sticking out of the rubbish bin and thought of going down to get it. She thought then of horror stories she had heard of people picking up diseases and viruses in hospital. "You wouldn't know who was reading it," she told herself.

Liam seemed to be coming under the influence of Cian and Abigail a bit too much for Sharon's liking. They were nice kids, mannerly and courteous but their father and mother had a different attitude to rearing children than Bill and herself. She thought of some of the things Liam had said about prayer, for instance. She had no problem with the others rearing their children anyway they wanted but they wanted Liam brought up as a Catholic. He could make up his mind to accept or reject that faith when he had grown up.

Sharon thought lovingly of her husband, Bill. They had seemed to drift apart a bit recently, but he was a good man, a good provider. She blamed her mother's sarcastic tongue for Bill's distance. Ann had a bee in her bonnet about him and never missed an opportunity to denigrate him. But Bill was steady, if unspectacular. They were never short of money. They would never be as fashionable as Eve and Adam but they were not trying to live their lives. Everything would be fine if her mother could just get better, even though she got on her daughter's nerves most of the time, despite how much she loved her.

Ann woke when Liam and Bill came to visit the hospital after their breakfast. She didn't have much choice as her grandson virtually climbed into bed on top of her in his effort to give her a hug. He was still thinking of the story he had heard in the church: "Did you know Grandma that you won't be able to take anything with you when you die?"

"What kind of a question is that to ask someone in hospital?" his mother said, but she couldn't help laughing when she heard the full story.

His grandmother was even more pleased: "Good boy, Liam. You've raised my heart. It's the first laugh I have heard since I was brought into this dungeon of a hospital." Ann seemed to have improved since she slept: "Is there anything to eat in this place?" she asked.

"The doctor said you will have to fast until you have the tests," Sharon told her. "It shouldn't be too long now."

Ann leaned out of the trolley in search of her handbag: "Get me my purse, Liam, until I send for a packet of those crisps you like. Salt and vinegar."

"You couldn't eat worse in the state you're in," her daughter told her. "What about the tests?"

"To hell with the tests. I'd say that crowd are just waiting for me to die so that they can do the post-mortem. That's the only test I'm likely to have done on me on a Sunday. In the meantime, I will die with the hunger."

"I'll see can I get you soup or something," Sharon said reluctantly. "I'll ask one of the nurses."

"Soup!" Anne snorted. "All they had here the last time was something that looked and smelt like the vomit one of the patients had coughed up. And maybe that is exactly what it was."

"You don't need to talk so loud," her daughter told her. "You are entertaining everyone in the corridor."

"Don't talk, don't eat, don't get off the trolley. Don't do anything except die," Ann chanted like a litany.

"Whatever was in those tablets last night must have cured you," Sharon remarked. "You are back to your old self again." She went to the nurses' station and a girl came along with soup after some time. The old woman allowed her grandson to spoon-feed her like a baby.

Bill advised Sharon to go home and sleep for the evening. He would stay and keep an eye on her mother. He would be home about nine o'clock and she could come in again if she wanted.

"I hope I am not dangerous driving, because I had no sleep," Sharon said. She got Liam to keep reminding her to stay awake, and he overdid that duty by advising her at every cross-roads to keep her eyes open.

As soon as his wife and son had left the hospital, Bill excused himself from Ann and went outside to call Eve on his mobile phone. When there was no reply, he sent a text to say the puppy was lost without his kitten and they would have to get together. He wondered had Adam become suspicious about their relationship or why should Eve cut him off like that. How could she be so close to him one day and so cold the next? Maybe that was how she was with Adam, too, that was the only way she could deal with deceiving him. What if they were back together?"

The last thing Bill wanted to do was to go back into that awful hospital corridor and spend hours talking to or being verbally abused by his mother-in-law. He needed time to clear his head and maybe she would be asleep when he went back in, if he was lucky. He crossed the road outside the hospital and went into the hotel bar there. He drank one pint of beer because he would be driving home later, but he felt better after it. It was more difficult than work, Bill thought, to be trying to satisfy two women, and the mother of one of them thrown in for good measure. Selling houses was easy by comparison.

"A long phone-call," was his mother-in-law's greeting when Bill returned to the hospital corridor.

"I couldn't get through the first time," he replied, "so I crossed over the road to go to the toilet in the hotel."

Ann sniffed: "I was thinking I got the smell of drink."

"I just had the one."

The old woman smiled: "I don't mind how much you drink. Frank, my poor husband, God be good to him, often had a few pints before facing me. I learned a long time ago that it's from the bottle men get their courage, with regard to women at least."

"I just wanted to get rid of the thirst," Bill said. "It had nothing to do with courage or the lack of it."

"Why would any man in his right mind be keeping company with an old hag in a hospital on a Sunday evening?" Ann asked. "Off you go and have a few pints for yourself. I won't say anything to Sharon."

"I'd take you up on your offer if I didn't have to drive home later. I'd be out of a job if the breathalyser was put on me on the way home."

Bill was so surprised when his mother-in-law placed a hand on his that he almost recoiled: "Won't you take good care of Sharon and Liam?" she said.

"Don't I always?"

"Sharon is not the strongest in the world and I would not like her to be hurt."

"As long as I..." Ann did not give him time to finish his sentence:

"I feel that I am not long for this world."

"Don't be talking like that."

"Look after..." The old woman's hand slipped off Bill's and she closed her eyes. He didn't know had she fallen asleep or what?

"Doctor, Nurse," Bill shouted.

XXII

Extract From Paul Godfool's Journal

One of the most difficult aspects of being a priest is changing from one parish to another. It is like being present at your own wake and funeral, without being in a coffin. There were times I would almost have preferred to be in a coffin, because I felt so lonely. Even today, despite all the scandals and bad publicity of recent years, much of it well earned, the high regard with which clergy are held at a local level is highlighted year after year at the time of clerical changes. Reading the local news items of provincial papers, the sense of people's grief is palpable, and it is not just the priest's themselves that are heartbroken.

This priest-people relationship is seldom recognised or commented on in the national media, but it is a tie strengthened by the sharing of both sorrow and joy over a period of years. While their paths might seldom even cross from week to week or year to year, people tend to know and feel that their priest is there for them, and particularly in times of tragedy and suffering. Journalists who do not move in such a world seldom understand this bond, or use it to balance their reporting on church and clerical matters.

The kind of sadness people have at the loss of a priest is of course far from that experienced at a time of death, but it is real. It is also usually broken by humour. A story is told of a convoy of horses and carts crossing the diocese many years ago to bring a priest from one parish to another. The cleric and his chattels were delivered, the men visited the local public house for refreshments. A local remarked on the high regard in which the priest must have been held to warrant such a long and arduous journey.

"When you have him half as long as we did," came the reply, "you'll feel like bringing him twice as far".

High profile cases such as the discovery that Bishop Eamon Casey and Fr. Michael Cleary had fathered children highlighted the basic mercy and forgiveness of people, who were both scandalised and understanding at the same time. While journalists went apoplectic in their efforts to get worshippers to condemn those involved, most people interviewed pointed to the good word done in other areas of life by those involved, and quoted Christ's maxim: "Let the one without sin cast the first stone."

People understand the humanity of their priest, and that there is no point in him pretending that he is other than he is. They see through him, but accept him. Some of the old saying people had as they kept a distance from their clergy sum up their recognition of his weakness. "Do what he says, not what he does," is one of them. Another: "Be neither with him nor against him. Give him his due and stay away from him" is a rough translation from the Irish. (*Ná bi leis agus ná bi ina n-aghaidh. Tabhair a chuid féin dó agus fan uaidh*)

This attitude summed up feelings of grudging respect as well as a fear that priest's had magical power apart from the strictly spiritual. This kind of belief among people was sometimes misused by clergy to help them maintain social control. The idea that a priest could do anything from striking a person dead to putting horns on their heads was not widely discouraged by many clergy. The doubt was always there that the "man of God" was not someone to be crossed.

This too was often relieved by humour as in the story of the priest who called on a man to catch his wild horse for him. Fearing injury, the man pretended not to hear. "Catch him," the priest said, "or I'll stick you to the ground". "If you have that much power," came the reply, "why don't you stick your mad horse to the ground".

XXIII

Paul Godfool did not feel like facing his colleague, Richard Scapegoat after Sunday mass. He needed fresh air and he decided to walk the mountain road until the tension he felt inside him had dissipated. He had shared a few whiskies with Richard the previous night and added to that when he found he could not sleep after going to bed with all the evening's talk going around and around in his head.

He was pleased that he had managed to say his masses without anyone obviously noticing that he had a hangover. One woman who came into the sacristy to have a mass-card signed remarked that he looked tired but she had her own charitable explanation: "Sure it's no wonder with all you have to do without any help." He made no effort to contradict her but her comment made him feel all the more guilty because of the real cause of his 'tiredness.'

Godfool drove his car to the foothills of the mountain. He parked in the viewing space overlooking the lake and began a steady walk uphill. There was no human to be seen and not many animals either, a few mountain sheep perched precariously on the slopes. He remembered the last time he had climbed to the top of the mountain to watch the setting sun. There were few better views in his estimation, great valleys stretching away to the coast, hills streams, mountain lakes which seemed to defy gravity, perched as they were away above sea level. There were fewer than a hundred houses in that vast area. Listening to some environmental commentators a person would get the impression that the country was in danger of being covered in concrete. That was certainly not true of area like this.

Croagh Patrick stood out from the other mountains and hills in the distance. It seemed slightly hump-backed from this angle, compared with the blue cone-shape it had when viewed from the place in which he had grown up. The last time he had been there it looked as if the sun was resting on the shoulder of the mountain, much as Atlas was supposed to have carried the earth in the old legends. It seemed then as if the sun was rolling down the mountain before disappearing behind the foothills, leaving Paul Godfool in the half-darkness, with barely enough time left to descend to his car in the gathering gloom.

Paul's mind wandered to the village in the glen behind the mountain which in many ways seemed more remote than the islands in which he had served earlier in his priesthood. He would visit the old and the housebound there with holy communion on the First Friday of the month. The first time he visited, he was apprehensive as many people might not have seen a bearded priest, but like most Irish people most of them had walked the world and the television set in the corner brought them the rest of it. He often told of how two of the older women competed with each other in the effort to give him whiskey. "And they say that priests have a tough life," he usually finished the story.

One woman told him later that she had not opened the door after seeing him through the window. "I thought you were the dog warden," she said, "and we hadn't a licence for any of the dogs. The same dogs were valuable animals among the hills as they saved much time and legwork gathering and herding sheep. Even the advent of the quad, a valuable asset to the sheep-farmer in that it could go where no other vehicle could, had not made the sheepdog a redundant species.

Paul Godfool paused by the mountain roadside to gaze out over the great lake below, which had been behind him as he climbed. It was said that the same lake was very deep and even though half the people from the county drank from it, not to speak of their animals, their showers and their toilets, its surface never lowered by more than a few metres. During a drought earlier in the year, Paul had joked with some of his parishioners that they would be out in the centre of what had been the lake yet, a cup in one hand and a kettle in the other as they tried to team enough water for a cup of tea. "As sure as it goes out a few feet from the shore, it will fill again in a matter of weeks," he was told.

Many of the mountain streams and waterfalls had slowed to a trickle at the time. Some dried up altogether. Paul found that strange in a place which he always associated with the sound of running water, and of course it did not last long. The rain was preceded by snow and sleet, driven by a gale which knocked trees and electricity poles, blackening out large areas of the county. As often happened when an inch of snow fell in the capital, it was a crisis. When much worse happened in the far west, it didn't matter a damn. "If I continue like this," Paul Godfool said to himself, "I will soon be as bad as Marcas McCabe for criticising the media."

When the snow melted, the rain came and it continued far longer than the dry spell that brought the drought. The streams were full again, making their own music as they hurtled to their destination. Water from hill, from bog and glen had soon filled the lake again to capacity, allowing it draw breath, its thirst sated. Looking around him, Paul admired the colours of the bog, colours he had never noticed in his youth. He felt that he was inclined to look at trees and bog-land with new eyes since finishing his sojourn on the offshore islands.

The islands on which he had lived had scarcely any trees because it was difficult for them to root on bare limestone, and if they managed that they had to face the full force of gale and storm. The mountain lowlands were full with every possible variety of tree and he sometimes stood looking at them and admired their beauty as if he had never seen a tree before.

Paul had grown up without a high regard for bogs and bog-lands. They were places in which people work hard to save turf, as peat is known in Ireland. What would eventually be used for fuel on winter fires had first to be cut, then spread, later footed in small stands of five or six sods with one or two across the top. As it dried further it was re-footed into bigger clamps, then drawn out to the roadside where it was stacked before being eventually drawn home and stacked again in a yard or put into a turf-shed, all hard and tedious work.

It was often joyful work, too, with different families coming together at lunch-time when a fire was lit, a pot or kettle of water boiled for tea-making. Sandwiches or brown bread was eaten with great relish in the hungry outdoors as stories were told and retold from year to year, with much banter and laughter. Despite that, Paul never felt that the bog was something you looked at or could ever imagine as beautiful.

It was the paintings of Dublin-born Brian Bourke who lived and worked in the west that changed Paul's view on bogs. When he had first seen those art-works, he thought the colours beautiful but were the result of artistic licence. Now that he lived among acres of bog, he could see where the colours came from, as they changed from season to season throughout the year.

As he faced up towards the mountain-top Paul let his eyes wander across the almost vertical potato ridges high above him, as he wondered how and human being with a spade could have managed to work in such gravity-defying conditions. People of the parish had different views on those ridges. Some said they were deliberately put there at a level the potato blight could not reach. Others said they were the work of people who had nowhere else to go after they were evicted from the low-lands. Such evictions were common in the area in the middle of the nineteenth century, with the people of one village, sixty-nine men women and children of all ages put out on the side of the road a couple of weeks before one Christmas.

Some of those evictions were for non-payment of rent, others because people would not send their children to schools set up by the local landlord in which the only religion taught was a fundamentalist Protestant version of Christianity. Paul Godfool was grateful the day had come that such sectarian division had evaporated, but the fact that such things happened had to be acknowledged and could not be air-brushed from history.

The pain and suffering caused by more recent church history could not be airbrushed or swept under the carpet, either. Efforts to hide or overlook clerical child abuse had gone on for too long, perpetrators warned and sent to another parish, diocese or country where they inevitably abused again. It was only in more recent times that anyone in authority had accepted responsibility. A Taoiseach or Prime Minister had lost his job because of perceived delays in dealing with one case. A President of the High Court, too, had to fall on a similar sword, but it was significant that for a long time, no bishop or abbot lost his job for similar reasons.

There were the excuses that they did not really understand paedophilia, or how to deal with it. In fairness, nobody knew much about child abuse at the time, Paul Godfool thought, but even in that kind of a situation it would have helped if a number of bishops had held up their hands, asked pardon for their ignorance of the subject, and resigned, because it had happened on their watch and nothing had been done about it. Government ministers in a similar situation were expected to and often did resign, not because they were at fault, but because something serious happened that their department should have been aware of and tried to prevent.

There were fine men on the bench of bishops and no doubt the extent of child abuse cut many of them to the quick. They were the ones at the coalface trying on the one hand to comfort the victims and their families, and at the same time trying to get the priest perpetrators a fair trial. Most of them were by nature conservative. That was what had them in the positions they were in and it was probably asking too much of them to make any radical gesture of reparation. One of their number walked like a pilgrim through the parishes of his diocese to ask people's forgiveness, and if anything, he appeared to be an embarrassment to his colleagues.

But then it was easy to blame the hierarchy of the church. He had kept his own head down because of his old friend, Richard Scapegoat's involvement. Ten or twenty years earlier, he would have been on the barricades, fighting every cause, as he had done during the contentious referenda of the eighties. He had taken the wrong side in all of them from a church point of view, often arguing that the church was defending the indefensible on matters such as the availability of civil divorce.

As he walked the hillside, Paul Godfool knew that he had to go back to his house and try to be at least civil to one of the priests convicted of child abuse. He realised now that was the reason he was out walking. He was reluctant to face Richard, but he had to face him. He had to face him with the kindness and compassion and forgiveness of Jesus Christ. Not for the first time he had to remind himself that his friend had paid his debt to society, and had his sins absolved by the church. He had served his prison sentence, and had now to face the sentence of being forever an outcast, a pariah, a social leper.

Paul Godfool tried to remove some of the weight from his mind by concentrating on other things. He had received a health warning earlier in the year when he attended a doctor for the first time in nearly forty years. He would not even have gone then except for life assurance reasons. His blood pressure was high so he was under orders to reduce his weight and aim for a lifestyle change. Porridge had replaced rashers for breakfast. Brown bread had replaced white, and he thought of cholesterol more than anything else as he made his purchases in the local shop or town supermarket.

"Here is somebody else out for the good of his health," Paul Godfool said to himself as he saw Adam Adams jogging steadily up the slope. While the priest knew him to see around the place, or bringing his children to football matches, he knew that he was not what one of his colleagues would call "gospel greedy."

"It's hard going against the hill," the priest said as Adam came by.

"You should know," came the reply as Adams struggled for breath. "It's all uphill in your job."

"I'm afraid we free-wheel downhill most of the time," Godfool answered lightly, just to make conversation.

"Adam looked at him intently: "Do ye ever give up on the bullshit?"

Taken aback, the priest asked: "What?"

"The bullshit, the hypocrisy, pretending everything is hunky-dory?"

"That's not the way I see it."

"Why have ye to have your finger in every pie? Why can't ye just let people be themselves?" Adam asked. "Especially now that ye haven't a leg to stand on after all that has happened in recent years."

"There were a couple of hundred people at mass this morning," the priest said, "and at least as many more last night. Do they not count?"

"How many young people? How many thinking people were among them?"

"I presume everyone that was there wanted to be there," the priest answered.

"You're on your last legs, and it's time ye recognised it."

The priest looked at his watch: "Could we discuss this some other time?"

"The dinner is ready, I suppose," Adam said sarcastically.

"I'm not trying to avoid you, but I do have a visitor… I'd love to talk more about this, because far too few people challenge me or my faith."

"A waste of time…" Whatever else Adams said was lost in the wind as he headed on up the hill. The priest shrugged, wondered what was really bothering him and decided he would try and put it behind him for the moment. "Sufficient for the day…" He was looking forward to taking things easy for the evening.

XXIV

Extract From Paul Godfool's Journal

Thirty years ago I wrote the following in a national magazine: "The younger generation with an instinct for what is basic and important are quietly discarding non-essential elements of traditional Catholicism, confession, Sunday Mass obligation, Church teachings on pre-marital sex, contraception, all of which will in twenty years most likely have gone the way of the Friday fast and the Latin Mass, once considered by many of us to be keystones of the faith."

I suggested that the Church would eventually accept the facts of life as she had always done: "Virtual non-attendance at confession by all age groups, apart from Christmas and Easter has already brought desperate efforts to introduce a relevant rite of penance. The only aspect of that rite likely to be relevant or effective is already a non-starter in Ireland, because the hierarchy has vetoed its use here." I referred here to general absolution. Officially this rite is only allowed in time of war or great natural disaster.

Before the article was published, I had been selected to go to the Diocesan Cathedral on Holy Thursday to collect the holy oils for the priest's in my local area. I got a letter from my bishop telling me not to go there, that a priest who fully accepted the teachings of the church would attend the chrism Mass and bring back the oil. Although Holy Thursday could be described as the birthday of the priesthood, I have never attended that Mass since, all the more so because a renewal of the vows of celibacy has seemingly been added to that ceremony.

It didn't help my case, of course, that the type of car used by the bishops of the region at the time had been mentioned in my article: "A

Christ preached, however sincerely, from a Lancia, Mercedes or Audi is an abomination to many, and a far cry from the Bethlehem stable and the Son of Man who had nowhere to lay his head. Is the image of a successful executive really necessary for members of the hierarchy?

The magazine in which the article was written was anathema to at least some bishops, but I had met the editor while visiting the Island, and I respected him as someone who would publish material that mainstream newspapers or magazines of the time would not. Thirty years later, it is even more difficult to have anything to do with religion other than denigrate it, published in the national media.

XXV

***"You have seduced me, Lord, and I have allowed
myself to be seduced" {Jer : 20:7}***

Paul Godfool was surprised to hear the sound of laughter from his sitting-room as he entered the presbytery. He recognised Richard Scapegoat's voice immediately, but who else was there? What had he told this person? What did the visitor know about the man staying with him? He told himself not to be paranoid, to be calm but careful as he entered the room.

Marcas McCabe rose from his armchair to shake his hand and to welcome him back "to your own house. Dickie and myself had a great conversation while I was waiting for you."

Paul looked at "Dickie" who indicated to him by a shake of his head that Marcas had no idea who he really was. "You are lucky," Richard Scapegoat said with a wink: "that you have people as intelligent and sophisticated as Marcas here in your parish, Father Paul."

Paul Godfool felt the tension he had felt when he came in dissipate with this kind of banter: "Is Marcas telling lies again?" he asked jokingly.

"Not a word of a lie," Marcas said, "but plenty of history."

"History, philosophy, theology," Richard said, rising from his chair: "I will leave you now, because I know that Marcas here has come to discuss a certain matter with Father Paul."

"I don't have a thing to say that you can't hear as well," Marcas said, "because it was the very same thing we were talking about between ourselves earlier."

"Would you mind if I readied a cup of tea?" Paul asked, "because I haven't had a drop since breakfast and my tongue is as dry as a bone. Will ye have a drop of tea or coffee?"

The others explained they had some earlier, Marcas adding his own piece of flattery: There you had the holy man saying masses and seeing to the sick all morning while we were in here chatting and joking." When Paul had his tea ready, Marcas invited both of them to his own and Nora's house for dinner that evening.

Richard looked at Paul, offering him an opportunity to refuse: "I doubt if you will have the time from what you were telling me." He then spoke directly to Marcas: "It mightn't be a bad idea to check it with herself?"

"There is no point in asking her," he answered, "until I find out first will the priest be free to come."

"I'm not sure yet," Paul answered tentatively, "but if I am, I will give a ring to Nora myself later."

Marcas gave all the encouragement he could: "Well I hope that you can come, because I have really enjoyed the conversation I have had with your colleague here. But that wasn't what brought me here, but to see is there anything we can do about that terrible programme that was on the TV last night."

"I told him we saw it," Richard explained.

Marcas shook his head gravely: "It came between me and my night's sleep. Nora didn't sleep a wink either, of course, with me twisting this way and that in the bed. In the end she told me to talk with the priest about it instead of driving her crazy. So that's what I came to discuss with you when mass was over.

"I was thinking about it earlier," Paul Godfool said, "and I decided to hold back thirty-seven euro of my television licence, one euro for every year since I was ordained."

Marcas was back to his flattery: "You must have been ordained when you were a child, because you don't look a day over the thirty-seven."

"Well, I am, and twenty-five more and I feel every minute of it," Paul Godfool replied.

"Why not refuse to pay any of it at all?" Richard asked.

"Because I have no issue with most of the programmes," Paul said. "In fact, I think some of them are great. But I don't like being insulted on prime-time TV."

"I'd be the first one to take the stand with you," Marcas commented, "only for Nora paid our licence when she was collecting the pension the last day." Speaking directly to Richard, he said: "She is of slightly nervous disposition and doesn't like to have bills hanging over us."

Paul Godfool was of the opinion that Marcas' reluctance to take a public stand had more to do with his association with the main political party in government than with the licence being paid. He tried to push him to do something himself rather than leave it all to others: "I'm drawing up a letter to send to the Director General of the TV station, and I think you should do the same."

"You're better with the pen than I am, Father."

Paul did not want to let him off so lightly: "Well why don't you bring it up at the next meeting of the cumann, the local party committee?"

Marcas made no promise: "Who knows but I might raise it with our local TD's as well?"

"I'm going to start writing this evening," Paul Godfool said. "Anything that is put on the long finger just doesn't get done."

"Couldn't you ask the European Parliament to investigate the TV station for bigotry?" Richard suggested. "Every citizen of the Union has a right to make that kind of petition."

"Isn't it strange too," Marcas said to his local priest, "that our visitor from the missions knows more about those things than either of us?"

"I saw it on Euronews," Scapegoat explained, not mentioning of course that it was in prison he had seen it.

"And is that available all over the world?" Marcas asked.

"It was only in recent days I saw it. There isn't much to do on a wet day in this country except to look at television."

"I'll bet they show more regard for religion where you are than they do on our lousy stations," Marcas said to Richard.

Scapegoat nodded and said: "I must say that I was pleasantly surprised when the last Pope was in the Holy Land that there was more coverage on some of the North African stations which were essentially Muslim than you would see here at home."

Marcas had nothing but pity for Pope John Paul: "The same poor man killed himself travelling all over the world. I get the impression that this man is a bit cuter and he knows how to mind himself."

Paul Godfool tried to be fair to the Irish TV stations: "In fairness our crowd went over the top a bit for the last Pope's funeral."

"I suppose they were just glad to be rid of him," Marcas said.

Richard Scapegoat had his own opinion on the matter: "I'd say they were trying to introduce a bit of balance because they had gone away overboard about the church in the years leading up to that."

Marcas was more cynical: "Not to speak of the allowances they got to spend a few days eating and drinking in Rome."

Richard showed his cynical side too: "You would pity Jesus, Mary and Joseph and all the other saints when the big TV star, John Paul the second arrived in heaven. He must have put all of the rest in the halfpenny place."

My biggest fault with those who write or speak about religion in the media," Marcas said, "is not only that they have no faith themselves, but they are bitterly opposed to it. To our great shame most of them were reared as Catholics and all that Christian doctrine was wasted on them."

Paul Godfool did not agree: "I think the biggest compliment we can pay our Catholic education system is that it has produced so many atheists and agnostics. From James Joyce to the present day none of them can say they were brainwashed or that religion was forced on them because they proved they were free to leave the church."

Richard was more interested in what Marcas had said about the teaching of Christian doctrine: "I'll bet not many of those who went to your school ended up as atheists or agnostics."

"It's true for you, even if I say so myself. I gave adequate time to the teaching of religion, unlike many present-day teachers who spend more time teaching science since it was introduced to the curriculum than they do to religion."

"More Darwin than Genesis?" Richard tried to get Marcas to rage even more about present day methods of teaching.

"The country is gone to the devil," Marcas replied, "and if we don't do something about it, nobody will. Fair play to this man here," he said about Paul Godfool. "At least he is going to take a stand about the way our religion was insulted last night."

Paul stood up: "Better action than words, and we won't do much about it if we stay sitting here."

Marcas got up to go: "good luck. I'll be off. Thanks for the tea and the talk. It's lovely to have an intelligent conversation. By the way don't forget the invitation to dinner. Nora will be disappointed if ye don't come."

Paul Godfool looked as Richard Scapegoat when Marcas had left: "Well, Dickie, you managed to keep your secret?"

"I had no intention of letting anyone in, but when he kept knocking, I thought it was some emergency, or that it was yourself and you had forgotten your keys or something."

"There is no harm in Marcas," Paul said lightly, "but when he starts talking, he is hard to stop."

"I can assume we won't be going to dinner?" Richard said.

Paul mused: "I wasn't keen at the start, but when I think of the amount of cooking it would save. I wouldn't like to give the impression either that something is being covered up."

"Is the wife as bad as himself in the talking department?" Richard asked: "Yap, yap yap, from morning till night."

"Nora is a lit calmer and quieter and she doesn't get all worked up about what is said on the radio or television." Godfool laughed: "I'll be as bad as him myself if I follow the course I laid out a while ago."

"You don't have to do it if you don't want to."

"That's true," Paul said, "but the best thing about announcing something publicly is that it puts pressure on you not to take the lazy way out and back down. I'll start on that letter as soon as this thing heats up," he said as he switched on his computer.

"You are dropping a huge hint to me, I imagine," Richard said, "to make myself scarce, get lost."

"It's not a private letter. Stay here if you like. Can't you read a Sunday paper or something? I don't mind what you do so long as you don't interrupt me when I am concentrating."

Richard moved towards the door of the room: "I might go out to the church and try to say a few prayers."

"You couldn't go to a better place." Paul thought of repeating the warning about talking to children, but decided not to rub his friend's nose in the dirt altogether. It was highly unlikely that there would be any children about on their own anyway.

When Richard reached the church, he went on his two knees just inside the door and stretched out his arms in the form of a crucifix. "Lord have mercy on me, a sinner," he said and he remained like that until his arms drooped with tiredness. He felt nothing. God must be a long way off, he thought. Spiritual directors had often said there is no need for talk in prayer, but he felt he wasn't getting anywhere with God. Why keep knocking when the door is closed, he wondered.

Scapegoat got up from his knees and walked around inside the church, stopping from time to time to look at some of the pictures in the Stations of the Cross. They were old pictures, imported from Italy a century earlier and the scenes of Jesus' suffering were graphic and striking, but Richard felt they did nothing to bring him closer to God. "maybe it's not him that's cold, but me," he said to himself. He stood then in the centre aisle in front of the altar and stood looking at the big cross on the wall behind it. It stood out as an image but it lacked strength. The figure of Jesus was too clean and neat for a man who had been subjected to about fifteen hours of torture. The Lord seemed to be in a comfortable sleep more than to have suffered a cruel death.

"Perhaps it is meant to be a resurrection cross," Scapegoat thought, but it was too sterile and sanctified for that. "It's just a dead man, a dead God, if you like," he said to himself. "It does nothing for me, but that is probably more the artist's fault than the fault of Jesus."

Seeing the door to the left of the altar open, Richard was surprised to find the sacristy door open. Priests were usually security conscious because of the value of sacred vessels and ancient chalices to thieves. These were more than likely locked in a safe, he thought, but the box of altar breads and bottle of wine were in open view.

Not having been allowed to celebrate mass in jail, Scapegoat had a sudden urge to say the words of consecration once again in the hope that they would hopefully kick-start his lost faith. He didn't bother with the preliminaries, or the readings. He poured wine into a glass and took one of the large breads in his hands. He said the words: "This is my body," and "This is my blood." He hadn't time for any more as he heard Paul Godfool's voice behind him ask: "What in the name of Jesus is going on here?"

"What do you think? I'm a priest. I'm saying mass."

"Why didn't you ask for the keys, get the chalice?" Paul asked.

"The urge just came on me. Anyway, why did you follow me. Did you expect to find me stripping some youngster?"

"Something like that," Godfool replied angrily. "I was told not to let you out of my sight for long. I started to get worried when you didn't come back.

"Who would ever have thought you would have become the priest's pet?"

"It's not on the bishop's behalf I am keeping an eye on you but on behalf of the children of the parish."

"On your own behalf," Richard countered, "in case anyone would find out what kind of a devil you are harbouring in the house."

Paul snapped back through his teeth: "Exactly. I have to protect myself as well. I'm the piggy in the middle here."

"You're a right friend alright."

"Friendship has its limits," Paul spat back.

"Obviously. You can't give a man fifteen minutes freedom after all the talk you have done about freedom all your life."

Paul measured out his words: "I made use of my freedom to make sure you did not compromise the freedom of innocent children, as you did in the past."

"Now we are talking. Now we are communicating. At last. But you haven't a clue what you are talking about. You never had to deal with that kind of urge, that kind of temptation."

"I didn't, and if I did, I don't know how I would react," Godfool answered. "But at this point in time it is about you we are talking. I am not the one who served time for raping children."

"That's court talk. I barely laid a hand on him," Richard said.

Paul was not going to let him away with that: "The evidence given in court gives the lie to that, as you know well."

"How do you know. You weren't there?"

"It was reported word for word in the daily papers," Paul retorted.

"So, you read the papers," came the sarcastic reply. "You took an interest in my case but not in me. You read up on the sin but ignored the sinner. Where were you for the past five years? That's the kind of friend you are, a fair day friend."

They were shouting at each other, and Paul Godfool looked from the sacristy to see was there anyone in the church before lowering his voice to say: "The very reason I never went near the prison is that I was disgusted with you. Having read what you did, I couldn't look you in the face, or couldn't look at the hands that did those things to children. You made me sick. You made me ashamed of you. All I wanted to do is vomit."

Richard was calmer but cold when he replied: "If that is how you feel why did you welcome me here yesterday?"

"To be quite honest I did not welcome you. I put up with you on the bishop's instructions." There was silence for a while before Paul continued: "But I admit that I am sorry and ashamed that I did not visit you in prison."

Richard nodded his head: "I know why…"

Paul continued: "I understand why you are angry about that, and it proves I am a poor friend, and a poor Christian. 'I was in prison and you never visited me' and all of that. You deserved better after all we went through together in the old days. I'm sorry I let you down."

"Forget about it. You are not the guilty one in all of this." It was as if the anger between them had fizzled away and left them drained. Richard said: "I'd love to give you a hiding for never going to see me, but that would be only to give some sort of relief to myself."

Paul Godfool reached out a tentative hand of friendship: "At our age, it shouldn't be any wonder that we have messed up in one way or another. I know your sins but you don't know mine."

"I could still hear your confession." Richard pointed out towards the confession box: "He hasn't taken that away from me yet."

Paul shook his head and smiled: "No thanks."

"Because you have no sin or because you don't want to tell me?"

"Both," Paul joked.

On their way back from the sacristy to the house, Richard said they wouldn't be able to go for dinner together after all that had been said.

"What choice have we?" Paul answered. "We will murder each other if we remain under the one roof all evening."

XXVI

Extract From Paul Godfool's Journal

Have you noticed how God seems to have relaxed, mellowed, grown old gracefully? Fear has been allowed to slip off the religious radar while hell-fire has burnt down to its embers. It's not that all that many people have turned from God. The numbers who pray (more than eighty per cent) are far higher than those who attend religious services. The God-relationship seems to have become more cosy, laid-back, and as far as I am concerned, that is the way it should be.

Of course, it is not God who has changed. We have. We no longer confuse upright with uptight. People who compare church attendance fifty years ago with the present day tend to forget that it is the churches themselves, and the Roman Catholic church in particular that have relaxed rules and regulations and allowed people make up their own minds in many areas, such as Lenten observance, fasting before holy communion, etc.

The people of God have flexed their own religious muscles in areas such as frequent confession and the church's official position on contraception, deciding themselves what is right and what is acceptable. Those decisions have taken place right across the board worldwide at the same time, like a tidal wave sweeping away all question, and as far as I am concerned, showing great common-sense.

Some describe this as 'a la carte Catholicism,' picking and choosing what you want from the religious menu. I don't think that is far removed from what Jesus did with regard to certain laws of his own religion which he thought were outmoded, strangling what they were intended for. Breaking the Sabbath, for instance in order to cure people is the most obvious. In matters like this, Jesus could be considered an 'a la carte Jew.'

In religion, as well as in all other areas of life, there is always tension between the letter and the spirit of the law, between law as shield and law as sword. Balance is needed. Law is there for protection more than for prosecution, or at least it should be. It is not that sanctions are not needed if laws are ignored, but they need to be sensible and in proportion. Law is certainly not meant for persecution and when it tips over that edge it goes into disrepute. When uptight is confused with upright we are in trouble.

I hope to leave my religious up-tightness with the rest of my religious baggage at the entrance to the Bethlehem stable this Christmas. I will offer it as my present instead of gold, frankincense and myrrh, because I think sweet Jesus is fragrant enough already. My baggage and yours are the baggage of real life, the cards that life has dealt us, nothing to be ashamed of, because real life is what this thing we call the Incarnation is about.

The Jesus we meet in the stable did not come among us to give us a cuddly feel-good factor so that we can pretend real life does not exist. Jesus was in-carn-ated, en-fleshed, human-ed in order to carry the baggage of real life, to 'take up his cross' as we put it and as he put it, to turn that instrument of death into an instrument of life. But that is a story for another day, for Easter Day to be precise.

Sufficient for Christmas day to soak up the wonder and the magic, to cuddle the baby Jesus and welcome him to our world. In welcoming Jesus, we welcome that world, and in welcoming that world we let go of the baggage that is keeping us from really entering the stable. So, what if Christmas has become too commercialised? So, what if the media have had one go too many at what we hold dear throughout the year? So, what if those attending Christmas mass don't darken a church door for another year? So, what if people of all religions and none climb aboard the Christmas bandwagon for a day? All are welcome. We don't own Jesus. Then again in a sense we do, not in a proprietorial way, but as one of our own flesh and blood, thanks to his mother, Mary.

Soon enough, we will be back to the real world, soon enough to see the shadow of the cross fall over Bethlehem, as Herod has the holy innocents taken out. We will move away, move on, our baggage a little lighter from having looked the baby Jesus in the face in the eyes of our minds. The grown-up Jesus will become our model. Jesus who was laid-back enough to enjoy social gatherings, food and drink, while strong and radical enough to take a stand against aspects of religion which he found to be oppressive. This led to much criticism and accusation and was part of the case against him at his trial, but he didn't mind taking the flak when he was doing what he thought was right.

The same Jesus constantly told his followers: "Do not be afraid. Behold the lilies of the field, etc." Relax, chill out, enjoy Christmas. What a dull world we would have without religious festivals, Christmas, Easter, Saint Patrick's Day, local patterns, christenings, weddings, carnivals in Rio or wherever, even November festivals in honour of ancestors. With all of those how did religion earn its reputation as a killjoy? A question for another day. Sufficient for this day... It wasn't God who needed to relax...

XXVII

After all the commotion caused by Bill Brown's plea for help for his mother-in-law, Ann, it turned out that she was not dead but in a deep sleep. Bill got the full force of her tongue when the doctors and nurses had checked her out:

"What kind of a bloody idiot are you, making a fool of me in front of everyone in the hospital?"

"I was trying to be helpful. Anyway, didn't it get a doctor to look at you?"

"If you had looked properly yourself, you would have known I was only asleep. I've heard about blind drunk… How many drinks had you over the road?"

"I only had the one."

"One too many. I suppose it was wishful thinking. You were hoping I'd wake up dead. I wouldn't mind but I was having the best sleep I had in a week."

Sharon and Liam arrived. Bill had called in a panic when he thought Ann was dead. He rang again when he discovered she was alive, but they were already on the way. The result of all the commotion was that Ann was moved into a ward when the next vacancy became available. She was well aware of what caused the vacancy:

"They are after moving me into a dead woman's bed. It would be as well for you to send for a coffin altogether and get it over with."

"Whatever else might be wrong with you, there is nothing wrong with your tongue," her daughter joked. "You look a lot better since you slept."

"I'll make a fine looking corpse alright."

"Isn't it great that you are not on that trolley anymore?" Sharon said.

Ann called her grandson: "Come over here, Liam, and give your grandmother a kiss."

Liam looked at Sharon and asked: "Do I have to?"

His mother seemed shocked: "What kind of a question is that and your poor grandmother on the broad of her back in the hospital?"

"Her breath was a bit sick the last time," Liam answered.

"Give your Granny a kiss this minute," his mother ordered.

"You smell alright now," was Liam's verdict. "You must be getting better."

"You're better than any doctor," his grandmother told him.

"I heard you were as thorny as a briar when the doctor woke you," Sharon said to her mother.

"What kind of a fool is that husband of yours? He woke me up from the first decent sleep I had in ages."

"He was sure you were dead," Sharon said.

"If he wasn't out drinking…"

Her daughter interrupted before Ann had time to finish her sentence: "He was out drinking when he was supposed to be looking after you? Well wait until I have a word with him when I get home."

"Have I let the cat out of the bag?" Ann asked. "Well, to be fair to him, it was me that told him to go across the street for a pint. I knew he was like a fish out of water out there in the corridor trying to keep talk with an ould wan like me. I didn't think he would be so blind as not to see the difference between sleep and death."

Sharon shook her head: "And I have let him drive home after all that drink."

"Don't be too hard on him," her mother said.

"The main thing is that you seem to be better and that you have got a right bed," Sharon commented.

Ann twisted around in the bed: "This bed isn't either right or left. There's a hollow in the middle of it where the last woman died. I was a lot better off out there in that corridor. At least I got a bit of sleep out there."

"You might sleep again if you closed your eyes," her daughter told her, "not to speak of your mouth."

"Do you hear her?" Ann asked Liam. "I hope you don't talk like that to your mother when you grow up."

Liam smiled at her: "I'll tell you how I go to sleep. I close my eyes and my mouth and I pretend that I am playing football and that I am the best player in the park and that I am scoring all the goals. Then I fall asleep unknown to myself."

"I never learned to play football," his grandmother told him, "and I am too old to start kicking now."

"Liam is only trying to be helpful," Sharon said. "You could imagine that you are knitting or something."

Her mother belittled her comment: "What do you know about knitting. And as for Liam I was only joking, but you wouldn't understand that because you never had a sense of humour."

Sharon was hurt: "Why do you always have to make little of me?"

"I'm only telling the truth. You were too serious all your life and you never saw the funny side of anything."

"I didn't," Sharon snapped, "because I had to put up with you."

"I had to put up with you, too."

Sharon gave money to Liam to go and buy a drink for himself in the dispenser. Then she said to her mother: "You shouldn't be talking like that in front of the child."

"I didn't start it. You called me a briar a while ago, but you are just as bad, reacting to everything I say."

"And I have plenty of reason to," Sharon replied. "I don't know whether I'm coming or going. I was just asleep when Bill called to say you were dead. Then he rang to say you were alive. Instead of being happy to see me when I came in, all you could do was attack and make little of me."

"It's that stupid husband of yours, thinking I was dead when I wasn't. No wonder I was all over the place. Could you blame me?" Ann put her head to one side then, like a little bird alert to danger. She said nothing for a while and then broke her silence: "Why is he always talking on that carry around phone, and who does he be talking to?"

"He is doing business, selling houses, making money so he can look after myself and Liam."

"They don't seem to give him a break even on a Sunday."

"He gets calls at all hours," Sharon said. "Sunday is the only day that some of his customers are free."

"He seems to be very great with some of them, all that soft talk."

"What are you trying to imply, mother?"

"I know men," Ann replied.

"How many do you know? As far as I can see the only man you ever knew was my father."

"That was enough."

"You're not trying to say he was unfaithful?" Sharon asked with wonder in her voice. "Sure, you were heartbroken when he died?"

"We were a long time together and I miss him terribly. But he was a man and he was like every man. You can't trust any of them."

Sharon probed as best she could: "What exactly are you trying to say? That I can't trust my husband?"

"Look after your husband," her mother said. "That is what I am saying and you are paying no heed to me. Look after him and keep an eye on him."

"We are talking about Bill here," said Sharon, exasperated. "Is there a better man or a better husband in Ireland?"

"Aren't you the lucky girl so?"

"Are you being sarcastic?" her daughter asked. "I never can tell."

Ann's voice took on a grave tone: "We learn things gradually as we go through life, or as they used to say in the old language, sense comes with age. I learned that as I went along, and it would be no harm if you learned it, too, before it is too late."

"Why can't you just say out exactly what you mean?" Sharon said.

"Why can't you see what is going on all around you?" was her mother's answer.

There was silence for a while until Sharon said: "I know that I am overweight because you have said it to me often enough. I know I was never good enough for you because I could not replace the little boy that was stillborn before I came along. Well get over it," she finished angrily.

There was sadness in Ann's eyes: "Did I ever say that I would have preferred anyone else in your place?"

"You didn't say it but you showed it. Even now you are much nicer to Liam than you are to me."

"Liam is a child. You are a grown woman, or at least I thought you were. It's the most natural thing in the world for a woman and her daughter to be at loggerheads. It's just human nature. It doesn't mean they don't love each other." Ann turned away from Sharon: "I'd like to have a rest now."

Sharon spoke to her mother's back: "I think you are losing your mind, that you are getting Alzheimer's or something."

"At least I have a mind to lose."

"That's it. I'm going." Sharon stood up and called to Liam that they were going home.

"I thought we were staying the evening with Grandma."

"There is a change of plan. She doesn't need us here."

XXVIII

Extract From Paul Godfool's Journal

"I fucking adore you." As Christmas greetings go, it was to say the least unusual. Still, I am a sucker for a compliment, so I sat at the wheel of my car as my admired leaned his elbows on the open window and delivered himself of some rambling comments about "the season to be jolly." He was a long way past jolly himself and the unshaven jaw, the loose tie and the piece of shirt hanging out over his trousers suggested he was on his way home from midnight mass at the time I was coming from the last mass of Christmas Day.

I have heard of football managers who give their players the 'hair-drier' treatment, but I would swear that the poteen breath that assailed my locks that morning was the start of the greying process. It was like methylated spirits without the colour, and it seemed to come from deep in a gut that smelt of something like the marinated droppings of a sick hen. Still, I could not complain. This was life in the raw, the reality of the incarnational theology about which I had tried to wax lyrical during three masses in the previous twelve hours. It mightn't have been 'publicans and sinners' but it certainly was shebeens and drinkers. And wasn't I supposed to be 'another Christ?'

This was Gaeltacht country, poteen country, free Ireland, a place in which the writ of Gael or Gaul or Rome (with either of its empires) never really ran. Neither Protestant Puritanism or Catholic Jansenism had gained a foothold here because their preachers did not speak 'the language that the stranger does not know' well enough. This is not to suggest that faith was absent. "God, Jesus, Mary" were on every lip, but it seemed more like a pre Pio Nono/Paul Cullen faith, maybe even a pre tridentine faith. A clergyperson like myself would be proudly presented with a glass of home produced poteen before breakfast at a station mass.

"Did Santa come?" was my response to the drunken ramblings that were going in one ear and out the other. It was a casual but in the circumstances a cruel and loaded question. I knew that a long-suffering wife and mother would have to be Father Christmas and everything else to their four children while Dad was out on his rounds. Nobody loved wife and children more than that man I was being told when I listened again. He was thinking about them all night and about how lucky he was to have them. He adored them. That was the only word for it. He fucking adored them.

What would really make his day he told me was for me to go home along with him. Herself would have the turkey ready and we would all have a few drinks. I did not fancy myself as a deflector or as a mudguard for his well-deserved flak, so I politely declined. I had been on the road night and day saying masses I told him. I was as tired as he was and had left a goose cooking in the oven while I was away. I would bring him a jar of goose-grease fore the arthritis and for the axle of the ass-cart before the seaweed would have to be gathered after the Spring tides. I spent the rest of the day wondering how that Christmas dinner went. A wife and children's faces swam in the eyes of my mind as they tried to make the best of a bad lot. "I'm dreaming of a fight Christmas" was one of the refrains running through my head.

A couple of parishes and a good few years later, I met that man in a shop in Galway and he greeted me like a long lost friend. They still missed me in the old place, he assured me, but himself more than anyone. I was the man who had saved his life. "I never saved anything except hay," I told him. "And money too, of course." The second part was not true, but who am I to try and change the legend of the greedy priest? "Do you not remember the day you gave me the pledge?" he asked. "It was on a Christmas morning and I had stayed out all night. Drinking the hard stuff... You saved my bacon. I went home and told herself you had put the pledge on me. Not a drop has crossed my lips from that day to this."

"Herself" joined us from further down the supermarket and she looked younger and healthier than she had been twenty years earlier. Life had been good to them, they told me. The children all went to college. Two were married and they had become grandparents for the third time that morning. They were just down from the maternity, buying a few presents. A big yellow note was pushed into my top pocket and no refusal would be brooked. "Thanks for everything..."

"I assured them that I had done nothing, and this was not false or any other kind of modesty. It was the truth. I certainly never "put the pledge" on someone pickled with poteen. But "don't change the legend" they say. Don't change the old cliché either: "God works in mysterious ways." It is not such a bad guilt trip to have to take credit I don't deserve.

XXIX

"It is man who breeds trouble for himself,
as surely as eagles fly to the height." [Job 5:7]

When Eve Adams was finished with the Sunday papers, she brought Cian and Abigail with her to give some space to her husband, Adam. They followed much the same pattern each weekend, Adam bringing the children for football on Saturday, Eve looking after them on Sunday morning. There were occasional exceptions. Some games were held on Sunday, for instance, but for the most part they followed the tried and trusted formula.

Eve brought the children to the wood that day and they enjoyed themselves running around and hiding behind trees. When they tired with that their mother set them the task of collecting as many different species of leaves that they could find. Many of the fallen leaves rustled beneath their feet, but they enjoyed separating them and comparing sizes and shapes. Many of the large pine trees had been felled at the time of the millennium with native Irish trees planted to replace them. Eve pointed out that the beech was not native to Ireland, but that was not to say that many of that variety had not found their way into the forest.

Eve concentrated as much as she could on what the children were doing and saying to keep her mind away from Bill Brown. She was fully determined the previous night to stay away from him but doubts had begun to creep into her mind since morning. Maybe she had made her decision too quickly. It wasn't that Adam and herself had not enjoyed each other's bodies the night before, but she had felt at the time that she was reliving the pleasure she had with Bill earlier in the evening while she was with her husband. She had heard it said in some film that the best cover-up in any affair was to give the person being cheated on the time of his or her life so that nothing would be suspected.

Eve blamed the amount of alcohol she had the previous night for the way she felt. It was not to first time that it had left her depressed. She hid those feelings from the children as best she could and as they walked or skipped along their enthusiasm and playfulness helped her feel much better. By the time they reached the waterfall in the heart of the wood, she head had cleared and she was telling the children to breathe deeply as the negative ions from the falling water helped raise a person's spirits.

"I thought negative is bad and positive is good," Abigail said.

"Not in this case," her mother told her. "Your Dad would know the scientific reasons far better than I do, but it is true that those kinds of ions make a person feel better. That is why a shower brightens you up more than a bath, it's something to do with the falling water."

"I didn't know why I preferred a shower," Cian said, "but I do now."

"You prefer it because it's quicker," Abigail interjected.

"You need a bath more than me because you are always dirty," her brother teased. "You are always tumbling in the park because you can't keep your feet properly."

Abigail picked up a fistful of soil and threw it at him: "You will have to wash now anyhow. They were expecting their mother to chide them for dirtying their clothes. Instead she joined in the fun and the three of them were bursting themselves laughing as they chased each other in and out between the trees, hurling mud and fallen leaves at whoever they could get nearest to.

"There will be baths and showers needed after this," Eve said when they stopped, breathless and tired from their game. "And the washing machine will be working overtime, but I hadn't as much fun in a long time. By the time they got back to the house, Bill hadn't figured in her thoughts for more than an hour. Almost against her will she allowed herself look at the texts on her mobile phone. There was a list of them from "sad puppy" imploring her to call him. He would not be able to live without her.

Eve had deleted all but one message when she noticed that he would be at home on his own for the next couple of hours, as Sharon and Liam were visiting the hospital. "Don't refuse, please" he had written. "You can't just finish it like this."

She called him to say that they would have to end it, but ended up in agreeing to call to his place. "I'll just have to square it with Adam, as I'm supposed to be minding the kids today."

Eve took a shower and put on a simple red dress before going into the conservatory where Adam was reading the Sunday papers. "Would you mind if we had a Chinese tonight?" she asked.

"Why?" he asked. "I thought you were the one that always wanted Sunday dinner to be special?"

"It will be special but I won't be cooking it. It's just that I heard that Sharon's mother was in hospital and I thought I might drop in to see how she is."

"I didn't know the two of you were that pally?"

"We're not," Eve said, "but Bill is your mate and all that."

"Are you taking the kids?"

"They would be bored out of their minds. Would you mind? They are tired after the wood and won't be any bother."

Adam waved his hand as if in blessing as he settled in front of a soccer match on the TV. "Don't be too long. The prospect of that crispy duck is beginning to make my teeth water."

Eve felt the kind of thrill she felt when going out as a teenager, excitement, anticipation and not a little apprehension. How would Bill react to her attempt to finish with him? How had she ever thought she could live without him? She reminded herself that they would need to be very careful. They had agreed that they would never meet in each other's homes, but on this occasion, that might be the safest option. She could say that she had heard that Sharon's mother was ill and she had call around to enquire how she was. Anyway, she could not stay long as she had to collect the Chinese dinner on her way home.

Eve parked her car right in front of Bill and Sharon's house to show that she had nothing to hide. Bill's enthusiasm and passion came as somewhat of a shock. As soon as she entered the house he was hugging and kissing her. His hands were all over her and he had her panties removed in a matter of seconds. He carried her into the kitchen and stretched her back on the kitchen table as he kissed her lips, her neck and her shoulders in an almost frenzied fashion.

"Have ye no bed in this house?" Eve asked laughingly between the kisses.

Bill paused long enough to say: "I'm an old-fashioned kind of a man. I like my meal on the table." It was as if the notion of meal gave him a different idea as his head went immediately beneath her dress and his tongue sent Eve into shudders of pleasure. What she wanted most of all was to have him inside her so she took his head between her hands and pulled him towards her. She unbuckled his belt as quickly as she could but as soon as she reached to guide him inside her his throbbing member exploded hot into her hand.

Bill was abject with shame: "That never happened before. I was just too wound up. I was so happy to see you again when I thought that I had lost you. I'm so sorry. Now I have ruined everything."

Eve put a finger to his lips: "Don't worry. You have just delayed things. All will be well and you will be twice as strong now that this load has been shifted." She reached for a tea-towel that was draped across one of the chairs beside the table and began to clean her hand.

Bill grabbed the cloth and threw it into the washing machine: "If Sharon finds this we are finished." He fumbled with the switches: "How do you get this thing going?" As he said so his trousers slipped down around his ankles and Eve laughed heartily at his predicament.

"What's the big joke?" Bill was still sensitive about his accident.

"It's just that I have never seen a bare-assed man trying to wash a tea-towel without washing powder, that doesn't know how to switch on the machine even. Give me that thing." She took the towel and rinsed it thoroughly under the tap. "What would really surprise Sharon is to find you using a machine you never used before to wash one little item. Now, could we go back to where we were without as much hurry on us this time?"

Bill tidied himself up and sat on the sofa, still ashamed of his messy attempt at love-making. Aoife sat on his knee and allowed her dress to slide up her thighs as if by accident. After a few minutes Bill began to caress her and then to kiss her slowly on the forehead, the eyes, the mouth, without the mad passion of his earlier efforts. As he slid his fingers between her thighs, Eve whispered in his ear: "Carry me down to the room."

"What?" was his surprised reaction.

Eve slid her fingers down along his cheekbone: "You are the brave giant, the mighty hero claiming his prize, and I am the innocent little princess waiting for the handsome prince to show his power."

Bill shook his head and pushed Eve away from him: "I can't"

"Why?" Eve asked. "Have you lost all desire because of that little spillage a while ago?"

"It's not that. I just can't do it to Sharon. We are bad enough as we are."

Eve looked at him as if he had insulted her: "You are with me, and all you can think of is Sharon?"

"It wouldn't be right to do it in our bed."

"You made your bed when you asked me here," Eve said. "Why the sudden fit of conscience when your hand was where it was a minute ago?"

"It's bad enough being unfaithful to Sharon. But in our own bed? That's close to treason."

Eve stood up and straightened her dress: "I know where we stand now. I am just a bit of fun. Your piece on the side. You are just as married to Sharon as you ever were. I get the message, loud and clear."

Bill held out his hands: "ah, Eve, don't be like that. You hardly thought we were going to let this destroy our marriages. Do you want to be separated from your children? Your way of living? Your life?"

Eve bowed her head and said quietly: "That is why I tried to break us up last night, because I was thinking of those very things, Adam, Cian Abigail, and believe it or not I was thinking of Sharon. And Liam. The five people who would suffer most on account of this. But when you texted me today, to say you wanted me. Me. I thought we could face the world together and take the flak, and work it all out like many a couple did before us. It would be difficult at the beginning, but we would have each other."

Bill reached out and held Eve's hands in his: "You know that's what I want too. Eventually. I want you and only you. My heart was broken when I woke up this morning to think we might never be together again. That's why I spent the morning texting you."

"You were just bulling," Eve said, "as you proved as soon as I got into the house. All you wanted was your oats."

"I could get that at home, but no, it was you I wanted, because you stir something inside me that I am not able to explain. Something nobody else ever stirred in me. You bring me alive in a way I could never imagine." Bill stretched out a hand to indicate his house, his life: "But I am not ready yet to leave all this. Liam most of all at the age he is. He would be devastated."

Eve shrugged: "I suppose I am not ready either. I want it all, I suppose. You, the kids, the life… I suppose I just got jealous when you mentioned Sharon."

Bill kissed her: "There is not the slightest reason for you to be jealous of Sharon. You are number one, by a long shot."

"That's what I find so hard to take, that you have a number two as well."

"So, have you," came the quick reply.

"That's true." Eve gave another shrug.

"Can we not continue as we are until the children are at least half reared?" Bill asked.

"It's not very satisfactory, but it is better than the alternative." They held each other and then kissed passionately. "Come on." Bill suggested: "Back to the room."

Eve lay back on the couch: "You were right earlier," she said. "It would not be right in your bed, but I'm telling you it is going to be right here this time, and more than right. It will be wonderful, because I have felt all day that I could not wait until we were together, locked into each other like two parts of some wonderful musical instrument." Eve held up her hand as Bill leaned over to kiss her: "Did I hear the noise of a car?"

"Oh, Jesus," Bill said. "Sharon is back."

XXX

Extract From Paul Godfool's Diary

I announced my epitaph to a startled world some years ago in my weekly column in a local newspaper. The article was a homage to the rasher and my epitaph read: "It was the fry made him die, but he died happy." Since then I have had a lifestyle conversion on the Lough Mask-us road. Porridge has replaced the breakfast fry and smoked salmon is the new rasher. Bacon, egg and sausage are gone and largely forgotten.

I find that the waiting room in the local doctor's surgery is one of the great levellers in life. Swords of Damocles click together and sparkle in the air above our heads as a motley gathering of all shapes and sizes await the call. The worry is almost palpable. Cancer of the breast, the bowel, the bladder, the cervix, the prostate, heart worries, blood pressure, children's ailments, unwanted pregnancies, unwanted miscarriages sit side by side with the just unwanted and make small talk or just read the magazines.

A three-year-old steps forward, points the finger at me and breaks the ice. "Holy God," she declares knowingly. There is a titter of laughter and I reply that the real Holy God is probably not amused. To the "You're far too modest, Father," I reply that I wish I was even "holy man." The child's grandmother says: "Aren't children innocent too?"

The man beside me in silage flavoured wellington boots looks at me as if I am a prize bullock and assures me that I have put on a "bit of condition" since he saw me last, and me hoping I had lost some weight because of the blood pressure. Attention shifts back to the weather until one of those who had shared the waiting room banter earlier comes from the surgery and leaves the building to murmers of: "They say he is riddled with it." There is no need to ask what "it" is.

I have been careful about which magazine to pick up since the last time when page after glossy page was of smaller and smaller sized lingerie. I even joked with the doctor that it was no wonder my blood pressure was so high, not so much because of what was on the pages but from the disapproving glances of some patients.

Then I find that I am the last one sitting and I pick up a "National Geographic." What a nice pickle to get into, I think, as I read that the body of Admiral Horatio Nelson was sent home from the Battle of Trafalger in a cask of brandy. What a way to go! It reminded me of flies I have found drowned in altar wine cruets that have been left uncovered. While saddened at their passing I consoled myself with the thought that at least they had happy deaths.

A story is told in a neighbouring parish of a priest who happened to come upon a road accident in which a heifer had been killed by a passing car. The distraught owner explained that he had just brought her to the bull for the very first time. The priest, relieved that no one had been killed or injured, tried to console the farmer with the immortal words: "At least she had that consolation before she died." By comparison poor Nelson was probably too far gone to appreciate what was all around him.

XXXI

"**The language used to describe a particular group of people was crass (for example in relation to priests, they are mainly white and mainly sh**e) It was unacceptable.**"

The Broadcasting Complaints Commission, 27th January 2005.

Nora McCabe had dinner ready when the two priests, Paul Godfool and Richard Scapegoat reached the house still known as "the master's cottage," although it was no longer, nor had it been for a long time a teacher's residence. Built more than a hundred years earlier at the same time as the local National School, the family had bought it from the parish before Marcas retired and renovated it to modern standards.

Knowing that the man of the house was a reformed alcoholic, the priests at first refused alcohol, but Nora poured them a whiskey each with the comment: "I don't want to be left drinking on my own, and what other satisfaction has a woman left at my time of life?"

"It is better not to answer that question," her husband smiled, "in deference to the two reverences."

"Have you no problem at all with others drinking?" Richard asked.

"I drank it while it was cheap," he answered, "so why should I object to someone who is not addicted having a few drinks? It would be a sad day for the world if a wife had to do without a drop because her husband was on the dry. He winked at their guests: "She is a much less cranky anyway when she has a drop on board."

"Look who is talking about being contrary," Nora retorted. "To tell you the truth I offered to give it up to make it easier for him to stay sober, but he insisted that I live my life in the way I wanted. So, I'm with Saint Paul on this one. Didn't he say that a little wine is good for the stomach."

"There she is again," Marcas commented with a twinkle: "She loves to show off what she learned on that Bible course."

Richard Scapegoat had a particular interest in addiction because of his own condition and he asked Marcas a version of the same question he had asked earlier that day as he tried to suss out how he dealt with it on a daily basis.

"The smell of what the three of you are drinking holds no attraction for me at this stage," Marcas answered, "if it ever did. I sometimes wonder had it more to do with company than with interest in a taste for the drink."

"Indeed, it did," his wife assured him, "because you have drunk it out of the droppings of a cow in the old days."

Marcas straightened himself up: "I would have done no such thing."

Richard looked as if he was afraid this couple were going to end up at each other's throats. Then he noticed Paul sitting comfortably with a little smile playing around the corners of his mouth. He obviously knew his parishioners.

Nora offered her opinion on the subject of addiction: "I think an addict is addicted to something all the time. If he gives up drink, for instance, he focuses big-time on something else."

Marcas winked at their visitors before addressing his wife: "Don't tell me that you are going to inform the visiting clergy about our private life."

"It would be easy to inform them about that," came her quick reply.

"Weren't ye blest with the rule of celibacy?" Marcas joked to the priests.

Paul Godfool said that he agreed with Nora with regard to addiction: "We see something the same with religion, in the zeal of the converted, or those who change from one religion to another."

Nora commented about Marcas: "This man never changed his religion but he buried himself deeper and deeper into it to the extent that he can't find any fault with our own church. You would need to be blind to accept every single thing about it in this day and age."

Richard agreed with her without giving any reason.

Marcas referred back to the discussion the three men had earlier: "We were in complete agreement about the bias and bigotry of the media, especially after what was said about priests last night."

"Father Paul put his pen where his mouth is," Richard said, "and he wrote to the relevant authorities."

"Watch that crowd," Nora said. "If they get a set on you, they will find a way to knife you."

"He is only telling the truth," Marcas said. "If clergy of other denominations were insulted in the same way there would be hell to pay. But they can treat the clergy of our church like…" He remembered his pledge against bad language: "like the proverbial."

Nora was more wary: "That crowd in the media will turn it to make it seem you are trying to defend the bad things that have happened in the church in recent years."

"You know as well as I do, Nora," her husband almost chided her, "that Father Paul here would not give help or comfort to any of those devils that were involved with interfering with children."

Paul Godfool glanced across at Richard Scapegoat, but he maintained a poker face through all of this before cleverly changing the subject by asking their hosts: "Were both of you teachers? Almost every teacher I ever met was married to one of their own profession."

"I wouldn't have the patience for it," Nora replied. "I found it hard enough to bring up two children. And of course, Marcas here was more childish than any of them."

"I was called "the master" everywhere except at home." Marcas said, before asking Richard: "Are the teachers where you are married to each other as well?"

"Some of the best teachers in the world were never trained," was his vague reply as he winked across at Paul.

Marcas was away with it: "It was like that here too at one stage. Many a young boy or girl in sixth class were asked to wait on and help the teacher. It was like an apprenticeship and the Department accepted them after a while."

"They were as good or better than those that came from the colleges," Nora added.

"I often thought the same about the priesthood," Richard said. "They should have a kind of apprenticeship instead of the big colleges. That was the way it was hundreds of years ago."

Marcas said he would have his doubts about that: "You would get one priest well able to pass on his theology. Some other old codger would set his apprentice astray altogether and teach him everything except the Catholic faith."

Richard suggested that an examination system could overcome that problem.

"More control," Paul Godfool commented.

"There would have to be some control," Marcas insisted, "or you would have every little Martin Luther in the country running around setting up his own church."

"I still think faith is more important than theology," Paul said. "You have people in every parish who are stand-out candidates for priesthood. If I was a bishop, I would ordain those if they had the support of their congregation."

Nora was taken by that suggestion: "I'd back that all the way. When you think of it, I'm sure many of those that abused children were very learned in theology, but that didn't stop them doing the dirty work."

Marcas held out his hands in part acknowledgment of the point made by his wife: "I'm sure there is a lot of truth in that, but what kind of sermons would we have if the student priests did not know their theology or their scripture?"

"What kind of sermons have we now?" Nora had asked the question before she remembered that the only priest that preached in their church for fifty Sundays of the year was in the company. "I'm sorry Father Paul," she said. "I'm not talking about you but about priests in general."

"Now the boot has been put in," Richard Scapegoat mocked.

Paul tried to shrug it off: "I know I am good at putting people to sleep, but that mightn't be such a bad thing, especially for those who suffer from insomnia."

"You are not the worst," Marcas told him. "You speak the word of God loud and clear, based on the readings of the day, even if you are a bit too liberal for some old folk like myself sometimes."

"How would you know?" Nora asked, "and you as deaf as the table over there unless your hearing aid is switched on." She explained to the others that the church microphone system interfered with Marcas' ear-piece and that he generally turned it off during mass.

"I'm only deaf when you are talking," Marcas assured his wife. Looking at his watch, he asked: "Will that dinner be burnt to death if we continue talking like this?"

Nora looked at the guest's drinking glasses: "I'm ready when all of you are."

"Can't they bring their glasses to the table," Marcas suggested. "They are slow drinkers, or is it that our malt whiskey is not as good as it used to be?"

Nora set aside the roast to settle and brought a big bowl of soup from the warming oven which she placed in the centre of the table for Marcas to dispense.

"Grace before meals," he said as he poured the soup. "Which of you holy men is going to say it?"

Richard suggested that in the era of women's liberation Nora should do the needful. Marcas had his own idea, asking Richard: "Why don't you say it yourself in the language of the people you work among?"

Paul thought his fellow cleric was caught out, but he remembered the words of the lord's prayer in Hebrew and he intoned the first line of it, hoping that Marcas' classical education had not extended that far.

"What does that mean in English?" Nora asked.

A spray of soup splattered from Richard's mouth as he could not contain his laughter as mock translated: "May the devil choke the lot of you."

"Whatever it means it can't be that," Marcas laughed before turning to Nora: "Wasn't I the lucky man to visit the presbytery this morning and encounter such engaging company?"

Nora pointed towards the roast lamb: "I'm sure our guests would prefer if you carved the joint instead of all the soft talk."

As their visitors finished their soup, Richard said to Nora: "You probably had half that meat earmarked for tomorrow's lunch. And here we are eating you out of house and home."

"No trouble at all," she said as she removed her apron: "I can enjoy this. My work is done for the day. I cook. He cleans up afterwards."

"We will do the clean-up tonight, won't we Paul?" Richard said. "It's the least we can do."

"No way," Nora replied, with a wink. "I'm not letting himself off the hook as easily as that."

"There is enough here to feed an army," Paul Godfool said as his plate was piled high with meat and vegetables. It will do me for a week. I wouldn't have to put a pan on the range at all this week if I didn't have to feed your man here."

"Are you suggesting that I am not capable of boiling an egg?" Richard said.

"Ye can come here again tomorrow for the lunch," Marcas suggested. "Can't they Nora?"

Paul Godfool took the pressure off Nora by stating immediately that they had plans made to tour around at times he would not be involved in parish duties.

"While you are tied up in the church, can't your mate come over here for a chat and a drink and a bite to eat if he wants?" Marcas suggested. "I'd like to hear more about the missions, from the horse's mouth as it were."

Richard Scapegoat made a vague promise to call again, but said he needed time to sleep and rest more than anything.

"They would prefer to be playing golf or something than to be here talking to two old codgers," Nora commented.

"I doubt if they play much golf on the missions," Marcas said. "It's far from golf those people were reared, though they probably have a few golf courses to attract tourists."

"The only principle I have left," Richard said, "is never to play golf. Not in this life anyway, whatever about in the great playing fields of the next world."

"Speaking of the next world," Marcas asked: "How do you see it? How do you imagine it?"

Nora was quickest to answer: "A place where men are women and women are men. As regards power and influence I mean."

"The question was directed to the men of God," Marcas said.

Nora laid down her knife and fork as if she was afraid she would use them on her husband: "Well, excuse me. I thought I was in the company, too, or are you just trying to prove my point? As it happens, I was joking, but it seems I have been put in my place, a woman's place, cooking and serving. Not to speak of bowing to my betters and saying: 'Yes, master.'"

Marcas laid aside his cutlery too: "We are trying to have a polite conversation here, not discussing the political implications of women's liberation. Anyway, I thought ye had stopped burning bras a long time ago."

Nora had a sudden burst of laughter: "It would be easy to burn some of the flimsy things they wear nowadays. Unless you are talking about the super-bras. There would be a lot of smoke out of them alright."

"Take it easy on the wine," Marcas said to her: "That kind of comment is hardly appropriate in the circumstances."

"But insulting women is, I suppose." Nora picked up her cutlery and got on with her dinner.

Marcas turned to Richard as if his wife was not present at all: "What is your picture of the heavens, Father?"

"A place where men listen to women," came the quick reply.

"Good man yourself." Nora gave him a clap on the back before topping up their guests and her own wine glasses.

"What about you, Father Paul?" Marcas continued his round of questioning.

"Something beyond our wildest dreams, because we don't have the ability to imagine it." He paused for a moment: "A place or state of being at least as different from this world as the life of the child in the womb is different from the world it enters."

"What about yourself?" Richard asked Marcas: "What is your heaven?"

"Contentment," he answered quietly, "because that must be the strongest desire of the human heart. It's what we pray for those who have gone before us whom we have loved dearly."

"It's men's heaven he is talking about," said Nora with a loud laugh, "because women can't be kept quiet. We always have the last word."

"It's a pity ye don't have the last word then," Marcas commented, "because you would shut up afterwards."

Richard made an effort to direct the conversation: "I don't know anything about the next life, but if you had an opportunity to do something important in this one, what would you do?"

Nora was the quickest off the mark: "I would put in a woman Pope, and she would soon sort out this church of ours."

"I'd put in a man as Pope," Marcas said with a smile, "to undo all the damage the woman Pope had done."

Paul looked at Richard: "What about you?"

"I would allow everyone do what they liked without being hogtied by the conservative forces of church and state."

"Interesting, although I do not agree with you," Marcas said: "What about our own priest? Father Paul?"

"What does the world need most?" he replied.

"To feed the hungry," Nora answered.

"Exactly, and to help the hungry feed themselves."

There was quiet for a while apart from the sounds of cutlery on delph. The subject retirement came up later, and Marcas mentioned that he was thinking of doing a course in computers in the local hall which had been advertised in the church newsletter: "Or would I be too old for that kind of thing?"

"There is no such thing as being too old," Richard said. "Why don't both of you do it? The Internet is amazing. You can get information on almost anything."

"For all his holy talk, I'd be afraid he would start looking at those dirty pictures that are supposed to be on it," Nora said. "He nearly crashed the car the last day when some young one in a miniskirt crossed the road."

"That is just human nature," Marcas replied, "and the day a man's eye isn't taken by a beautiful girl, he is finished. That is not to say he has any intention of doing anything about it. You can look at the menu, as they used to say."

"You wouldn't just look at the menu," commented Nora. "You would have the meal as well if anyone was stupid enough to give it to you."

Marcas replied: "All I could do at this stage is look."

Nora was not finished yet: "We have all heard of men who were led astray by pornographic pictures on the Internet and the damage they did to children on account of it. What was your man's name in Belgium?"

"This would be different," Richard said. "You would be there beside him to watch what he was doing and to advise him. There is an awful lot of good stuff on the Internet, about the Bible and everything."

"I think I will stick to my knitting," was Nora's comment. "It would be a recipe for murder if the two of us were looking at the one computer. The television is bad enough."

They all sat around on the big leather sofas afterwards. Despite the priest's offers to clean up and wash up, their hosts were having none of it. "What else have we to do in the morning?" Marcas asked. "That's the beauty of retirement."

"Was it good manners to leave so early?" Richard Scapegoat asked on their way back to the presbytery in the car.

"They are not getting any younger," Paul replied, "and I have had a long day myself, and a lot to do tomorrow, too."

"It wasn't a bad night."

"The meal was great," Paul answered.

"The conversation was not bad either."

"I was wondering does Nora suspect something," Paul mused. "She brought up child abuse a couple of times."

Richard had his own view on that: "I think she would be too courteous to broach the subject if she knew anything."

"You took it all in your stride anyhow."

"What did you expect? A public confession?"

"There is no need to be so defensive," Paul answered. "I was not finding fault, so much as admiring how steady your nerves are."

Richard got in his own dig: "Do you often drive home at night after having so much to drink?"

"It's only a couple of miles, and I didn't have that much to drink."

"I'd say we are both well over the limit," Richard said, "between whiskey and wine. They certainly were generous hosts."

"It's not the worst crime in the world."

"Still if they were to put the bag on you, or worse again if you had an accident?"

Paul Godfool was in no mood for such criticism: "They would take away my driver's licence, or even put me in prison. Sure, you could advise me about conditions there."

XXXII

Extract From Paul Godfool's Journal

After much body and soul searching recently, I deduced what is wrong with me, or at least one of the things wrong with me. I suffer from dessert deficiency in general, and from profiterole deprivation in particular. This condition has arisen from having to leave wedding receptions early. In some cases, I have been unable to attend such gatherings at all this year, due to distance, Saturday evening masses, evening meetings, or rehearsals for other weddings.

In so far as desserts are concerned the profiterole is the new "Baked Alaska". Sometimes referred to as "baked elastic" and not always without reason, this was the most popular dessert in my early priestly ministry. It was a big deal at that time, so much so that I suspect some couples got married for the sake of the sumptuous dessert. Those were the days before three-month's notice and other restrictions led to more serious thought being put into marriage, other than what was promised in its immediate aftermath. I remember couples arriving at the presbytery door and telling me: "We are getting married on Saturday week." Amazingly, thankfully, most are still together as invitations back to twenty-fifth anniversaries attest.

The magic and the mystery of this particular dessert was deepened by having the lights switched off and the baked Alaska carried in flames to the table. I must confess to having committed the sins of covetousness and gluttony many times in respect to that after dinner offering. Baked Alaska seemed to disappear completely from the radar as a new generation of chefs took over, a class of cook I would tend to refer to as "the dribblers and the dusters."

Dribbling was something babies and soccer players did in my youth. Now it is the preserve of the chef, with oil dribbled on salads, chocolate dribbled on desserts and all kind of obscure hieroglyphics drawn on plates with coloured fruit dribbles. What isn't dribbled on is dusted, with flour or sugar or condiments. We have come a long way from the day the duster was referred to in Irish households as "the rag." It was generally the remains of a well-worn and long discarded garment pressed into service when no longer useful for the purpose for which it was woven, but still capable of absorbing liquid or gathering dust.

Another of my favourite desserts is the old-fashioned jelly and ice-cream. This I am lucky enough to partake of at christening and first holy communion parties in a local hostelry. They say that they provide it for the children, but I notice that it is one area in which many adults, including myself "become like little children." It is one of those tastes that takes me back and reminds me of long lost youth, but it does not completely take away my profiterole hankering.

The obvious answer to my dessert deficiency problems is to go out and buy a container of ready-made profiteroles in a Supermarket and bring them home to gorge on, but that is completely missing the point. The joy of the hotel dessert is that it is handed up to you, usually with a fork so that a person cannot consume too much cream, runny chocolate or other cholesterol increasing dribble. The finished plate looks like a Picasso painting. Best of all is the fact that the oversized plate has not to be carried to sink or dish-washer by the satisfied guest afterwards.

With regard to having dinners handed up to you, I recall a story told to me by a man in Conamara many years ago about the free beef made available during the economic war between Ireland and the United Kingdom in the thirties of the last century. As far as this man was concerned the free beef was the making of Eamon De Valera as a politician. It was not just that he took on the might of the then formidable British Empire, but he provided free beef for his followers. As miracles go, this bettered the five loaves and two fishes story in the Bible, but that was mainly because the man concerned hated fish, because it was the staple diet of his youth.

The Conamara man recalled how his mother put all seven pounds of beef in a pot that hung on a crane above the fire. She added potatoes and onions and let it boil away. The man, his two brothers, and their mother consumed the massive stew in one go. They then sat down and smoked their pipes until they fell asleep. Now that was happiness. It makes me hope for the day the present government might declare another economic war and provide us all with profiteroles to help us cope with dessert deficiency.

XXXIII

*"Test me, probe me, Lord, put me to the test,
loins and heart." [Ps 26:2]*

The last thing Sharon Brown wanted when she returned, with her son, Liam, tired and stressed after visiting her mother in the hospital was to find anyone other than her husband, Bill in the house. Eve Adams sat opposite her husband at the kitchen table in a designer dress. For a woman who never had a hair out of place, she looked as if she had been out in the wind. Sharon greeted them perfunctorily before flopping on the couch as if her legs had collapsed beneath her. "Make me a cup of tea, good man," she said to Bill.

"How is your mother?" Eve asked. "Adam heard she was in hospital and I ran over to enquire about her."

"Would you like a crisp?" Liam proffered his packet of potato crisps in Eve's direction.

His mother reacted angrily: "Where are your manners? Eve is speaking to me. How often have I told you not to interrupt when grown-ups are talking?"

"I'm sorry," Liam replied: "I thought it was good manners to share my chips."

"You're fine," Eve assured him. "You have a lot more manners than my two. I will have a crisp or two, if you have them to spare."

Sharon apologised to their visitor: "Everything in the house is upside down since my mother went into hospital. What is that wet towel doing there?" She took the towel Eve had rinsed earlier and threw it into the washing machine, before asking Eve: "Would you like a cup of tea or coffee? Something stronger?"

"No thanks, Sharon." Eve explained that she was on her way to pick up a Chinese meal for the family. Sharon had started to tell of her mother's ordeal on the hospital trolley when Liam interrupted again: "I love Chinese, but we only have it an odd time because my Mam thinks that it is not healthy."

"What did I say about interrupting grown-ups?" his mother asked sternly.

"I'm sorry," Liam said and he hung his head.

"I wonder are those healthier than Chinese," Eve said, as she took another crisp. She asked Sharon: "Would it help if I was to take Liam for the night and he could have a Chinese with Abigail and Cian?"

"Yes, yes." Liam jumped up and down in delight. "Say yes, Mam and Dad." They looked at each other and agreed.

"Hurry up," Liam said to Eve after he had thanked his parents.

"What did your Mam say about manners?" Bill said. "Get your sport's bag and put in some clean clothes."

"It will give you a chance to catch some sleep," Eve was saying to Sharon, "after the ordeal you had in the hospital."

"I'm so grateful, Eve. You are a real friend."

"Isn't that what friends are for?" Eve looked across at Bill who did not meet her eyes. "Why don't I drop him off to school with my own in the morning?"

Bill and Sharon went to the front door to wave them off, joking about the full bag Liam had brought with him as if he was going away for a month. As soon as the others had left, Sharon turned into her husband's arms and asked him to give her the biggest hug ever. "I need it after all I have been through with mother. She is just impossible."

Bill caressed her as best he could, rubbing his hands around her back and shoulders, feeling a mixture of guilt and inadequacy: "Your shoulders are very tense," he said.

Sharon took one of his hands and led him over to sit beside her on the couch: "If she is dead in the morning, I'll never forgive myself for walking away from her in the hospital, but she is so cruel, the way she treats me."

"Maybe it's something else that is coming on her," Bill said. "She wasn't always that contrary."

There was always tension between us, though some say that is natural between mother and daughter," Sharon answered. "I did mention Alzheimers when she said something particularly hurtful to me."

Bill shook his head from side to side: "Is it fair to say that to an old person? It's probably their greatest fear."

"She deserved it after the way she treated me. She was getting at me from the time I got to the hospital, worrying was she going to die. Well she didn't die. She just turned into an old witch, like one of the characters in those books Liam has."

Bill tried to console her: "It was a stressful weekend for you."

Sharon continued as if she had not heard him: "If mother isn't going out of her mind, I am, because I don't know whether I'm coming or going."

Bill put his arm across her shoulder: "The best thing you can do is go to bed and not open an eye until Liam comes home from school tomorrow."

"I have to go in to see her again in the morning, even though it will probably turn into another biting session. I've heard of love-hate relationships, but this must be the ultimate in them."

Bill looked at his watch: "If you go to bed now you could have more than twelve hours sleep. That should refresh you and you will be able for your mother or anything else life throws at you."

"Come with me."

Bill answered as if the invitation had come as a shock: "To bed you mean. You don't mean…?"

Sharon didn't allow him finish his question as she stopped his words with a kiss. "It might seem strange, with my mother in hospital and everything, but I just want your strong arms around me. I feel so lonely these days."

"You were hardly lonely with that crowd around you in the hospital corridor?"

"I feel we have lost something of the way we were. You were able to turn my night into day with your love. That's what I was thinking of in that corridor among the trolleys. That's what I need now, and to sleep like an angel afterwards."

Bill sounded sheepish and embarrassed: "I don't know can I turn it on just like that."

"We are not in a hurry. Liam is being cared for. The night is ours. I'm going for a bath and I will be waiting in the bed. I'll bet that is the best offer you had all day."

Bill remained on the couch while Sharon was in the bathroom. What would she think, he wondered, if he was to tell her that he had two better offers that day, that he had made a mess of the first, and that she had almost interrupted the second? He wondered was his earlier failure psychological, due to guilt or as some kind of punishment from the gods. "Was he going to fail again now? Not if I pretend to myself I am with Eve," he thought.

Bill removed his shoes and socks, almost as if he was preparing to play a match. He left them by the couch and went into the bathroom to join his wife in the shower.

"We haven't done this since we were on honeymoon." Sharon welcomed him with big generous kisses: "I was able to jump up on you that time, but I would probably put you out through the glass door now." She took his hand and they went to the bedroom, trailing water on the tiled floor. They sat beside each other on the bed and kissed as if they were just getting to know each other.

"Will you take me in your mouth?" Bill said.

Sharon backed away slightly as if in disgust: "What?"

"It would make me harder. I would last longer."

"It's not right."

"Just a little and I'll go inside then."

Sharon licked him lightly with her tongue."

"That's lovely. Again. That's beautiful."

Bill entered his wife, an image of Eve in his mind and they had the longest session of intercourse they ever had. Sharon moaned with pleasure as she tightened her legs around her husband. He had a moment of panic when he remembered her legs had strengthened from jogging. For an awful moment he felt she was going to break his back. The ridiculous thought of how he would explain that to Eve occurred to him, but his pleasure was carrying him away now as he ploughed deeper and deeper. Sharon's legs loosened and seemed to just open wide as her pleasure carried her away. Bill wondered was he cursed with an incurable erection that would go on forever, but then the explosion came. When he opened his eyes, Sharon was looking at him with a big smile on her face.

"I don't know what has come over you," she said in admiration, "but I hope it is not long until it happens again."

Bill kissed her tenderly: "I hope I didn't offend you by asking you to do that."

"It was well worth it. What brought that into your mind?"

"Something I read in a magazine," Bill said lightly.

"I never thought you would be reading about the likes of that."

Bill continued with his casual approach: "Maybe it was on the radio I heard it. You know those programmes on how to improve your personal life."

"You will have to tell me when that programme is on again. I am sure that I have a lot to learn," Sharon said.

"Not after what we have just done."

"Did you think things were getting boring between us or what?" Sharon asked.

"It had nothing to do with anything like that. It came on the radio or whatever, and for once I thought their so-called expert made a bit of sense."

Sharon rubbed her hand in a circular motion on her stomach area: "You can try out those theories anytime. Now if you like."

"You know as well as I do that you need sleep more than anything," her husband said, "after the couple of days you have put in."

"I was never as wide awake in my life. I could keep doing that all night."

"A man is different," Bill said. "All he is able to do afterwards is turn over and fall asleep."

Despite her talk Sharon was soon asleep with Bill's arms around her. He carefully disentangled himself and went outside to call Eve. He had forgotten that she would be at dinner but was still surprised by the coldness of her voice when she answered. He realised Adam was present when she spoke as if to a telesales assistant: "No, I don't want to change to a different telephone company and you have a cheek to ring on a Sunday evening. Have you never heard of the day of rest?" He heard Adam offer to have a word with her caller, but she immediately clicked off. Bill felt guilty and unfaithful to Eve because he had made love to his wife. At the same time, he felt guilty for thinking of Eve while he was with Sharon. There is no easy way to do this, he thought. He went inside and switched on the round-up of that day's sport to try and take his mind away from all of it.

XXXIV

Extract From Paul Godfool's Journal

I sometimes wonder have we got the song of the angels in Bethlehem wrong all down through the years. Could it be that instead of "peace on earth" they were actually singing "PC on earth?" PC in this context does not refer to personal computer, but to political correctness. This means being so careful in our speech and writing that we do not offend anyone. On the other hand, it can be used as a convenient way to sideline the deity and to airbrush God from our consciousness.

God has become a fierce embarrassment to many people in this country. It raises the question of whether we should try and have Christmas without God or Jesus or the rest of them in order to please the PC brigade. A controversy about the inclusion of the word crib in an advertisement on the National Radio and TV station led me to try and think of a way to tell the Christmas story without offending anyone, and especially those most sensitive of souls, journalists in the national media who have a major problem with religion, the poor dears.

What have you left if you leave out words like God, Jesus, Saviour, crib, etcetera? I would suggest that God be renamed "The Great Unmentionable," so that we can talk about him/her without mentioning names. This would make Jesus "The Little Unmentionable." Swaddling clothes can become a baby-gro, crib a hay-box or more realistically in this day and age, a bale of silage.

Angels could be called "fly-by-nights," although I am bound to be reassured that they fly by day as well. Shepherds could be called quad-drivers and the three wise men "Boy camel-racers." That would have the

Christmas – I apologise, I should say "The Little-Unmentionable-mas" story going something like this: "A long time ago in Bethlehem there was this Jewish bloke and his girlfriend on their way to sign on for some kind of big people count. The stupid government had sent them all back to where their people came from to see how many of them were in it. The young couple could not find any place to stay in BnB's hotels, hostels or anything. They had to camp out in this kind of old shed with animals and manure and everything. Gross.

That was where your one had her baby and it was like all a bit weird. She was not much more than a slip of a girl herself and she claimed it was The Great Unmentionable that had her knocked up. She didn't mind like – she loved her little baby. When she had the baby cleaned up and put in a baby-gro didn't these fly-by-nights start circling around above them making out the baby was a big deal. Then didn't a crowd of sheep minders turn up on their quads or whatever to see what all the fuss was about. They swallowed the story, hook, line and stinker (the silage). Other blokes on camels turned up with perfume to help get rid of the smell, but that old story is still as sweet as ever."

XXXV

**"Why did I not die in the womb, That I didn't
die as I was being born?" [Job 3:11]**

"I cannot understand why those sales-people are trying to sell things day and night," Eve Adams said as she laid her mobile phone aside. She wondered what had got into Bill that he had called so casually at a time Adam would be present at their evening meal. The thought then struck her that Liam may have forgotten something, but in a case like that his father would ring on the land-line. It would seem strange to Adam that Bill would have her mobile number. Her mind was in such a state of confusion that she did not even notice that Adam was speaking to her from the other side of the dinner-table.

"Hello, hello!" Abigail waved a finger back and over in front of her mother: "Is there anyone in?"

Cian and Liam enjoyed this and started to say: "Hello, hello," themselves.

Eve joined in the fun when she realised what was going on: "Is there anyone in? I'm in." She apologised to Adam for the fact that her mind had wandered: "I wasn't listening properly because I was mad with that sales crowd for interrupting our dinner."

"I suppose they don't know what day it is here or that it is bad manners to interrupt our dinner. They are probably ringing from Hong Kong. A lot of that telesales business is in the far east nowadays."

Eve laughed: "It is appropriate enough if they are ringing from Hong Kong. They might have got a smell of the Chinese."

"Don't be daft, Mum," Cian said. "You can't smell anything on the phone."

Abigail answered him: "She is only joking. Duh."

Cian put out his tongue at her: "Are you trying to show off in front of your boyfriend?"

"I don't have a boyfriend. I hate boys."

"Why is Liam here so?" her brother asked.

Eve intervened: "Stop fighting. Liam is here because his grandmother is in hospital and I am minding him to give his mother a break."

Cian put on a funny accent: "And he likes to be here with Abby." He tried to make a rhyme: "Abby and Liam, it's only a dream."

"I thought Liam was your friend," Eve said to Cian, before telling their visitor: "Take no notice of Cian."

Cian giggled: "Liam always wants to sit beside Abby at school. I think they are in love or something."

"One more word out of you, young man," his mother said sternly, "and you will be going to your room."

"Why don't ye go and have a game of pool or something?" Adam took money from his pocket. "Five euro for the winner." The three children ran off excitedly to the pool-room.

"Who says you can't buy peace?" Adam said to Eve as they rested on the arm-chairs after the children had gone. "Cheap at the price. Five euro."

"Until they start fighting about the game," his wife answered. "Those kids are so competitive."

"Ours certainly are," Adam said. "Isn't that a good thing?"

"I think Liam is a bit softer," Eve commented.

"What would you expect? He is his father's son."

"Do you think Bill is soft?" Eve asked.

"He was a bit like that on the football pitch."

"He must be tough enough to be a successful businessman."

Adam shrugged: "Successful in the good times. Easy. The real test will come now that we have the down-turn."

Eve reached for the magazine section of one of the Sunday papers, as if talk of Bill was just a pastime. Adam switched on a sports channel on TV. It was like a typical Sunday evening but Eve hardly saw what was in front of her as she flicked from page to page. She was thinking that bringing Liam home with her had been a clever move. Adam would have no reason to suspect visits to Bill and Sharon's house if it had to do with the children.

Eve was already thinking that she would have an excuse to go there the following day to drop off Liam's overnight bag.

Eve was still upset with Bill for calling at such an awkward time. What if Adam had taken the phone from her hand in order to give a piece of his mind to the supposed sales-person? Too close for comfort. They would have to be more careful. Feelings do not always sense danger, she thought. She continued to flick through the magazine before breaking the silence:

"I never saw so many holiday homes for sale as there are this week."

"People are trying to free up money because of the credit crunch," Adam said. "And they probably want to get out now in case prices plummet."

"Does that mean we could be in trouble with the new scheme in Lanzarote?"

Adam smiled smugly: "They were sold off the plans. The contracts are signed so we don't really have anything to lose."

"I know you got the deposits, but what if people can't come up with the rest of the money?" Eve asked.

"Not our problem. We might postpone the next phase until we see how things are going. I will have a word with Bill about it one of the days."

"By the way," Eve asked casually, "do the two of you still intend to go out there for that working holiday?"

"It is not a holiday," Adam said testily, "and right now I am too busy with work. It is a pity you are not prepared to go out with him."

"I have thought about what you said the last day," Eve said carefully. "If it helps the project… I would be terrified though that I might make a mistake and you would be so angry with me."

Adam shook his head: "You used to be so self-confident. You know as much about it as I do. Can't you e-mail the plans to me to be checked? And we have a good solicitor. Bill will be there, too. All you have to do is sign on behalf of both of us. It would take a great weight off my mind."

"So long as I don't make a mess of it." Eve was already thinking of sunny beaches, the pool, the shops, a week with Bill all to herself.

"You will be fine," her husband insisted. "I'd love to see you getting more involved. You seem so distracted lately."

"Maybe I have too much time on my hands now that the children are virtually able to look after themselves."

"I will mention it to Bill tomorrow," Adam said.

"With the way Sharon's mother is, he mightn't be able to go anywhere."

"Life must go on," was Adam's reply. "Sharon's mother will be at home or in the grave in a couple of weeks."

Eve looked at him to see was this meant as a joke: "That isn't a nice thing to say about the poor woman."

"It's true, though. I'm a realist. I have no wish to bury the woman, but you must admit she is no chicken. Whether his mother-in-law is alive or dead, Bill will not be tied down forever. That is all I am saying. Lanzarote is less than five hours away. Can't he be back for the funeral if anything happens?"

"You are so cold," his wife said. She was thinking at the same time that was what would surely happen, God's revenge on Bill and herself after their scheming and unfaithfulness.

"Why do you say I am cold?" Bill asked.

"There is more involved with Ann dying than Bill being at the funeral. He would want to be there for Sharon while her mother was sick or on her death bed."

Adam shrugged his shoulders: "I don't know are they as great with each other as you seem to think."

"What makes you think that?"

"It was something he said while we were at soccer yesterday," Adam replied.

Eve put on a sarcastic tone: "I was forgetting that both of you are new men, that you discuss your private lives and your feelings and everything. You are as bad as two old women"

"I felt Bill was not happy with his lot."

"Did he actually say that?" Eve asked.

"Not in so any words, but we "new men" are able to read between the lines."

"The lines around his eyes or the ones on his forehead?" Eve wondered.

Adam responded: "I read that they are not together very often, if you know what I mean."

"Isn't it you that is very diplomatic," Eve said, "when what you mean is that the poor man is not getting his hole as often or as well as he would like. Wouldn't you pity the poor man."

"Some say that is the first thing that suffers when a couple are not getting along," Adam said.

Eve looked at him as if he hadn't got a clue: "So it all depends on sex? According to the new men that know all about the human condition and who get most of their information from American TV programmes. Doctor this and Counseller that."

"You are missing the point," Adam said. "I was just trying to say that Bill would find the time to go to Lanzarote, and it ended up in all this silly talk."

"Lanzarote!" Eve said the word as if it disgusted her.

"What is wrong with Lanzarote?" Adam asked.

"All of the Canary island holiday thing just makes me sick. Lager louts and layabouts."

Adam looked directly at her: "Not every part of the islands is like that or we wouldn't be involved in developments there. Anyway, isn't it part of Spain, and I thought Spain was your favourite place in the world?"

"I am not staying in the same hotel as Bill," Eve said.

"You don't need to. Just think pool and shops and a very small amount of work on the project."

Eve was thinking of Bill's arms around her in the pool, romantic dinners and full nights spent together: "Give Bill a call tomorrow," she said casually, "but don't forget to ask about Sharon's mother first. Pretend you have some heart."

"I'm all heart, me," Adam laughed. "Full of heart and soul and intelligence and an eye for a business opportunity. And full of love for my wife." He held out his arms.

"Don't even think of it tonight," Eve said, "and a visitor under our roof."

"What difference does that make?" Adam asked. "We don't want to wake Cian or Abigail either, but that never stopped us."

"Ours would sleep through anything in their own beds, but remember Liam might not settle in a strange house. And he will probably be worried about his grandmother."

Adam was in boastful mood: "That is part of our marriage that has always been healthy. We never get bored with each other's bodies."

Eve tried to hide her sarcasm as she replied: "And if that is right, everything else is alright."

"Alright is not the word," Adam said. "Last night was sensational."

Eve bowed dramatically: "Pleased to be of service, master."

Adam pointed to the door of the pool-room: "Only for the children are in there I would want to do it right here in front of the fire. I have only to look at you in that dress with the slits at the side. The same dress would not be left on you long if I wasn't afraid the children would burst in."

"It's not your tongue that is talking now," Eve smiled, aroused by his talk.

Adam licked his lips: "This tongue can do more than talk."

"Stop," Eve said, "or you will have me tearing the clothes off you." She playfully hid her head behind a newspaper, peeping out like a child.

Adam changed the subject: "I will ring Bill so, tomorrow and tell him to organise that trip to Lanzarote, as long as Sharon's mother is alright."

"That is a quick change from what we were discussing," Eve replied. Business is the most important thing to you."

"I had to talk about something else in case I would burst out of my trousers."

"Why is there always an obstacle when people are hot?" Eve wondered.

"It is a long night yet, and some say anticipation is the best part."

Eve was emphatic: "Whoever said that knows nothing about it." They were silent for a while before Eve said: "It will be strange to be overseas without you. I will miss you."

"It is only for a week."

"There would be very little sunshine at this time of the year."

"So it is skin colour that his really upsetting you," Adam said playfully. "You have nothing to worry about. The sun shines there all year. It is on the same level as the Sahara."

"Tanning has nothing to do with it," Eve replied. "You can get that from a bottle. But I will put up with it. I will go through with it."

Adam teased her: "Poor thing. I would give anything to be free to spend a week over there. Sun myself, play golf, eat fish, drink wine, do a little business in the cool of the evening after siesta. It is not the worst job in the world to have to do."

"I know, but I don't play golf. I would be gone from you and the kids. The pool will be too cold. I won't understand a word on the television. How am I going to pass the time?"

"Have you ever heard of shopping?" Adam asked with light sarcasm. "Has it not helped you pass the time on other days?"

Eve dismissed that argument: "We are not talking Paris or Milan here."

"As for TV," Adam assured her. "They have Sky and many English language films on their own channels."

"There is nothing worse than looking at the same news channel every half-hour all day," Eve said. "Where were we that had only CNN in English? If there is such a thing as hell, that must be it."

Adam spoke bluntly: "Don't bother, if you don't want to go."

"It's not that I won't do it, just that it will be so boring."

"It would pass the time if you shared a meal with Bill in the evening."

Eve twisted her face in a kind of scowl: "I would prefer to enjoy my dinner, thank you."

"He is not that bad."

"I'm not saying he is," Eve answered, "but it is hard to keep conversation with someone you have nothing in common with. I'm not into sport."

"It's not that he is a complete stranger," Adam said. "I didn't notice any tension between you when we were on holiday last year."

"But you were there and Sharon, and Liam as well as our kids to keep the conversation going. I will eat by myself. I will have that much comfort."

"Speak to him like you would speak to me," her husband said. "Chat to him like we are chatting now."

Eve winked: "Are you giving me carte blanche? He wouldn't know what hit him if I pretended he was you. It would shock him so much that he would have a heart attack on the spot."

"You know as well as I do that is not what I mean. I would say that he is the last man in the world you would be interested in," Adam said. "But Bill is alright. He is slow and steady and old-fashioned, conservative in his ideas, but he is not a bad fellow. I would have no worry about you being over there as long as Bill was on the island."

"Why would you be worried about me anyway?" Eve asked.

"You know the way things happen. Someone snatches your handbag. A person can be very vulnerable if they know nobody."

"I wouldn't like to be depending on Bill," Eve said, dismissively. "Anyway, it's only for a week. I will survive it."

"Enjoy it as much as you can," Adam advised, but he was not thinking of the kind of enjoyment Eve had in mind.

XXXVI

Extract From Paul Godfool's Journal

"What is all the fuss about one-off housing?" I ask myself when visiting some of the great valleys that hide behind the local hills. I know one into which you could fit Dublin, Galway and Belfast, and still have room for Sligo, Limerick and Cork. The idea that rural Ireland is in danger of becoming a concrete jungle is quickly given the lie by such vast areas which are virtually empty of human habitation. Ten national schools have closed within twenty square miles of me in the past thirty years. The place is far more in danger of reverting completely to nature than to being swamped by one-off houses. Houses mean people, and a few white specs of housing in a massive landscape takes nothing away as far as I am concerned.

The extent to which ecology is in danger of going eco-loco was brought home to me last year by reports in the national papers that a man I had known in my first island posting was prosecuted and fined for turning a piece of rock into arable land in the traditional island way. I used to watch in admiration and amazement as people virtually made something out of nothing, made arable land from rock. Sand and seaweed were scattered on the bare limestone. Every handful of soil that could be garnered from the roadside or anywhere else was added. Ridges were made and the finest of flowery potatoes grown. Now this has become a crime. Ok, the pensioner in question should have got permission from some bureaucrat, but the very idea that an old man should be hounded in this manner and forced to return a few square yards of rock to its original state beggars belief when we see what developers get away with. Eco-loco-ism is becoming the ultimate political correctness.

For the first time in almost two hundred years, this area is not being devastated by emigration. This is the first generation of young people who do not have to, or want to go to live in Chicago or Croydon or Sydney. Most want to settle down and to rear families in the area in which they grew up. Many parents are willing to supply them with sites to help reduce the costs of housing, but planning authorities seem to bend over backwards to make this as difficult as possible. Continental Europeans, by contrast who want to build holiday homes in the area seem to have little difficulty in obtaining planning permission.

I suspect this has less to do with discrimination than with people's ability to deal bureaucracy (bureau-crazy?) While we tend to throw up our hands in frustration, deliver ourselves of a few curses and give up when refused permission, our continental cousins do not let go of the bone. They reapply, make a few changes here and there, wear down the planners as much as anything else, but each application costs more money.

Some excuses used for the refusal of planning permission have entered local legend. I am particularly taken by the one that a house near the shore would disturb those looking in from the lake. Do they mean the fish or the fishermen and women? I cannot imagine fisher-folk being too worried by what is on the shore unless the fishing is bad and they are in foul humour. Neither had I realised that a scavenging pike would be so sensitive as to be disturbed by a building on the shore. Perhaps we could supply them with tinted glasses.

I'm all for environmental protection and traipse down regularly to the bottle bank. (I'm not telling you with how many bottles.) I avoid aerosols, only light a fire outdoors on the traditional bonfire night, Saint John's Eve. I support national and European legislation in this area as long as it is common sense, eco-sense rather than eco-loco.

Mention of the bottle bank reminds me of a man I knew in an earlier parish who regularly (religiously) collected altar wine bottles from beside a church sacristy. I thought he was engaged in some kind of recycling until a neighbour of his presented me with a bottle of poteen. Most of the label had been removed except the line which read: "Approved by the Irish bishops."

XXXVII

"The Broadcasting Complaint's Commission upheld eleven complaints about RTÉ output. Eight of these complaints were about one programme, The Late Late Show, broadcast on 22nd October 2004 which featured the comedian, Tommy Tiernan. This programme was judged to have breached impartiality and taste and decency."

RTÉ and the Broadcasting Complaint's Commission 2005 Annual Report

Time passed. Looking back on that period later the image Paul Godfool had was of the hands of a clock racing around in an old black and white film to give the impression of time passing while little happened. Christmas and the New Year came and went. Paul was busy with the usual ceremonies, and apart from Marcas McCabe wondering why he got no help from "the missioner" in his priestly work, it was as if Richard Scapegoat was staying in the presbytery unknown to the world.

It was not that the community was unaware that Richard was there. They often walked together on the mountainside or went for trips in Paul's car, but nobody noticed or commented on the fact that this was the priest convicted in a high-profile court case more than five years earlier. Richard's appearance had also changed in the meantime. The lock of hair that he was once at great pains to comb across his head was gone, leaving a bald pate.

The tension between the two men dissipated gradually as they drifted into a "live and let live" mode. It came as a surprise to Paul to realise one evening as they prepared a meal together in the kitchen, that he would miss his old pal's company when he left. It was not that he had any talk of leaving. The bishop had given no hint, though Paul expected to have a chat with him after the chrism mass on Holy Thursday. He was happy enough to continue with the existing situation until then.

The two priests worked side by side in the small walled garden at the rear of the presbytery at times Paul was free of priestly duties. They carried sea-weed in plastic bags in the boot of Paul's car and spread it between the lines of string they had stretched across the ground to mark the shape of potato and vegetable ridges. Although Paul had grown up at home with potato drills, he had learned how to make ridges in the old-fashioned way while on the islands. Few enough local farmers grew potatoes even for their own use anymore, as they were available washed, clean and cheap in local shops and supermarkets.

"It won't be long until people are back to the old ways again," Paul said one evening as they straightened their backs after a couple of hours of steady digging.

"Wishful thinking. Nostalgia," was Richard's reply. "You just want to see things return to the way they used to be."

"I heard in a recent report that thirty per cent of householders in England are growing their own in back gardens and allotments."

"It's just a fashion," Richard said. "They are watching too many television programmes about cookery and gardening.

"It's partly the expense but even more so because they don't know what chemicals have been put on the vegetables in the shops."

Richard pointed to the work they had done: "Yours will certainly be organic, but we will have a power of weeding to do later in the year."

Paul noted the "we" but let it go. "Isn't this a lovely little sun-trap," he said about the walled garden.

"I suppose it was built with cheap labour at a time when the clergy were aping the gentry. That explains why the so-called celibate priest had the biggest house in every village." He told a story he had heard of a priest who went to the United States a century earlier to raise money from his parish's many emigrants to build a church and a presbytery. There was an open day when the house was built to allow parishioners see the inside of the new house. A number of women reached a room near the top of the stairs and marvelled at the fittings. The bath was fairly obvious. The basin was at a level that might have different uses, but the big question was about the bowl on the floor. One lady who liked to show she was a woman of the world declared: "That is for washing the towels."

"The day has thankfully come," Paul commented, "that most houses in the parish are larger than those of the clergy."

They were interrupted by the postman with Paul Godfool's mail. He sifted through them in the garden although his hands were soiled. He opened the one that was clearly from An Post who administer TV licences. The County Postmaster had returned the cheque from which he had removed one euro for every year spent as a priest. The letter was friendly but firm. He had sympathy for the case in question but needed to receive all of the payment or he would have passed the matter on to be dealt with by the courts.

This came as little surprise. The Director General of the TV station had written earlier expressing regret that the programme in question had offended him but not giving anything away. He sounded like a football manager expressing regret that an opposing player was injured but at the same time supporting the player who had put in the boot. It had all happened in the name of comedy and people had to learn to take a joke. In fairness, though, he had given the name and address of the Broadcasting Complaints Commission if Paul wanted to make a formal submission.

After receiving that letter, Godfool was tempted to let the matter drop, but then came a letter from the programme's producer which made no effort to deal with the matters raised. It was little more than a generalised sop sent to mollify complainants, a classic example of saying nothing in a longwinded way. Paul wrote back to both explaining that he could not afford to sue the station but hoped to have his day in court when prosecuted for not paying his full television licence.

"Am I daft to be making an issue of this at all?" he asked Richard Scapegoat after showing him the Postmaster's letter.

"My only regret is that I am not in a position to support you."

Paul put the letter as well as the others that had come in that day's post under a stone to keep them from blowing away in the wind before getting back to work on the garden: "I'm too old for this crack," he said. "I would be better off to keep my mouth shut."

It's a pity Jesus Christ didn't keep his mouth shut, too, or he wouldn't have ended up on that silly cross." Richard said, sarcastically. "Think of all the trouble he would have saved the human race."

"There is a big difference between my little protest and what Christ did."

"If I hadn't shat in my own well I would back you to the hilt," Richard assured him. "I am jealous that you are still free to take a stand. That is my own fault, but if I was in your place, I would have a go. What have you to lose? A good parish? The people's approval? The bishop's friendship? Do what you need to do, what you have to do."

"The very word Jesus said to Judas before he went out to betray him: 'What you have to do, do quickly.'"

"It's up to you," Scapegoat said. "Pull out if you don't have the bottle."

"I have to weigh up all the implications."

"You mean me?" Richard said. "I am the millstone around your neck?"

"It's not just you. It would put this place in the news. I remember what Nora McCabe said about bringing the media down on your back. I'm not sure the community would be too pleased with that."

"The community will back you whatever you decide. I have no doubt about that. Unless you run naked up and down the street, maybe."

"That would waken them up alright," Paul smiled, "to see the emperor without his clothes."

"They could see worse."

"You can imagine the tabloid headline if they find out that you have stayed here: "Protest priest's secret visitor."

"Tell it like it would really be," Scapegoat said: "Prorest priest harbours paedophile."

"I don't want to draw trouble like that down on you for the sake of a little argument about a television licence."

Richard spoke quietly: "What you really mean is that you do not want to bring that trouble on yourself either, and I understand that. But don't let that stop you. I am long enough here already. Too long, maybe. I will ask the fox to find me a safe den in some corner or another."

"It would be much easier for me to keep my mouth shut and not draw any trouble on either of us."

"You were no more than a shadow of your former self when I came here," Richard said. "You were like a man who had given up on life, but you seem alive again since you decided to make that protest. Don't give that up."

"What will you do?" Paul asked.

"Don't worry about me. I am not your problem. I am nothing if not resilient. Didn't I survive the past five years? I am not your responsibility even though you seem to look on me like that for the past while, the stray dog that needs looking after. Well it's time for me to start looking after myself and facing my own situation."

"Don't be daft," Paul said with more confidence than he felt. "You can stay here as long as you like and I'll take whatever flack that comes."

"You've done enough. You have given me enough time to begin to find my feet. I came here to hide really, but a man can't stay hidden forever."

XXXVIII

Extract From Paul Godfool's Journal

I see Jesus as a butterfly in those heady days after Easter, cocoon cracked, shell open, tomb empty. He flits from flower to flower, freed of the constraints of space and time, appearing here and there to bewildered apostles and disciples, bringing joy, but also bringing doubt and disbelief. Has he really done it? This is too far-fetched. To take on death and win. Risen, glorified, unrestrained, unrestricted. There has to be a catch somewhere.

Our attitude to the resurrection comes down to faith. We believe it or we don't. We can't prove it, but we can provide some evidence. There is the empty tomb, Thomas fingering the nail-holes in his hands and feet, the evidence of witnesses so taken by it all that they were willing to give their lives for their beliefs, and most of them did. But sceptics still say that it was all a con-job. He didn't actually die, and if he did the body was stolen. Maybe someone else was crucified in his place. Those arguments might carry as much weight in a legal tribunal or a court of law. Judge and jury would have a lot of thinking to do.

The nearest thing we have to prove of the resurrection is the change that came over the apostles and disciples between Calvary and Pentecost. What caused those craven cowards, most of whom denied Jesus and fled when he was apprehended to go out into the streets fifty days later proclaiming that he had risen from the dead. It takes a lot to change a mind, to change an attitude. What changed them?

That was then and this is now and I remain convinced despite Thomas-like doubts from time to time. I have staked my life on those beliefs and

I do not regret it. If I discover I was wrong when I reach the next world, not to worry. I will face that when it comes. Clay and worm do not bother me because I won't know the difference. For now, I can honestly say in the creed: "I believe in the resurrection of the body and the life of the world to come."

Easter is about life, life that is stronger than death. It is about the indomitable soul or spirit that is in us. This is not some wishy-washy ghostly spirit like a plume of smoke that we cannot grasp. Easter is about the resurrection of the person, body and soul, glorified, as different from what we are now as is the butterfly from the caterpillar in the cocoon. Still the same basic being, though.

If someone was to come back from the other side to tell of the new life, I suspect that we would not know what they were talking about, because we do not have the imagination to grasp it. The Easter stories give us a few hints. Jesus still has the holes in his hands and feet, but he can come and go despite locked doors, walls, distances. The caterpillar has been butterflied. Alleluia.

XXXIX

Bill Brown and Eve Adams managed to keep their affair secret through Christmas and away out into the new year. They had a glorious week in Lanzarote. Living as man and wife in so far as they could. They were like a couple on honeymoon more than anything else. Apart from dealing with the business matters, which were their excuse for being there, they enjoyed beautiful meals, good wine, shopping, walks and tours, not to speak of the pleasure and passion they shared with each other.

Eve had chosen the Occidental Hotel in Teguise Grand Playa from the Internet before the left home. Bill was supposed to be staying in the Los Jameos in Metagorde close to where the development he and Adam were involved in near Puerto Del Carmen. Although he had paid for his room in advance, he seldom stayed there, joking with Eve that he was like the man who got a return ticket to Galway and walked home, later boasting to friends that he had played a great trick on the railway company.

Bill had hired a car and he usually left for his own hotel for breakfast early in the morning in case Sharon would call his hotel room instead of his mobile phone. He rang home as often as possible to reduce her need to ring, but there was always the possibility of an emergency because of her mother's condition. When Sharon warned him of the cost of the calls, he said he was charging them to the company and would get tax relief.

Generally speaking, Eve had breakfast sent to her room or she rose late to avail of an even larger selection of foods served in the breakfast room until ten-thirty. She availed of the morning sunshine until nearly midday, using a high factor cream and taking care to avoid the hottest part of the day. She finished her morning with a swim in the heated pool, followed by a light lunch, after which she took a taxi to one of the local villages or to the main town, Arrecife.

Puerto De Carmen might have had a bigger population, especially when swelled by tourists but Arrecife was a much nicer place to shop in Eve's opinion. The size of the shops as well as the standard of the goods on sale came as a pleasant surprise, Zara, Ferrer, Ravelo. She had planned to get presents in good time for Adam, Cian and Abigail, and not be caught for last-minute purchases like the evening she had little choice except buy them footballs.

On the streets between those relatively expensive shops Eve saw more signs of poverty than anywhere else on the island. She came across three people begging in less than half an hour. She gave each a little change and was surprised at the warmth of their gratitude, as if the little she gave them was more than what they got from most people. Her mind moved quickly on to other business when she saw a shop called Momu Woman which had a liquidation sale advertised with reductions from fifty to seventy per cent. Eve bought most of the clothes she wanted herself there and took a taxi back to the hotel, tired but happy.

Bill was stretched on one of the beds in her room when she returned. "Where were you?" he asked in a surly voice.

"You sound just like a husband," Eve replied.

Bill seemed to be in a sulk: "I came here early so that we could spend more time together. I began to get worried when I couldn't find you."

"I thought that was what we had mobiles for," Eve answered.

"All I got was a taped message in Spanish."

"Sorry, I forgot to recharge. Anyway you hardly thought I was going to spend the day cooped up in this room."

Bill said he thought she would be there when he returned.

Eve put on a pandering tone: "Ah, you missed me. Well, I am here now. At your pleasure, sir." She went over to the bed to give him a kiss.

Bill turned away: "I'm tired."

"You are not in the humour, you mean. What have I done on you?"

"Nothing. It's just... I was working all day."

"Had you trouble with the contractor or what?" Eve asked.

Bill sighed: "You know yourself."

"I don't know, but I can guess," Eve said. "Was it Sharon bitching on the phone?"

"The way she goes on you would think she has an awful lot to do. Liam, her mother. I'd like to see her if she was trying to sell houses in a recession."

Eve answered lightly: "She is probably feeling sorry for herself and thinking you are having a great time. Lovely meals, sun, sea, sand… She doesn't know about the rest, I hope."

"She forgets all about the work part of it," Bill replied.

Eve did not want anything to interfere with her own happy mood: "Well she is right if she thinks you are having a great time. So am I, and let us make the best of it while we have it."

"Just as well she knows nothing about us," Bill said gloomily.

It was not clear whether Eve was joking or serious when she answered: "Maybe she does."

Bill dismissed the idea: "How could she?"

"Women's intuition."

Bill sat upright in the bed: "She can hardly intuit what we are doing so far from home."

"Feelings have nothing to do with distance," Eve said.

"Do you feel like that about Adam since you came here?"

"He is such a steady plodder that I don't worry about him. Anyway, I called him earlier on the hotel phone."

"Did he ask anything about the business?"

"I told him I had hardly seen you and that I had an appointment to meet you tomorrow at midday when I came back from the beach. Whatever needs to be signed will be arranged then, I said."

"That was all?" Bill asked.

"He was more interested in the cologne he wanted me to buy."

Bill sounded depressed. "We are as we ate, and you are buying presents for your husband."

"I hope you are buying for Sharon and Liam and his grandmother, or the intuition will really be working overtime when you get back."

"I suppose you are right," Bill answered wearily, "but it might be stretching things too far to buy something for the old lady."

"Why?" Eve asked.

"I never bought her anything before, so they might get suspicious. I was wondering was she on to me already from some things she said when she was in hospital."

"It was different when she was in her own house, but now that she is staying with you, it might soften her up," Eve suggested.

Bill managed a little smile at last: "It would take acid to soften that one up. Maybe you are right. But you will have to help me to pick something."

"I will for the Granny or for Liam, but you will have to choose for Sharon yourself."

"She likes perfume." Bill said.

Eve laid down the law: "Not the same one as me."

"Don't worry. I am not likely to mix up the two of you."

Eve took her cigarettes and went out on the balcony as smoking was forbidden in the rooms. She spent some time looking out across the sea. When she stubbed out her cigarette and returned to the room she suggested: "Why don't we go downstairs early and have a few drinks before dinner? This old room would depress anyone."

Downstairs, they sat outside but in the shelter of the building as there was a sea-breeze from the other direction. They sipped their drinks slowly and only spoke now and again. There were still children splashing around in the small pool and some grown-ups in the heated one in which Eve had swam earlier. All three pools contained sea water, possibly because of the scarcity of fresh water on the island or maybe because it was healthier and more buoyant for swimmers.

Bill began to talk of business and the price of houses and apartments. Eve barely listened, her mind on the enjoyment Cian and Abigail would have in those pools and from the hotel's other facilities. She missed them and from the first time since she arrived on the island. She admitted to herself that she missed Adam, too. She found Bill boring, something she had never noticed when they just used to be together for a couple of hours at a time. He never seemed to talk of anything but business, unlike Adam who was interested in the arts and politics as well as sport.

Feeling that perhaps she was to blame for the boredom, Eve decided to listen carefully to Bill who was talking about prices in Puerto Del Carmen, one bedroom apartments from as little as e120,000, with up to e200,000 for a three bedroom duplex. He turned to her accusingly and said: "You are not listening to a word I am saying."

"That's not fair," she replied as she gave him back his figures word for word, pleased with herself that she had listened to that much.

Bill tried to take the sting out of things: "You are not just beautiful but clever as well."

"Could we leave the rest of the homework until tomorrow," Eve asked, "and enjoy the rest of the evening?"

"We will leave it until the day after tomorrow," Bill answered, "because I am taking tomorrow off completely so that we can spend the day together. I have booked us on a coach to tour the volcanoes."

Eve was delighted and both were in good form during their evening meal. There was a group of Brazilian dancers on stage in the spacious hotel lobby afterwards, full of life and athleticism, wearing nothing except g-strings and feathers. Eve joked later that it was those nubile bodies that made Bill so horny, as they made love on the floor of their room as soon as they entered the door.

The guide on the bus the following day was from the island. He spoke very good English and had worked in that capacity for ten years. He gave them a history of volcanic activity right up to one of the most violent outbreaks which had covered the island in lava and ash in 1824. Even now red-hot lava could be seen and he promised to show them examples later. His warped sense of humour did little to settle the stomach of any tourist that felt queasy as he stated that another earthquake could erupt at any time beneath their bus for instance. High among the hills with no roadside protection and drops of hundreds of metres to the valleys below, the guide announced that the bus-driver's wife had left him that morning and that he felt suicidal. Political correctness was not one of his strong points, Bill remarked, as Eve clung, frightened to his arm.

"We are going to suffer," she kept repeating. "We are going to suffer for all we have done wrong."

Bill assured her that the roads were good, the bus new and as far as he knew there had never been an accident with any of the tour buses.

Eve was not convinced: "There is always a first time."

A green lake formed by water entering through an air-pocket in the lava was shown to them in passing and they were then brought to see a salt-farm. Salt-water was pumped ashore by windmills, the water gradually evaporating in the sun, leaving a thick salt residue. The most interesting aspect of their journey was a heritage centre designed by Canaries' architect, Cesar Manrique. It was a circular building with lots of glass, and as well as history, tea, coffee and other refreshments were available. Before going inside, their guide poured a bucket of water into a hole in the dried lava, the water spraying up immediately like a geyser. Inside the building, halves of chickens were roasting over hot lava.

Eve enjoyed none of this as her legs were like jelly with fear. Back in the bus, she clung with one hand to her seat and with the other to Bill's elbow. She kept her eyes shut while the bus circled the hills on their way back to level ground, promising God she would never sleep with any man except Adam, if he brought her safely back to her family. Those promises were quickly forgotten when they came to an area on the edge of the national park where they were able to go for camel rides. They had pictures taken with the camels and their drivers as well as with both of them on wooden straddles on one of the animal's backs.

"We will have to be careful about those pictures," Bill said when they were back in the bus, "or the cat will be out of the bag."

"There is nothing too intimate about them," Eve answered. "They will go to show our innocence, that we have nothing to hide. They know we were in Lanzarote. We just got our pictures taken with a camel here."

Bill shook his head: "I don't think Sharon would be best pleased to see us laughing and messing about like that."

Eve was tempted to say: "Pity about her." Instead she asked with a hint of sarcasm: "Is life at home without you still getting her down?"

"Not at all," was Bill's reply. "She was in great humour the last time I rang. She brought Liam and her mother to the bingo and they won a hundred euro."

"Good for them. It's not just us that are hitting the jackpot." Bill looked at Eve as if he was not amused but he let it go.

There was a simple meal for everyone on the bus in a village called Yaiza, one of the few places to escape the ravages of volcanic action which meant that the little church there had survived for about three hundred years. The local priest at the time wrote a graphic account of the spread of the lava all over the island. His parishioners had enough, however and most immigrated to South America. Bill and Eve learned this from a brochure in the building when they visited the church in the half-hour they had to spare after the meal. There were interesting pictures of Jesus and his mother Mary as well as other saints they had never heard of. They lit candles and stood them in the box of sand in front of Mary's shrine.

"I wonder what she thinks of the two of us," Eve whispered so that other passengers from the bus would not hear her.

"Didn't soma saint say that God is love," Bill replied. "He would understand."

"He mightn't understand why we are hurting and betraying others."

"But are we really?" Bill asked lamely, "when they don't know about it."

Eve didn't answer until they had left the church and were some distance from the other bus passengers: "I would say that God is putting on the biggest pair of boots he has to kick our backsides as far away from heaven as he can."

Bill made no comment on that. He sat on a wall and spent five minutes writing a text on his phone while she wandered about in the sun. When he finished texting, she said: "You can't even go half a day without getting in touch with them at home."

The ding on her own phone told Eve she had a text. Her face broke into a smile as she read it. It was from Bill to say that the red flower growing among the lava reminded him of their love. The bloom sprouted in its precarious position on the burnt earth despite many difficulties. Eve's heart softened and she went over and kissed him tenderly.

"Isn't it strange," Bill remarked as the bus moved through the barren countryside, "that we have not seen cow or calf, sheep or lamb, goat or kid, donkey or horse since we arrived."

"What I have seen since morning reminds me of only one place," Eve remarked, "and that is hell."

"And I suppose I'm the devil that brought you here," Bill said playfully.

"Only an angel from heaven could send me the text I got from you in that little village," Eve replied: "I will treasure it forever."

"Do not," Bill answered. "Delete it immediately. What if Adam sees it?"

"I will when we are ready to go home. After that I will just treasure it in my heart."

The final stop on the tour brought them to a vineyard which reflected the indomitable spirit of the human being and of a particular type of vine. Each plant grew up through the lava and ashes and was protected by a small wall. Samples of the wine produced were available in the winery, with bottles available for those who wished to buy them. The circles of stone and ashes around the vines reminded Bill of pictures he had seen of moonscapes, but both were amazed that anything of value could be produced in such a climate.

XL

Extract From Paul Godfool's Journal

Spitting was virtually an art-form when I was growing up. People of my vintage would remember old people (those who were the age I am now) sitting around a blazing fire on a winter's night. Neighbours would have gathered to share news or tell stories. There would be murmers of conversation and contented silences broken only by the sizzle of a spit from the flames. Tobacco chewers were the chief exponents of this art and as children we used to try and shape our tongues in similar fashion to create a good spit, but not with much success. It was a skill that obviously took many years and tons of plug tobacco to perfect.

Of course it was considered bad manners if the children were caught imitating the grown-ups. Life was not fair in the good old days either. Occasionally a tobacco chewers spit would fall short but the only collateral damage was a splash resembling a sick hen's dropping on the concrete floor. This would lead to a re-telling of the story of the priest who always carried a tube of mustard in his top pocket, to spice up the sausages at breakfast after a station mass. Seeing the offending mess on his plate and not knowing where it came from, the woman of the house wiped it off with a sweep of her apron and the words: "Those hens are awful for going up on the table." I learned when in college that the same story was told in every parish in the country.

The only people allowed to spit with impunity nowadays seem to be the millionaire footballers we see on our television screens. Their skill is usually in their feet rather than in their tongues. Unlike the perfectly formed tobacco spit of old, the new football-star ones are chewing-gum related, no doubt hoping that the manufacturer's logo is seen on TV in a slow-motion shot between the time it leaves the mouth and reaches the grass. Football players would no doubt be red-carded and suspended if the raw nicotine of the chewed tobacco used by spitters in the old days was found in their systems.

If random drug testing had been applied in Post Offices in days gone by, there would have been plenty of red cards for pensioners, male and female. Nicotine was imbibed not just from cigarette and pipe smoking, but from snuff as well. The phrase: "thrown about like snuff at a wake" obviously originated from just such a practice. One of my memories of snuff has to do with helping to camouflage snuff-blackened fingers in the rosary beads after the death of the first person I anointed.

It was in the islands too that I saw one of the happiest deaths I have witnessed, a woman dying with cancer whose last request was for her pipe and she literally passed away in a puff of smoke. I take the point that she might have lived longer if she avoided tobacco altogether, but her peaceful death is an abiding memory. Jesus Christ used spittle in curing a man born blind according to Saint John, the evangelist. Let us not write off the old spit completely yet.

XLI

"Have you eyes that do not see, ears that do not hear? [Mk 8:18]

Liam Brown was delighted that his grandmother had come to live with his family after she was sent home from hospital, but his mother and father were finding the going tough. The old woman was constantly saying that she would prefer to be at home in her own little house, Sharon telling her she was not able to care for herself: "That was the cause of your problems in the first place. The doctor said you were run down more than anything."

Bill stayed away from the house as much as he could, pretending he was working when with Eve, telling Sharon that it was her mother's sharp tongue that kept him away from home so much. He said he would prefer to be in the office until after his mother-in-law went to bed. Ann, the woman in question, was civil when talking to him, but she never missed an opportunity to question her daughter about why he worked so much or stayed out so late.

"You must have your fortune made since the start of the year," she said to Bill one evening he was home relatively early in order to spend a while playing football with Liam. "How many houses have you sold so far?"

"Four or five," Bill said casually as he glanced through one of Liam's school homework.

"Is that around here or does it include that place you were on your holidays?" Ann asked.

"It wasn't a holiday," Bill insisted for the umpteenth time. "Many of the houses over there are still in the planning stage. They were sold off the plans but all we have got out of them at this stage is the deposits."

Ann was looking at her fingers: "Five or six houses sold. What do you be doing for the rest of the time?"

Sharon intervened in support of her husband: "His work is not like trying to sell a cow at a fair. There is a lot of work involved in selling houses, especially when there are so many on the market."

"What do you know about it?" was her mother's scathing answer. "You never did a days work in your life. Or you never sold anything either."

"I wish I could sell you," Sharon answered angrily. "I don't work, you say. What have I been doing all day? Who took the pissy sheets off your bed? Who cleaned the house? Who got the dinner? You don't have to be employed to spend your day doing thankless work."

"I never asked you to do anything in your life," her mother said plaintively, "and I wouldn't be here at all if you let me go back to my own lovely little house."

Bill tried to be diplomatic as he spoke directly to his mother-in-law: "Why don't you come to the office some day and I will show you what I do?"

Ann laughed it off: "I'd be some sight in the office, pretending to be your secretary. Don't you know well I was only joking?"

"There doesn't be much fun in your jokes most of the time," Sharon said, "but bitching and biting."

Ann indicated Liam with a wave of her hand: "That's nice talk in front of the child, calling your mother an old bitch." The boy's interest seemed to be on what was on TV more than what they were talking about'

Her daughter answered: "You can twist it any way you like. I didn't call you a bitch. I said your talk was bitching."

"Same thing," Ann commented.

Bill stood up: "I have just remembered that there is somebody calling to see me later and that I have to have to have papers ready to sign."

His mother-in-law obviously did not believe a word he said: "Is it in the office or in the public house you have this important meeting?"

Bill answered proudly: "Perhaps you have not noticed that I haven't had a drink of any kind since I came home from Lanzarote."

"No wonder you are so contrary," Ann commented. Bill and Sharon gave each other an "I give up" look.

"You are after driving him away," Sharon said to her mother after Bill had gone. "You complain when he is not here and you drive him out when he is."

"He wouldn't have gone if he didn't want to go," was her mother's opinion.

That reply remained in Sharon's mind as she went about her work, and for the first time she allowed herself to ask in her own mind and heart: "what if she is right?" The thought scared her but drove her to take action. She decided to follow Bill and find out the truth. She told her mother she was going out for a breath of fresh air to clear her head. "Would you look after Liam for a while?"

"They say it is dangerous for a woman to go out walking by herself at night," Ann said, "but take no notice of me. I'm only your mother and nobody takes heed of the likes of me."

"Don't worry," Sharon said. "I will just drive down to the little pier by the lake and take the breeze. I will stand by the car and jump in if I see any danger."

"Into the water?" Liam was suddenly all attention.

Sharon laughed: "No way, silly. Into the car."

Her mother seemed a little worried: "Wouldn't it be better if you brought Liam with you?"

"He has to finish his homework when that programme is over. Anyway I have my mobile. She told Liam to ring her immediately if his grandmother got sick.

"Which of us is minding the other?" Ann asked her grandson.

Sharon felt foolish and in some way unfaithful to Bill that she could even doubt him, but she sat into the old car all the same and drove towards his office. She was delighted to see light in the office windows and the BMW parked outside. Of course, what he said was true. Why did she allow her witch of a mother to sew doubts in her mind? She was about to drive away when it occurred to her to initiate something that had been awkward to do since her mother came to live with them.

Sharon parked around the corner from Bill's office and through the window as she passed she saw that he was on the phone, talking and laughing. "See you soon, so," he was saying as she opened the office door.

He seemed to get a shock and hung up the phone as if it was hot. "What is it? Is there something wrong at home?"

"There is nothing wrong that we can't put right," Sharon said, mischievously as she went from window to window pulling the blinds. She then clicked the door locked before going over to give her husband a big kiss on the lips.

"What about Liam and your mother?"

"They are minding each other, and we won't be too long, that is if all you have been saving up inside for the past few weeks doesn't last forever."

"But I have work to do. There is someone coming." Bill had just arranged for Eve to call around when Cian and Abigail went to bed. What if she was to walk in and find him shagging his wife? His one consolation was that she might notice Sharon's old car outside and stay away.

"Put the work, put the world on hold," Sharon was saying as she opened his flies: "See, I haven't forgotten. I know how to really get you going" She pushed him back on the desk: "If what they say in the soaps is true there is no better place to do it than on a desk." Bill decided to let her get on with it, get it over with. Eve would be at least half an hour and he would have Sharon out of the office by then. His heart was not in it and neither was the rest of him. Sharon failed to rouse him. Bill sat up and buttoned his trousers: "It's just not working," he said. "It all happened too quickly. Why don't we take it easy and do things in our own time later?"

"I can't do anything right," Sharon said.

Bill tried to console her: "It was a great idea, but you were ready and I wasn't. I had work on my mind and I was afraid a customer might just walk in."

"At this time of the night?" Sharon asked.

"When the light is on the office is open as far as people are concerned."

"You are expecting a customer?"

Bill explained: "That was why I was on the phone when you came in." He looked at his watch: "It will be another ten minutes anyway."

At that moment Eve Adams was peering in by the side of the closed blinds wondering what Sharon was doing there. Did she really see her adjusting her bra?

"I'm out of here," she said to herself as she hurried back to her car.

XLII

Extract From Paul Godfool's Diary

When I grow up I want to be God. It is not that I want to take over from the present, future, and eternal incumbent, who is doing a fine job. I just want to be a bigger part of the life of God. I'm part of that life already, but I only play a bit-part, struggling around the edges, and barely hanging on to the hem of God's garment. It is my own fault that I am not giving it everything, but I do intend to get down to it one of the days, not unlike Saint Augustine's: "Make me pure, Lord, but not yet."

I've had the God-gene in me from the beginning, the gene of immortality, eternity. I am in a sense God-cloned, being made, as the scriptures say "in God's image." Cloning implies sameness, but then you would expect God's clones to be different. I am a chip off the old God-block, chipped off, but connected through my spiritual DNA.

Daft and playful as this sounds, it makes good theological sense to me. In any understanding of what we call incarnation, of God becoming human in the person of Jesus, God is one of our own, our own flesh and blood. We are expected to look on others as God's children as each has the dignity and importance of Christ. We are not just rational animals, human-ed animals but divine-d animals as well.

Did we create God or vice versa? This is one of the world's great questions, and as you might expect I have hung my coat on the vice versa. God is the ultimate creator. We share that creativity. Do we really have enough imagination to dream up God? Even if we did would we imagine something as bizarre as God's son being crucified and rising from the dead? We would be too cute, too soft for that. We would want something more realistic, something less raw and savage. The idea of suffering Jesus would not be politically correct unless it has to be.

In all of this, your guess is as good as mine. God's greatest gift is freedom, or if you don't believe in God it is our gift. Either way we can make up our own minds, take it or leave it. I've taken it, nailed my colours to the cross. If I have been duped or have fooled myself, so what? I have enjoyed the roller-coaster ride of faith. I wanted it all, this world and the next, and the fact that we can contemplate eternity means for me that we have the ability to reach beyond the world, the stars, and the universe. The sky is not the limit.

XLIII

*"Nobody should have to pay to be called a sh**te on RTÉ."*
Headline on an article in the Connaught Telegraph,
18th December 2004.

The non-stop ringing of the phone wakened Richard Scapegoat. The noise stopped every few moments but began again almost immediately. He got up, left his room and knocked hard at the door of Paul Godfool's. It was then he remembered that Paul had mass at the other side of the parish that morning and had said something about visiting a school afterwards.

Richard picked up the receiver. A stressed Nora McCabe told him she needed a priest immediately. "Marcas was dead or dying. Why wasn't Father Paul answering his phone?"

Richard answered that he was at mass.

"The last thing Marcas would want is to die without a priest. Won't you do?" Nora said.

Richard tried to buy time: "Did the doctor say he is on the way out?" He remembered from his own experience that someone for whom the last rites were called, were already dead but people would not say so. Was this some kind of superstition? It didn't matter now. He had something more urgent to deal with. The bishop had told him not to be involved in the administration of church sacraments without his permission until further notice. "I don't know where Father Paul has left the holy oils," he answered lamely.

Nora knew exactly where they were: "They are in the same safe as the chalices and the key is in the little box to the right of the cross."

Richard tried another avenue of escape: "I don't have a car or anything and it will take me more than half an hour to walk it."

"There will be one of the neighbours at the door in ten minutes," Nora told him, leaving down the phone.

Richard thought he had little option to comply with Nora's request, whatever about the bishop. He was still a priest, even if he was a bad one. In a case of emergency any priest of whatever standing could administer the sacraments. He was coming out of the sacristy pulling an old soutane of Paul's around him when the car arrived outside to collect him.

Richard was grateful that the woman driver was so respectful of the blessed sacrament he carried that she made no conversation on their short journey. The last thing he needed was questioning. By the time they reached the house, Marcas was sitting up in bed asking what was all the trouble about.

"You had passed out on the bed when I brought you the tea," Nora explained, and I couldn't get a response of any kind out of you."

"What were you trying to wake me for when I was having a pleasant dream and nothing to wake up for but another boring day?"

"You were as cold as ice, and I was thinking of the trouble you had before with your heart."

"I was cold because you pulled all the blankets off me," Marcas complained. "Like you do every night."

Richard felt he was off the hook now that Marcas was sitting up but he was not getting away that easily: "You better put the holy oil on me now, Father, seeing that you are here, and in case I don't wake up at all the next time."

"Everyone gets better when they are anointed," the woman who had collected Richard said. "For a while anyhow."

"I'm as well to go to confession as well when I am at it," Marcas suggested. "Instead of telling my tales to Father Paul. It is a lot easier to confess to someone you don't meet every day." Using all his school-masterish authority he ordered his wife and neighbours out of the room "until my sins are told and forgiven, recounted and shriven" as he put it. He tried to remember a biblical quotation: "Although my sins are like scarlet, you will make them as white as wool." "Isn't that it?"

Richard thought to say something about black sheep but this was not the time or the place. He administered sacraments as best he could for the first time in over five years. By the time he was finished, the doctor had arrived and Marcas was proclaiming that he was never as "well oiled" as he was with the holy oils.

Under a new cover scheme to give doctors time off the local doctor was away from Friday evening until midday Monday. A doctor who lived twenty-five miles away was covering a vast area with a scattered population. When he examined Marcas and was having a cup of tea in the sitting room, he looked intensely at Richard and said: "I know your face from someplace."

Before he had time to answer, Nora said that he was a priest home from the missions and they were lucky to have him in the parish that morning.

The doctor was still curious: "Where were you before you went on the missions?"

Richard felt the colour rising in his face as he thought his cover was blown: "In college, I was in the same class as Father Paul who is based here."

The doctor shook his head: "I could swear that I saw you somewhere. Maybe your picture was in the paper?"

"I'm not that famous," Richard joked but the words nearly stuck in his throat. He was a happy man when the doctor left and they all sat around Marcas' bed as if it was a wake with the corpse sitting up and talking. One story led to another about priests, patients and sick calls. Richard told a story of an old woman who sent for the priest about once a month late at night. He had to saddle his horse and ride for miles across the bogs to get to her house. She asked him every time: "Will I die tonight, Father?" he assured her that she wouldn't. Then one night he had enough and when she asked: "Will I die tonight, Father?" he answered: "Not tonight but you will the next time." She never sent for him again and he was dead and buried long before she was.

Richard sat back and allowed the others talk of days long gone and priests they had known in the parish. The doctor had given him a shock. He had little doubt that it was the photo published in the national newspapers after his conviction that was in the doctor's mind. He was sure now that it was time to leave. The latest word he had from the bishop was that he was looking for a flat in a convent for retired nuns in which he could stay "until Rome makes its judgment."

This was as much as acknowledging that he would be laicised, as was the custom with the latest Pope. That had made him even more reluctant to anoint Marcas, as he was not sure what his status was. It was an ironic thought that Marcas would arrive in the next life to find he had been anointed and given holy communion for his last journey by a rogue priest who had been convicted of child abuse. He was so caught up in his own thoughts that he did not realise that Nora was addressing him. He had to ask her to please repeat her question.

"Would you like a lift back to the presbytery, Father? Or will you wait with us here for the breakfast?"

"Wait, wait," Marcas said. "Can't Father Paul call and collect you after a while when he has his duties done. He might have a bit of breakfast, too."

The neighbours who had gathered to show support were gradually leaving one by one, until Richard Scapegoat was there on his own with Marcas and Nora. Paul Godfool arrived in a hurry soon afterwards. He had checked his messages when he came out of the school and there was a list of them from Nora telling him Marcas was seriously ill. He was surprised to find Richard sitting on an easy chair in conversation with the supposedly dying man and his wife.

Marcas praised Richard as "this wonderful missioner who anointed me and got me ready for my last journey." He finished with a little joke: "A journey that I was too stubborn to take."

Paul teased him: "Do you regret now that you were not taken away by the angels to God's right hand?"

"There would be nothing wrong with it," Marcas replied. "I was ready to go but God mustn't want me yet. And of course I didn't want to leave Nora and the family."

Nora laughed: "So long as you didn't try to take me with you. Sure you would probably have found another old lady to fighting with up there."

"There is only one woman I ever wanted," her husband replied, "and that's the vow I made before the altar many years ago, that I would love you and be faithful "till death do us part."

Nora winked at her visitors: "Isn't that it? You were nearly off the hook this morning. You were free to have another old hag on the other side."

"I don't believe that there is any old hag in heaven," Marcas said solemnly, "but that everyone there has a glorious body like our saviour had when he rose from the dead."

"There you are now," Nora said. "You missed your chance to get yourself a glorious young one. If it is all you say it is on the other side I will be looking forward to seeing all the fine stumps of men."

"Don't forget that you are a married woman," Marcas reminded her. "We may have said "till death do us part" the day we married, but as far as I was concerned it was for all eternity."

"And there was I thinking of the fun I would have on the other side," Nora said in mock disappointment.

By the time they were finishing breakfast, they were back to Marcas' favourite theme, the media. He mentioned a survey he had read in the paper which showed that nearly ninety percent of the population said that they believed in God. "How is it?" Marcas asked, "that it is the other ten percent that have no religion and no respect for God or man that are in charge of the media."

"Where are the other nine?" said Richard Scapegoat, almost to himself, quoting the words of Jesus when only one of ten whom he had healed came back to say thanks."

"The other nine are us," Marcas said, "the ones who keep our mouths shut and let them get away with it. If Jesus was around now, how would he look at the media. He would condemn them like he condemned the Pharisees – whited sepulchres."

"There are a lot who look at the holy Joes and holy Marys like that," Nora chimed in. "Like the Scribes and Pharisees."

"Today's scribes are certainly a shower of Pharisees," Marcas said. "Pharisees with a capital F if I may say so."

Nora turned to the theme of Jesus: "If Jesus was around today, he would have the media in his pocket. They would take to him like ducks to water because they couldn't but see the good in him."

"He would be a hero for a while," Marcas answered, "but then they would say that he and Mary Magadalene were lovers and they would pull him down and sink his face in the mud. It would be worse than the crucifixion itself."

Richard returned to the results of the survey about belief in God: "It amazed me that so many claim to believe, but not just that, to acknowledge it in answer to a question in a survey. Especially now that faith is not fashionable."

"Can you trust any of those surveys?" Marcas asked. "We have all seen them at election times."

Paul Godfool tried to inject some humour into the proceedings: "Isn't God lucky that he doesn't have to stand for election or take heed of opinion polls?"

Nora laughed: "He doesn't mind so long as he is number one all of the time."

"Opinion polls are not that far from the mark," Richard insisted, "three percent either way. Those figures were remarkable, especially when they were backed up by the results of the census. Eighty-seven percent had themselves down as Catholic, even though many of those do not practice. Still it creates a great challenge for the church to try and reach them."

Marcas had his own view on the matter: "Don't forget that it is in Allah many in this country believe at the moment."

"And other in Jehovah," his wife said. "What harm? Isn't it all the one God?"

"It makes it all the more strange," Marcas commented, "that the media can pretend that not alone is God dead but he is buried as well."

"There is life in the old God yet," Richard said.

Marcas spoke directly to Paul Godfool: "That's a point well worth making if they bring you to court about your television licence."

"It's all arranged," Paul answered. "The Bangharda stopped me this morning to tell me to be in court next Wednesday"

"Our woman?" Marcas asked. "That one that doesn't look fourteen years old? What's her name?" He answered his own question: "Sheila McCormack."

"The very one," Paul answered. "Very civil and very professional she was, courteous but ready to fulfil the law without fear or favour."

Marcas was not pleased: "The cheek of the little whipper-snapper. That wouldn't happen in days gone by. I'm tempted to write to the Minister. There are places more remote than this that she could be sent to to cool her heels."

"She was just doing her job," Paul Godfool said.

Marcas was not finished on the subject. "Well it's a bad job it is. Hasn't she little to do and all the crime there is in the country?"

Nora corrected him: "Doesn't Father Paul want to go to jail? That little girl is only helping him to do what he wants."

"There was a day that they would get a Guard from town to do dirty work like that," Marcas remarked. "She will live to regret it."

"The old days are gone," Nora pronounced. "The times have changed, and changed for the better, thanks be to God."

Marcas did not agree with that either: "The changes have come too fast. We are not able to keep up with them."

"Some people mightn't be able to keep up," Nora said pointedly, "but does anyone want to back to the old life? Poverty, TB, emigration, not to mention the child abuse and all that has come out in the last few years."

"But the people had strong faith." Marcas pointed at the TV set in the corner: "And they didn't have the bigot box running down what they believed in every night of the week."

"What good is a religion you can't question?" his wife asked. "Life is a lot healthier than it was then."

"Marcas saw little point in continuing an argument he was not going to win: "We are gone away from the point we should be discussing," he said. Addressing Paul Godfool, he asked: "Will all this be too much for you?"

"I hear it's a woman Judge as well as a woman Guard," he answered. "Women are in charge everywhere but in the church."

"Will you get fair play from those women?" Marcas asked.

Paul answered with another question: "Is there any reason why I shouldn't?"

"If they are women's libbers," Marcas said, "you could be in trouble. They might be anti-church."

"You would prefer to see them scrubbing and cleaning," his wife said, rather than being up there on the bench making judgments. Well it's not the church we are talking about now."

"Nobody said anything about scrubbing," Marcas said, disdainfully. "I am making a valid point about the Judge's agenda, or to be more accurate in this case, the Justice's agenda."

"What does it matter what the agenda is?" Nora asked, "so long as they send him to jail. Isn't that what he wants? It is the only way he is going to get publicity. Good luck to you," she said to Paul. "But watch the journalists. They will be the ones with the agenda."

On the way back to the presbytery in Paul's car, Richard Scapegoat apologised for breaking one of the rules laid down for him when he arrived in the parish: "I know that I was not supposed to administer the sacraments, but I felt I was caught between the devil and the deep blue sea. How could I refuse? How could I explain such a refusal? Was I supposed to say I am suspended and expose the whole sorry mess?"

"You are still a priest," Paul answered, "and as far as I am concerned you did the right thing."

"The fox won't see it like that."

"Who is going to tell him?" Godfool asked. "I'm glad you were there when they could not reach me." After driving in silence for a while, he remarked: "It is almost as if it was meant to be. I had no sick call for six months, maybe, because many people are in hospital now by the time they need anointing. The one call I get, I can't be reached on the phone."

"It wasn't your fault," Richard said. "You were there within the hour anyway."

"You were there first, as if the Lord himself had sent you."

"I'm not sure that God is that great with me."

"You did what you had to do," Paul said, quoting the Old Testament: "A priest forever, according to the order of Melchisidec." I don't believe that Pope or bishop can take that away from you."

XLIV

Extract From Paul Godfool's Journal

Nobody deserved the Couch Potato Of The Year more than my humble self, so I shook hands with myself and presented the award without ever rising from the comfortable corner of my sitting-room sofa. No fuss, no speeches, just a dignified ceremony to mark my tear as superstar couch-supporter. There are awards every year for those who sweat and strain to be the best at some sport or another while little recognition is given to the supine supported stretched on the sofa, zapping from one sport to another from morning 'till night. I have designed an award which will be available annually if not broken in the meantime.

The cup, or more accurately, the pot in question is both decorative and practical. It is round in shape, red and green in colour to represent my native county, a gallon in capacity and it has a lid to prevent odours escaping when not in use. The pot is an interim measure while I am waiting the patent I have requested for the en-suite sitting-room.

Like all great inventors, I cannot understand why this has not been thought of before now. How often had a goal been scored or a record broken at the very moment nature called and the couch potato has left the room? How often has a commentator delivered a mind-blowing analysis while you thought the ad-break had given you a moment's respite? The obvious solution is the en-suite sitting-room with kitchen facilities, or until that is patented, the portable parlour pot in the colours of your favourite team.

People tend to look on the Suite Spud or Couch Potato as lazy louts who never get any exercise. They forget that we run every race, jump for every ball, crunch into every scrum, dodge every uppercut, jockey in every steeplechase, and leap over every hurdle, not to speak of celebrating with the winners and weeping with the losers, a huge emotional strain after every contest.

I think I have designed the perfect pad for the Couch Potato, with not just the toilet facilities, but the fridge, the microwave and a range of wheelie-bins within easy reach. Who said we were slobs? We can re-cycle with the best of them. The age of chivalry might be dead but the age of convenience has arrived.

XLV

*"Trouble is coming to them, for they have strayed from me,
Ruin on them for they have rebelled against me." [Hosea 7:13]*

Bill Brown could not understand why Eve Adams would not return his calls or even text him. He did not know why she had not come to his office as arranged on the night Sharon had arrived unexpectedly, and embarrassedly. He presumed that Eve had seen Sharon's car, or seen herself leave his office, but why could she just not tell him that by text or phone? Bill's first instinct on such occasions was to presume that Adam had found out about himself and Eve, that there had been a row and that she promised to break off the affair.

If that was to happen, Bill half hoped that Sharon would just walk out and the two of them would go to live together. It wouldn't be easy, of course, especially for Liam, but he would get over it like many another youngsters. What Bill did know for sure was that he did not love Sharon anymore and that her mother, Ann was driving him mad. There would be a certain release and a freedom in not having to hide anymore, but the heartache involved for all concerned would be considerable.

When he had failed to get a reply from Eve for two days in a row, Bill called Eve's house. When she answered, he asked in a whisper was Adam there.

He recognised the heavy irony in her voice: "My husband and I are in the middle of something at the moment, making love, actually. Could you call us back after we are finished with the orgasms? Or should that be singular if we manage to come together?"

"Sarcasm doesn't become you." Bill said, "or crudeness either."

"I'm only doing what you were doing with your wife the other night when I looked into your office," Eve replied.

"We were not doing anything. How did I know she was going to arrive in at that time of the night when I arranged to meet you a short time later? I stopped her, didn't let her do anything."

Eve became even more sarcastic: "Was there a button gone in your flies that she was trying to sew on with her tongue?"

Bill wondered how much Eve had seen: "I can assure you nothing happened and we have not been together since I got back from Lanzarote. I have the excuse that her mother is in the next room."

"I never heard such a lame excuse." Eve went silent then as if she half-believed him and didn't know what to say next.

Bill saw a chink of light at the end of the tunnel and told her his heart had been broken for the previous two days because she had not answered his calls.

"You are lucky that it is not your head that is broken," Eve said. "I was tempted to walk in the door and tell Sharon everything."

"I'm glad that you didn't."

"It wasn't for you but for myself that I didn't," she replied. "To see her there at the time we were supposed to be together. I haven't stopped crying for two days. The children are asking me what is wrong. Adam thinks it's PMT."

"I can assure you nothing happened between Sharon and myself that night. If you look at it from my point of view you will see that I am right. I was hardly going to invite you to the office and be there with Sharon ten minutes earlier. I'm not that much of a dog."

"I know that sounds logical, but I haven't seen much logic for two days," Eve said. Bill was afraid she was going to start crying on the phone.

"When can you meet me?" he asked.

"Is that a good idea?"

"The whole episode the last night was a misunderstanding," Bill said. "I know how much you hurt and I just want to put my arms around you and show you how much I love you."

Eve gave a little skit of laughter: "Is that all you want to show me?"

"That too, but we will have to go somewhere where Sharon or anyone else won't be anywhere near us. We are living too close to the edge lately. We are going to get caught sooner or later."

"Why don't you come here?" Eve asked.

"Talk of close to the edge."

"Adam is at work and the kids are at school. Bring over the plans for the apartments in Lanzarote, and if anyone comes around we will be looking at those."

It was into the games room Eve took Bill when he arrived because it was in the centre of the house and had no window other than a roof light. They were in each other's arms immediately, removing clothes as quickly as they could while kissing passionately at the same time. Bill stopped suddenly: "You did not lock the door?"

Eve explained that that room had no lock but she had bolted the front door and the Yale lock on the backdoor could only be opened from the inside. "Don't worry, we will not be disturbed."

Bill was nervous: "What if Adam comes back and finds the front door locked with me inside? It will look very strange."

"He is always telling me to lock the front door, for safety and security reasons. I'll say I must have bolted it as well from habit."

Bill shook his head: "I don't know."

"Adam is a creature of habit," Eve said. "He never leaves work before five o' clock in the evening."

Her lover was not convinced: "Sharon never came to the office until the other night either. There is always a first time."

Eve dismissed his concerns: "Lightning never strikes twice."

"That is not technically correct." Bill said.

"Did you come here to give me a lesson in meteorology or to make love to me?" Eve asked impatiently.

Bill glanced at the fluorescent bulbs overhead: "We should at least switch off the light. It makes me feel naked and exposed."

"That is because you are going to be naked and exposed in a minute." Eve went over and switched off the lights. As she put her arms around him she said: "You are full of tension and stress."

"What would you expect after what happened the last night?"

"Lie back there and I will take away your stress," Eve promised. They fell asleep in each other's arms on the pool table when they had obtained their pleasure.

The switching on of the overhead light wakened Bill and Eve. As they blinked awake they saw Cian, Abigail and Liam standing at the door of the pool-room looking at them as if they had seen ghosts. They had entered the house by the bathroom window when neither Cian nor Abigail's keys could open the front door.

"Where did ye come out of?" Eve asked confusedly, half-asleep and half-awake as she scrambled to gather up clothes to cover her nakedness.

"Liam!" Bill called after his son who was heading quickly towards the bathroom door. He leaped from the table and started to put on his clothes in haste. It was like a nightmare when he found one trouser-leg was caught in the other and he tripped and fell while trying to pull them up on his legs and follow his son at the same time. He put his socks in a pocket, forced his bare feet into his shoes and ran after Liam to the bathroom. The window was open and his son gone. Bill got a glimpse of him as he ran down the avenue towards the big gates. He called after Liam but his son kept running.

Abigail answered Eve's question about how they got into the house even though it seemed that neither she nor Cian could bear to look at their mother. "We came in through the bathroom window to give you a surprise. We didn't know that Liam's Daddy was here."

"This is not what it seems…" Eve could hardly believe that she was trying to make such a stupid excuse, but she had to say something to try and limit the damage even though that was probably too late. By now Bill had the front door unbolted and he got in his car and tried to follow Liam. He drove in the direction of their own home but turned back after a mile when he was sure his son could not run that far in such a short time. He began to drive the highways and byways around the village in the hope of finding him.

Liam did not know what to make of what he had seen in the games-room and he had ran headlong from his friend's house without any sense of purpose or direction other than to just get out of there. He left the road and hid in a clump of furze when he heard his father's car from around the turn in the road. He hid there for a long time, his knees up against his chest, his head hanging down. It was as if he could not feel the furze needles which pressed against him on all sides.

Liam wanted his mother, but at the same time he did not want to go home. He took his new mobile phone from his pocket and looked at it. He was about to ring home but didn't know what to say so he switched off the phone altogether. Everything had happened so quickly that he did not know what was going on. What he did know was that what he had seen on that pool table was not right. He knew his mother would be raging with his father if she knew about it. There would be a lot of shouting and screeching and his grandmother would have her say, too. He didn't want to hear any of it.

Liam was in two minds. He didn't want to say anything about, or even think about what he had seen. His father and his mother especially had always told him to tell the truth. How could he hide it because his mother always knew when he was trying to keep a secret? He would do anything, he thought, if he could go back to the way that life was before he saw those naked bodies twisted together on the pool table like two great lumps of white meat you would see in the butchers.

Cian, Abigail and himself had been getting on well on their way home from school, Liam thought. The other two were not picking on each other and arguing as they usually did. The schoolmaster had let them go home early because the heating system failed. There was a rumour that one of the pupils had driven a nail into the plastic tank and the oil had slowly drained away. Parents were usually informed in such circumstances, but it seemed that neither Eve nor Adam could be reached on their mobiles, while Sharon had said that Liam could walk with Cian and Abigail to their house which was much nearer the school than her own and Bill's. "Liam was having a sleep-over there last night." She explained, "so Eve will be expecting all three of them."

They thought that going in through the bathroom window would be an adventure. They could have rung the door-bell when the children's keys failed to open the front door but then Abigail noticed the bathroom window was open. They used a trick they had seen in a film. Liam bent down and Cian helped Abigail climb onto his back and reach the window. The two boys pushed her legs while she slid through the narrow opening. Cian then bent down for Liam to climb over him while Abigail pulled from inside. Liam and Abigail then pulled Cian's hands while he climbed up with his feet against the wall.

They were having great fun but the fun came to a swift end when they reached the poolroom. Liam had not felt so bad since his grandfather's death and that nothing short of his grandmother's passing could make him feel so bad again. No unless something happened his father and mother, of course, but they were not of dying age as far as he was concerned. Liam felt he would love to cry, but he was so shaken by what had happened that no tear came.

How long he huddled there, Liam did not know. Then he heard a rustle in the undergrowth and he saw a rat looking at him with no fear. He jumped up and ran for dear life. He saw the church in front of him and decided to go in there. He intended to say a prayer but when he knelt down he did not know what to ask God for. He felt he had a problem that not even God would be able to solve. But at least there would be no rats in the church.

XLVI

Extract From Paul Godfool's Journal

"Isn't God the right waster!" That is the kind of statement I sometimes use to catch the attention of a congregation. I have to qualify it quickly, of course, before some people start heading for the exits: "Yes, I knew those words would raise hackles, get a few backs up, but don't worry. I am on your side. I love God too, and the only waste I accuse God of is being wasteful with love, of loving us beyond our means of reciprocation, of loving us to death, often in spite of ourselves.

God is profligate, prodigal, extravagant, wasteful, and unrepentant when it comes to loving us. It is as if God can't take no for an answer, can't accept the fact that much of what goes on between us is one-way traffic. The love-tap is turned on and the love-flow runneth over and around us even when we ourselves are turned off, and turned off big-time quite often.

The love of God is manifest most of all at Easter as we follow the God-son, Jesus on Calvary's road. No picnic. Torture, blood, sweat, tears, spittle, follow betrayal, rejection, fear in those last eighteen hours of Jesus' life, but the physical pain was probably nowhere near as profound as the psychological. Here is a man on his last legs emotionally and physically, betrayed, denied, denounced, disfigured, defiled, despairing, depressed, dismayed, destroyed.

The most poignant words of the week are heard in Jesus heartrending cry of despair from the cross: "My God, my God, why have you deserted me?" Quoting a psalm that summed up what he felt Jesus probably echoed the cry of this age more than any other. The Love-God was not visible even to his own son, just as he seemed to have gone missing earlier in

Gethsemane's garden when Jesus tried to dodge death with the prayer: "Let this chalice pass."

Then from the very depths of despair Jesus managed the faith and hope, maybe even the desperation to call once more on God: "Not my will but thine be done." And later on the cross: "Into your hands, O Lord, I commend my spirit."

I think of the despair, the dark side Jesus faced is partly summed up in the phrase: "He descended into hell." It tells us God's love is often tough love, that even though we are not expected to go looking for the cross, realities of life and death have to be faced rather than sidestepped. But God's love is there through and in spite of the pain, generous, extravagant, overflowing, wasteful but never wasted.

XLVII

"It is RTÉ's view that satire is legitimate and plays an important role in society as a vehicle which holds up to examination all aspects of life. The inclusion of the Catholic Church in Tommy Tiernan's performance is therefore not exceptional."

Jim Jennings, Acting Producer, *The Late Late Show*.

Paul Godfool felt a mixture of elation and disappointment on his way home from court. He was delighted that the Justice had ruled that he did not have a duty to pay his television licence in the circumstance. "Satire is one thing, insult another," she had said, throwing out the case. His regret stemmed from the fact that it was all over so quickly and without fuss. The publicity he had hoped to gain by going to prison in order to embarrass the national television station just fizzled away. He smiled ruefully to himself at the thought that he was probably the only person in Ireland at that moment who regretted that he was not being sent to prison.

There was a sense in which the case was not over, Paul felt, in that it had implications for TV services in the country. Their authorities would surely appeal it to higher courts as many might refuse to pay licences for similar reasons. The national station was vulnerable in that the refusal of even a hundred thousand households who felt insulted by some form of what they considered blasphemy could cause serious funding problems. "It should make them realise they can't just trample on people's deeply held convictions," he said to himself.

As he drove along the winding mountainy road, Paul Godfool had time to sift the days happenings in his mind. He had sat for two hours in the courtroom, as case after case was dealt with in swift and business-like fashion. There seemed to be agreement between solicitors on both sides, the Justice and the Gardaí on many of the cases and they were processed without delay. Those contested were dealt with courteously but firmly, particularly those that had to do with violence in the home.

"This is real life," Godfool thought, as each case came and went like small dramas on stage. "Where does my incarnational theology fit in here?" As the day went on he realised the importance of solicitors in the process and began to regret that he had not got someone to represent him. "What does it matter?" he thought then: "I am not going to pay the fine anyway." He was in such a small daydream when he heard his own name being called. Surprised that he was so nervous as he stood in front of what he considered an extremely young woman for her position in the bench, he stammered and stuttered through his reasons for not paying a full licence, thinking how trivial this was in the light of cases he had just observed.

When the Justice had glanced through the correspondence he had received from the TV station and an article he had written about it in the local paper, she said: "I agree completely with you. Nobody should have to pay a licence to be called a sh**te on TV. Next case." Paul was heading for the exit in a matter of seconds. He had meant to say he would like to go to prison to highlight the case, but it was all over and done with just like that.

Paul Godfool had no more time to consider the matter as his mobile phone rang and a hysterical Sharon Brown told him her son Liam had gone missing shortly after going home from school. The phone reception was poor in the hills and he pulled the car into a space left for a turf-stack to hear her properly. "Have you called the Guards?" he asked.

"The local girl is away at court," Sharon answered. "They said he has probably just wandered off to kick a ball somewhere, but he has just got a new phone and he is not answering it..." Her voice tailed off and he could hear her stifling the tears.

Paul tried to offer words of comfort: "They wouldn't have allowed him have the phone switched on at school. Maybe he just forgot to switch it on because it is still new to him."

"He could walk in the door any minute, but you hear so many stories. Will you ask anyone you see to look out for him, and spread the word from the altar? Haven't you mass at six?"

"I'm sure he will be found long before then," the priest assured her. "I'll be back in twenty minutes and we will get people organised to search for him."

Paul Godfool felt a cold sweat breaking out on the back of his neck after the phone conversation ended. "Richard," he thought. "He wouldn't…" But how could he be so sure? He knew that it was his duty to inform the Gardaí immediately so he rang the direct line of BanGharda Shiela McCormack who had brought him to court that morning. "We are on to it," she said. "We are on our way from town and the areas around the church and your house are the first places we will search." Paul rang his own house in an effort to speak with Richard Scapegoat, but there was no reply other than his own voice on the answering machine. He drove as quickly as it was safe to do on the mountain road, and the first sight he saw as he entered the church grounds was Richard walking between the rose-beds with Liam, apparently deep in conversation.

"At least they are out in the open," he thought, "but what has happened since Liam left school?" He was about to phone Sharon to tell her Liam was by the church but inside a matter of seconds a police car had arrived with Sharon in the back seat. She rushed over and smothered Liam in a hug. Two Gardai led Richard Scapegoat to the squad-car as he asked: "What in the name of God is going on here?"

Paul shook his head: "I thought you would have more sense."

"There is a big misunderstanding here," Richard was saying as a Guard laid a hand on his head to help him into the back seat without hitting his forehead against the door-frame.

"I saw him crying in the church," Richard was saying. I tried to help. I did nothing wrong."

"That is what you said the last time too," Paul Godfool answered. "I told you to have nothing to do with children."

XLVIII

Extract From Paul Godfool's Journal

I just can't write anything today. I have nothing to say.

XLIX

*"**Wherever the corpse is, there will the vultures gather.**" [Mt 24:28]*

The only time Sharon Brown spoke to her husband was when she threw some bed clothes into the spare room and told him: "This is not over yet, and I doubt if it ever will, but you can stay here for a while. For Liam's sake.

Although she was not speaking to her husband directly, Sharon never missed an opportunity to curse and insult him under her breath when Liam was not present. Liam was quite pleased to be kept home from school while the trauma he had gone through was being assessed and dealt with by a child psychologist. He lay comfortably beneath a blanket on the sofa while Sharon brought him whatever his taste-buds or his stomach desired. Bill was tempted to say that all that sweet stuff was not healthy, but he kept his head down and his mouth shut. The one consolation he had was that his mother and mother-in-law had to keep their mouths shut, too, about what had happened, while Liam was in the company.

What surprised Bill most was that his mother-in-law was not as sarcastic to him or as hurtful to her daughter as she usually was. He wondered had it something to do with the mellowing some sufferers of senility attain as they get older. She was probably happy in the knowledge that this marriage she had loathed from the beginning was effectively over. At least she tried to keep conversation going at the dinner table even though Sharon refused to speak to her husband. Liam was allowed to eat his meal from the coffee table between the sofa and the fire.

The old woman talked of Lent in her young days. She may not have been able to remember much of what happened the previous day, but she had no trouble remembering what happened in her youth. She talked of black tea and dry bread, of food being rationed to what was described as "one full meal and two collations." The number of eggs or the amount of meat a person was allowed eat was laid out in church regulations. Priests from religious orders came on "missions" preaching about the evils of poteen more than anything else, even though, the old woman said, many of them were fond of the hard stuff themselves.

Bill tried to keep the conversation going. Anything was better than silence as far as he was concerned: "Ye weren't allowed to go to dances either, I'm told?"

"Don't be talking about allowed. There were no dances to go to, but we had dramas and other pastimes," Ann answered. "Companies came around every year and set up big tents on the fair-green."

"Were the plays any good?" Bill asked. He felt he had never had such a civil conversation with his mother-in-law before. Sharon sat at the end of the table and picked at her dinner with her fork.

"We had Shakespeare. "The Merchant of Ennis," even though we weren't allowed to dance the "siege of Ennis." And "Lady Macbeth," a right bitch that one. The one I liked best was "Murder in The Red Barn."

"Country people always enjoyed that kind of a story, plenty of blood and guts and a bit of a mystery to be solved," Bill said. His wife looked at him momentarily with a hatred he had not previously seen in her eyes.

The old woman continued: "The Song of Bernadette" was lovely. It brought tears to my eyes every time I saw it. They always had a few funny sketches after a sad play, so that people would come back for a laugh the next night."

The only time Sharon spoke was to ask Liam was he alright. She was answered with a "Ssssh, I'm watching this."

"The poor little mite," his grandmother said. There was silence around the table for a while, a silence broken by a little ring that indicated Bill had a text message. Bill had not had any contact from Eve since Liam went missing so he guessed it was not from her, even though he assumed Sharon suspected it was. He checked his text, reading aloud as he did so that a couple requested that he show them a house the following day.

"It's that yellow house in the middle of the village," Bill said, "the one with the bay windows." Neither woman at the table commented, as if they did not believe a word he spoke any more. Bill excused himself and went to the small room in which he had slept for the previous couple of nights. He felt that a jail cell must be something like this, and in a way he thought of himself as doing his time, paying for his indiscretion. He had done wrong and was prepared to take the consequences, hoping that good behaviour would wear down Sharon's resolve to keep him at a distance.

Lying back on the narrow bed, his shoes kicked off, Bill felt a certain relief that his secret was out. He was obviously in worse trouble than he had ever been in his life, but he was still alive and under his own roof. Liam was his trump card. Sharon would not throw him out for that reason alone. He would probably never be close to his wife again, but in practice they had been close for a very long time. He could stay with Sharon and live without her at the same time. As long as he was not separated from his son.

Bill knew that he would have a difficult time making up to Liam for what he had seen. But then Liam was innocent for his age and may not have understood what he saw. Bill shuddered when he thought of what he would have felt if he had seen his own father naked, never mind with a woman other than his mother. He decided to encourage Sharon to get on-going counselling for Liam, whatever the cost. That would show he wanted to put things right.

As for Eve… He would miss the pleasure and the passion, but was it worth the cost? The stress and pressure had been getting too much, and he had not slept as well for ages as he had in the spare room since being exiled there. Would Eve get back with Adam? He could see her just taking off and going to live in Spain or the Canary Islands, taking a lover from time to time as it suited her. That thought made him jealous for a moment, but he dismissed it when he thought of how much he had lost by trying to have it all.

Bill fell asleep for a while, and it was the slow murmur of talk in the room next to him that wakened him. Would Sharon have been so brazen as to have brought a lover to their bed as revenge? There was only one voice, her voice. His heart went out to her when he thought she was praying, saying a rosary or something. Listening more carefully he heard a long low stream of curses directed at him. One of them referred to the cloth tied around the head of a corpse to keep the mouth closed after death, the marbh fáisc, and a cold shiver ran down his spine.

At the other side of the wall between them, his wife thought she was losing her mind. She had never felt so angry before in her life. She had experienced much anger with her mother because of the way she treated her, but this was much different. This was cold, calculating anger that made her feel that she understood why someone would take a knife and stab their sleeping partner. Only the thought of Liam kept her from doing just that now.

Her one consolation was that Liam was alright. His disappearance, short as it was, had shaken her to the core. Was he really alright? He might be having a nightmare at this very moment, she thought. An innocent poor boy had been exposed to something worse than pornography. He had been thrown into a place worse than a dung-pit, a dark immoral place. He had seen his own father stripped with that bitch Eve who had pretended to be her friend. How long had it being going on? A week, a month, a year? She remembered now how they had gone abroad ostensibly to work. Sharon thought she would love to find out the truth, but that would mean asking Bill. She wondered would she ever speak to him again. All she wanted was to hurt him as much or more as he had hurt her.

Sharon thought of going to Bill's room with a kettle of boiling water and pouring it on his genitals as he slept. That would lessen his desire for quite some time. But she was the one who would end up in prison. It would be nearly worth it. But where would that leave Liam? He was the most important person in all of this. She couldn't do anything that would make his life worse than it was.

Did that mean that she was going to have to stay with Bill? A question without an answer. She would put up with the pretence for Liam's sake. But that was all it would be. Pretence. Bill would be made to suffer every day of his life. She would see to that. That was probably the best revenge of all. Stay with him. Hurt him day after day. With her tongue. Remind him what he did, what he lost, how much he hurt her. The harm he did to their son. Leaving him would be too easy. That would let him off the hook. It would give him an excuse to go back to the bitch. He would be going nowhere except to the hell she created for him, Sharon thought.

L

Extract From Paul Godfool's Journal

Writing can be a chore when life is or seems to be going against us. I'm struggling at the moment to put one word after another. This is all the more frustrating as I know that I wrote a lovely article during a dream last night, but could I remember a word of it when I woke up this morning? I remember being pleased with myself, happy in the knowledge that this chore had been done for another week. But I just could not download a word from my dream-brain, so I have to start all over again.

Words and ideas come much easier one day rather than another. I sometimes come back from a walk with words tumbling from my fingers. Another day, such as today, it is a matter of building one word on another, building a word-wall without being sure of what shape the wall will take. We begin with a scattering of stones in the shape of words, words of different sizes, shapes and textures. There is a certain amount of trial and error, building up and knocking down before the word-wall takes on the shape we want.

This is particularly true of writing on a computer or word processor, the main difference being that the wall starts at the top rather than at the bottom of the screen. As I step back now to survey my handiwork, I am pleased to see that I am about half way through the job in hand without really saying anything at all. What is important from my point of view is that I am fighting my way through my writer's block.

Unknown to myself, I may have managed to say more than I intended as it is often the chance remark that strikes a chord. I will have some success if dragging myself through what is a chore for me today helps someone else struggling to write. The message is – hang in there. Keep making the hard yards. Keep putting one word-stone on top of or below another, and hope that the end product will turn out better than the sum of the parts. I look again at the bottom of the page and see that I am getting closer. Two more paragraphs and the job is done.

In sporting parlance, we are often told that the good team is the one that wins while playing badly. In every walk of life, there are days that are a struggle, others in which we walk on air and everything seems to come easily. If we sit back and wait for those days, very little gets done. The pressure of a deadline often means that we have to drag a dead-head along on tired shoulders to come up with what needs to be produced on the day.

It will not surprise me if last night's dream article comes from its hiding place as soon as I finish this one. If so, that is the time to strike while the iron is hot and the ink flowing, and have an easy week next week with no deadline to meet. In the meantime a snatch of a poem from my schooldays runs through my mind: "Say not the struggle naught availeth. The struggle is what gets things done. The easy road is there for very few.

***"Where do these wars and battles between
yourselves first start?" [James 4:1]***

Marcas McCabe did not speak to Father Paul Godfool the first time they met after the news broke that the priest who had been staying with him was a convicted paedophile. He shook his head from side to side and walked past the priest without a greeting after Sunday mass. Godfool followed him and said: "Marcas, there is something I want to say to you."

Marcas paused and without looking back at the priest, said: "Say what you have to say."

"I'm sorry, Marcas."

Marcas turned around and looked him straight in the eye: "Sorry because you were caught? Sorry because your sordid little secret is out? Or sorry because you brought that devil out of hell into my house to sit at my table, and to eat and drink in our company. I feel our house is tarnished because of you."

The priest tried to make an excuse: "I was not allowed to tell anyone."

"Did someone put a gun to your head?" Marcas asked.

"I accepted him against my will because my bishop asked me to."

The retired teacher looked at him with what seemed like hate in his eyes: "You often went against the will of your bishop in the past when it suited you. Isn't that how you made your name?"

"I had to take him in because he used to be my friend," Paul Godfool said plaintively.

"And he is no longer your friend because you got caught out? No priest that ever lived in this parish disappointed me as much as you have done. I respected you. I admired you. I would nearly go so far as to say that I loved you. But all I have for you now is contempt." Marcas looked as if he was about to spit.

The priest shrugged his shoulders: "What can I say?"

"Nothing. Say nothing to me anyway. Do you know I was thinking of giving up going to mass altogether? That was until I thought priests come and go but God is there forever." Marcas was virtually shaking with anger: "It was not on account of you that I came to mass today but because of whatever little faith I have left."

"I know," Paul Godfool said quietly.

"You don't know," Marcas snapped. "You have no idea how much you have upset me and the rest of your parishioners."

Paul Godfool pointed to the people getting into their cars outside the church: "Nobody told me that they are as upset as you say they are."

Marcas spat out his answer: "People here have manners. They always had. Nobody is going to tell the local priest that he has let them down badly. But I know it and I know that there has been no other subject of conversation in the area since it all came to light."

Paul Godfool thought it was time to stand up for himself: "But he did nothing to the boy. Richard I mean. The Guards say he has no case to answer. They knew he was here because the bishop told them. They were keeping an eye on him so that he would be of no danger to anyone."

Marcas looked at him more in sorrow than in anger: "You are even more stupid than I thought. The point is that that convicted criminal was harboured here in the parish by you without anyone's knowledge or consent."

"I couldn't tell anyone because the press would be down on top of us like a ton of bricks." The priest decided to cut his losses as he seemed to be digging his own grave even deeper.

"You are the one who let the cuckoo enter the nest, who let the devil into the garden," Marcas said with contempt.

"You have no idea how reluctant I was, how much I argued with the bishop not to send him. It was just a temporary measure until he found someplace else suitable."

"There is no place suitable for the likes of him," was Marcas' opinion.

"He has served his sentence, taken his punishment," the priest argued. "Unless you put him to death, he has to live somewhere."

"That somewhere doesn't have to be here. Castration wouldn't be good enough for the likes of him." The old man's anger seemed to be coming to the boil again: "I don't know… The world, the church, everything is going to the devil." Marcas walked away as if he had the weight of the world on his shoulders.

Paul Godfool went to his house, where he listened to his messages in the hope of hearing something from Richard Scapegoat. The inanimate voice on the machine told him that he had no message. He had rung the bishop the night before to check if he had heard anything. No. It was as if he had disappeared without a trace. Paul Godfool plonked himself in front of the television to see could he find a match or a film that would take his mind off his troubles for a while.

XLII

Extract From Paul Godfool's Journal

I often turn to the psalms when I can find no other consolation. Living where I do the words: "I lift up my eyes to the mountains," always inspires me. It as if the very act of raising your eyes to the hills raises the soul.

Some psalms can be off-putting, especially when there are references to people, places or happenings which have little relevance to the present day. Places like Massah and Meribah mean little to us but they probably had the same resonance to people two thousand years ago as the Yellow Ford, Kinsale or Boolavogue have in our conscious and subconscious memories.

Psalms like "The Lord is my Shepherd" are as meaningful now as when composed and are favourites at funeral masses because of the expression of God's care and concern even when we are passing through the valley of the shadow of death. The De Profundis too, which I learned in Latin as a mass server reminds us that "With God is found forgiveness.

"The constant sound of quiet water slipping down the hills recalls the lines: "Near restful waters he leads me to revive my drooping spirit. Many psalms seem to have been composed by those on the lookout at night, from the campfires of shepherds to the walls of fortresses. They speak of God our guard, the one who protects us, the one who looks out for us, who is with us night and day, above us and below us protecting us from evil. Not unlike our own "Saint Patrick's Breastplate."

Right now I need all the support I can get.

LIII

"One day making enquiries is better than two searching."

Irish Proverb.

Adam Adams did not understand what had befallen him. He felt guilty although he had done nothing wrong. His wife Eve had an affair with his best friend and now she had disappeared. She answered neither phone nor text. She did not even enquire about the children. He found that he himself was cranky and impatient with Cian and Abigail even though they had done nothing to deserve that kind of treatment. He was drinking too much and generally felt that his life was falling apart. Adam thought of a programme he had seen about homeless people and had thought that the person who said it could happen to anyone was mad. Right now he felt that day was not far away from himself if the bad luck that had dogged him lately was to continue. Even though he didn't believe in that kind of thing it was as if some devil or evil spirit had come into his life.

Adam sat in his car outside his house, drinking a bottle of whiskey. He had never done anything like that before. It was not that he intended to drive anywhere but he was afraid one of the children would get up during the night and find him drinking. He had told them to go to bed at the usual time, that he had some work to do in the car. The lap-top lead for the electric plug was broken, he said so he needed to plug it into the cigarette lighter in the car.

The children were driving him daft with their constant questioning about where their mother was. How did he know? He exploded in anger at last and said things about Eve he should not have said in front of them, even if they were true. Up until then he had considered himself good about the house and well able to ready a good meal. He found he was useless when he had to do all the house-work as well as his office work. He felt that it would not take much more for him to break down altogether.

Adam thought of other women, beauties he could pursue now that his marriage was seemingly over. Nobody would blame him after the way in which he was cuckolded. But those women who were attractive to him when he was married didn't seem to matter now that he was free. He didn't want any of them. He wanted his own life back, or as near as possible as he could get to that. Himself, Eve and the kids. They were his life and he was left without a life now.

Could he forgive Eve? Adam didn't know. Would he welcome her home? He didn't know. He rang her mobile one more time and left a garbled message because the beep caught him unawares. At least she would know he called, would know that he tried. That was unless the phone was in a rubbish bin somewhere. He turned on the radio but the lively music did not suit his mood. Changing to another station he found a political programme. That would usually interest him, but not tonight. It had nothing to do with his life as it was now.

The other big story that had come to light because of what had happened with Eve and Bill flashed through Adam's mind, the paedophile that was staying in the priest's house. Hadn't he told Bill that none of them were to be trusted? The same Bill was not to be trusted himself, as he had found out to his cost. He didn't know what to think of Father Paul Godfool. It was clear that local people liked and respected him, though many were angry with him for harbouring that rotten paedophile.

"I don't know anything about anything anymore," Bill said to himself as he watched the lights being switched off in his children's rooms. He left the car and brought what remained in the whiskey bottle into the house. He sat for a while in front of the television but the day's news did not impinge on his consciousness. Nothing mattered any more. The big world no longer interested him because his own little world was in a mess.

Adam had never given much thought to killing himself and when he thought of it now he put the idea aside. It would be easy, especially when he was as drunk as he was now. How many did it while in a similar state would regret it next day if they lived to see the dawn? Adam tried to put the very thought of taking his own life out of his mind. He could not do that to his children, but it worried him that he even considered the idea.

He went to the bathroom and splashed water on his face. He decided to face his personal problems as he would face a problem at work, logically and methodically. He had to think of a plan and follow it through. But what plan? The first step would seem to be to try and find out where Eve was. What had she in mind? Separation? Divorce? Reconciliation? They would have to talk. For the children's sake at least. He could not look after them on his own. Married or separated she would have to help. He was useless without her.

Adam tried to think things through, his hands on the bathroom sink, his head hanging down. He raised his eyes and looked at his puffy eyes in the mirror before asking himself what does a man do when he is trying to find a lost wife. He calls the Guards. Why hadn't he thought of that? But he couldn't call while he was drunk. They would either take no heed of him or think he had harmed her. He would call first thing in the morning. Adam went to the bed which hadn't been made since the last night Eve had slept beside him. For the first time in days he fell into a deep, if disturbed sleep.

LIV

Extract From Paul Godfool's Journal

ooking through the annual Diocesan priestly changes is for me a bit like checking the newspaper obituaries to find out if I am still alive. I am delighted to find that I am not listed, even if at this particular time it might come as somewhat of a relief. Change is traumatic for both priests and people in a parish. Tributes paid to priests who are being changed in the local newspapers in recent weeks show high levels of appreciation and affection in an age in which this profession is often denigrated, and has, admittedly earned much of that opprobrium.

People are big enough not to tar all with the same brush no matter what tabloids or even self-styled quality newspapers write, or radio and TV programmes say. They look behind the headlines and the sweeping statements to what their priests do in the ordinary grind of every day. This understanding, broadmindedness and continuing support is greatly appreciated by clergy.

Right now a number of parishes and church areas are feeling the pain of cutbacks and the loss of a resident priest. Other places are bracing themselves for a similar loss next time around. It is generally accepted that the number of priests available to the Irish church will be much smaller than it has been for the past hundred years or so.

This is not necessarily a bad thing as it leads people to take responsibility for and ownership of their church. We still have more priests than we had two hundred years ago when the population was much higher and clergy had none of the means of transport and communication we have now.

Most did not even have churches until Catholic Emancipation took effect after 1829.

I find a strong feeling among Catholics that the official church is looking at everything except the obvious means of dealing with the present shortage of priests. Can the Bishop's and priestly gatherings not hear the people crying out – "for Christ's sake" - take a serious look at the question of women priests, for reasons of equality of the sexes more than to fill a shortage. Married clergy is another option that is studiously avoided in Rome and elsewhere.

I think it is time for committed lay people (Bishops and priests won't do it) to organise a professional opinion poll on this subject and present the findings to the Pope. Collaborative ministry between people and priest is welcome and has already lifted burdens from our shoulders, but priests will still be needed if people wish to have mass and holy communion as many still desire. We do not have to give in and accept the supposed inevitable. It is time to take our clerical, Episcopal and pontifical heads out of the sand.

LV

Eve Adams got into her car and drove before her the evening she and Bill were discovered on the pool table. She did not know where she was going. Anywhere except where she was. She had made the biggest mistake in her life and could see no way of putting things right. But she did not want to even think of that, just drive and drive to the end of the road or until a juggernaut crushed herself and her car like a matchbox. Eve opened the windows and turned the radio music so high that it was difficult to think. Cars hooted their horns because she was driving so quickly and erratically. She replied by waving two fingers out the window.

Eve slowed down a little as the mad adrenalin rush eased. She noticed on a road-sign at a crossroads that she was less than ten miles from the city. As night was falling she decided to book into the first hotel that had a vacancy. The young man with little English that greeted her in the first hotel she entered looked askance at this woman with blurred eye-shadow who had no bag or suitcase. "Wait moment," he said, and he went over to a girl who was on the phone in reception.

When this girl was finished taking a booking, she came over and said: "Tell me it is none of my business, but there is a woman's refuge less than half a mile from here."

"You are right," Eve answered. "It is not your business." She relented when she realised the girl wanted to be helpful. "Sorry," Eve wiped an eye with the back of her hand. "The break-up of a relationship..."

"Who are you telling?" the girl said. "We have all gone through it, but we manage to pull through it."

"So long as you don't tell me there are more fish in the sea." It surprised Eve to find she was smiling in spite of how she felt.

"There are certainly plenty of sharks."

As the girl was booking her in, Eve noticed an advertisement for flights to the islands at the mouth of the bay. She decided to go there the following day when she had bought clothes, cosmetics, and a carrier bag. It would give her a chance to get away from it all and try to think things through. She ordered a double gin and tonic to be sent to her room and she had slept for thirteen hours when two members of staff arrived in the morning with her breakfast.

When Eve had her shopping done she made her way to the airstrip. It had not occurred to her to book in advance and she had to wait four hours to avail of a cancellation. She did not mind which island she was going to, as she had no idea of the differences between them. The Middle Island was as good as any, she thought, as it had the only vacancy that day. While waiting for her flight Eve walked a nearby beach letting the sea-breeze blow through her hair. She tried not to think of Bill, Adam, Cian, Abigail or anyone else.

Eve had never been on such a small aeroplane. It reminded her of a minibus with wings. She enjoyed the view as they chugged out over the bay, although she got a start the couple of times the plane seemed to bounce in an air-pocket. It didn't ease her anxiety that they had to land in both of the other islands before reaching her destination. It's a bit of an adventure, she thought. "Wait until I tell Abby and Cian." The terrible thought that she might never see them again dawned on her then.

The plane journey and the other landings kept Eve from thinking too deeply of her problems. She had not booked a place to stay but a land-rover brought her to a house close to the chapel in the centre of the island. A kind lady showed her to her room and then gave her one of the largest and most wholesome meals she had ever eaten. What pleased Eve most of all was that she did not pry, did not ask any personal questions.

When Eve went for a walk after dinner, she felt that she was in another world altogether. It did not look any different. Houses were like houses on the mainland. The church looked like a country chapel, but there was an atmosphere in the place she had never previously experienced. There was a quietness and a calm. "It was God that brought me here," Eve said aloud to herself as she headed towards the chapel.

There was a magic about that building too, Eve thought, if magic was the right word to associate with religion. She had heard the term "odour of sanctity" in her youth. Her classmates in the convent school used to joke that it was a nun's fart. But there was a smell here Eve did not recognise, a smell of wood mixed with incense, the smell of the sea as well, maybe, the smell of tears shed for young men who had drowned. It was then that she noticed the sunshine through the stained glass windows. The colours and stylised images told her immediately that they were the Work of Harry Clarke. Suddenly, Eve threw herself on her knees before the altar of the quiet church and asked God to help her, to guide her and above all to bring her contentment.

LVI

Extract From Paul Godfool's Journal

As I write this, I am in imminent danger of quacking up. This is due to the eggsorbitant number of duck-eggs I have been presented with lately by parishioners. It is as if people are showing support after recent traumas in their own quiet way. My only problem is that all this duck-egging is in danger of driving my cholesterol through the roof. I have been assured that duck-eggs do not effect cholesterol but suspect that this information may have come from a quack rather than from a real doctor.

Eggs have long been associated with Easter, because they represent new life, and each life in the human, the animal, the fish and the reptile world begins with an egg. The chocolate Easter egg may not carry quite the same significance though it too can give an energy surge.

We don't know which came first, the chicken or the egg, but we know that even the morning cock-crow was associated with the resurrection in Irish folklore. The crow of the cock was supposed to say: "Tá Mac Na hOige Slán" – The Virgin's son is safe (or free). Other stories had a cooking cockerel leaping from a boiling pot to proclaim that "Christ is Alive."

All of those associations come to mind as I quack open yet another sitting duck-egg for my breakfast. I think of the story of the ugly duckling and wonder is this egging it the kind of beauty treatment that will turn me into a swan. In my eggsasperation, I look in the mirror to discover that apart from the whitening feathers about my face, this particular drake will always be a duck. But who wants to look like a big goose anyway?

LVII

"What God has joined together, let no-one put asunder." [Mt 19:6]

The words "Life is hell" went through the mind of Paul Godfool many times in those days. He felt the community among whom he worked was distracted and distraught and there was little he could do about it. Humpty Dumpty had fallen from the wall and there was no way in which it could be replaced. He remembered a time when a clergyman like him could mediate with people who had marriage difficulties, but those days were in the past. He had lost confidence and the church to which he belonged had lost even more confidence.

He had seen difficult days in the past, days in which island communities were split down the middle over matters like where a pier should be built. People of strong character and opinion stood on opposing sides, and it often took a death or a drowning to make them realise that there are things more important than disputes. It was at times like that real neighbourliness was experienced. The present situation in his parish was different. Couples were separated, marriages collapsed, children suffering. "What could he do but pray?" he asked himself, as if that was a strange question for a priest.

Father Godfool knew that good days would come again as surely as the sun shines after rain, or as happy days come when the black cloud of depression lifts. "But how do you get from this to that?" was the question he asked himself as he sat in the church during exposition of the blessed sacrament. He wondered were the mostly older women who shared the holy hours in front of the exposed holy communion praying for the broken community as well as for their families in Chicago or Sydney, not to speak of those nearer home.

Their priest felt that he would certainly not doubt the power of the prayer of those women to heal the wounds of their people. It would be easy to belittle them and their prayer as a waste of time. They were women of the world who had lived often tough lives, reared large families and maintained a good humour and dignity even when times were most difficult. If God owed anyone anything, Paul Godfool thought, it was those women. But then, he reminded himself, God is not supposed to owe anyone anything. He shook his head, feeling confused by too much of that kind of learned theology, as he asked God to get it sorted: "Over to you, Lord. I can do nothing on my own."

Paul Godfool felt better when he felt that he had lifted the burdens of life from his own shoulders and landed them on God's. When the people had gone home and the church was closed, he went home and poured himself a glass of whiskey. He was just in time for the nine o'clock television news. Suddenly there was a loud knocking on the front window. His first thought was of the many people who lived on their own throughout the country who had been attacked and robbed. Surely a parishioner would ring the doorbell or knock on the front door.

Paul Godfool reached for a hatchet he kept beside the front door in order to defend himself if threatened or attacked, before slipping back the bolt and opening the door. He dropped the axe when he saw who was there: "Adam!" he said. "Come in." The priest beckoned towards his sitting room: "Would you like a drink?"

"Drink is not the cure for everything," Adam answered before noticing the glass beside the priest's chair. "I didn't mean anything…"

"I know. Are you sure? It can ease the nerves."

"I'm mixed up enough and I am driving anyway." Adam hung his head for a moment as if this was one of the most difficult things he ever had to do. Then he asked the priest to get his wife back for him.

"What can I do?"

"Just get her back. I thought your crowd were in favour of marriage."

"It's a long time since anyone asked me to do something like that," the priest said, as he searched his mind for the right thing to say.

"You are the only one I can think of…" Adam too was searching for words. "It wasn't easy for me to come here, because I actually hate the church. But you seem to have something about you. Some kind of influence, something people respect. Not touching the cap respect, but respect for you."

The priest shook his head slowly: "I don't know."

"Are you refusing me?" Adam asked aggressively.

"No, but I'm not so sure about the influence. That, or I have lost my confidence. There are other services, Family Life, for instance that deal with marriage problems. Priests try to stay out of people's private lives."

Adam showed his frustration: "In the name of God... Fuck what others do. I'm looking for your help. Don't refuse me."

The priest threw what was left in his glass back his throat and stood up: "Ok, I'll try. I will do my best. Where is she? Is she still with Bill Brown?"

"Bill the bollocks is back with his wife and family and the injured party here," Adam tapped his own chest, "is left to mind the children as well as to earn a living. I have to pay for their lust, or whatever you call it."

"Has Eve been in touch?" the priest asked.

"No, I would say she is too ashamed."

"Did she ring the kids?"

Adam shook his head.

"Don't be expecting too much," Paul Godfool said.

"I'm not expecting anything, but I want her to know she can come home."

"Do you know where she is?"

"The Guards said she was out on an island, but she came in this evening and she is staying in a hotel in the city."

"Let's go," the priest said.

"You mean now?"

"You're driving. I've been drinking."

LVIII

Extract From Paul Godfool's Journal

When we, Irish, were colonised by the British, we were colonised good. Or bad, depending on how you look at it. Ok, I know that is not good grammar, but what do you expect from a colonised subject writing in an acquired language? What really left us a beaten docket was the taking away of our language. The words were taken out of our mouths. The re-acquisition of some of the national territory failed to alleviate that beaten-ness and broken-ness which is still part of our make-up.

We didn't just lose a language. We lost a mind-set, a thought process, a way of thinking and speaking, a unique Irish-ness. We did not lose it completely as we still speak an Irish-English, and Irish poets and writers have carved their own niche in this language, just as other former colonial peoples have in theirs. How many Booker prize winners in the past ten years are English-English? We lost centuries of ideas along with our confidence. We lost an outlook on life, of understanding of the world, of spirituality, of prayer, of poetry, of home-grown philosophy, of justifiable pride in who we used to be. We were really conquered.

I see this conquered-ness in people who are ashamed of the Irish language, who cringe when they hear even a few token words, who wish that Gaelic would just go away and let us get on with being little Brits or Europeans or Americans. I don't blame them for what is not their fault so much as regret the failure of years of schooling to put even the rudiments of the national language back into their mouths.

I have no problem with English. It was my first language. I talk it, write in it every day, and it would be a handicap for any Irish person not to be able to speak or understand it. That does not mean we cannot take pride in the language of our own people. It is not the only badge of Irishness, but it is the one that marks us out most as a different nation.

LIX

A great crowd of people had gathered around the mass-rock in Gleann na Cuaiche on one of the finest days of summer. Young and old were there, rich and poor as well as many who had not darkened a church door for years. The mass on the bare rock stirred emotions that ran deep in the community, days of hunger and eviction, days they were not allowed to practice their religion, days their ancestors had risked their lives to stand for God and for his glory.

Liam Brown was the mass-server. His parents, Sharon and Bill were towards the front of the crowd with Sharon's mother, Ann in a wheelchair. The Adams family had brought little stools to sit on, and they sat well away from the Browns. Marcas McCabe was on one of the chairs brought from the community centre for senior citizens. His wife Nora had refused a chair, so that an "old person" could have it.

Father Paul Godfool spoke of an account written by a French writer who visited the area about two hundred years previously. He had witnessed people gathering for mass at that very mass-rock in the glen. During the consecration people had shouted: "Croch suas é" "Raise it up," as the priest raised the communion host and chalice. It was not clear at this point in time what exactly was meant, to speak louder, perhaps, or to raise their Lord in the appearance of bread and wine so that they could see him properly. Either way, it was an act of faith, he said.

The priest lost the rhythm of his speech when he noticed a figure wearing a hood at the back of the crowd. It was a strange sight on such a fine day. He had not seen or heard from Richard Scapegoat since the day he had been bundled unceremoniously into the back of a Garda car. He knew he was freed soon afterwards, but he had never gone back to the presbytery to collect his bag. Was it he who was at the back of the crowd like a ghost at a party, or a dark cloud in an otherwise clear sky? Maybe it was not him at all.

Paul Godfool gave a little cough to cover the interruption in his speech. When he looked again for the hooded figure he, or maybe she, was nowhere to be seen.

ABOUT THE AUTHOR

Pádraig Standún is a bestselling Irish language (Gaelic) author, with ten novels published, some of which are available in English, German, Polish and Romanian. He works as a Roman Catholic priest in the west of Ireland.

www.ingramcontent.com/pod-product-compliance
Lightning Source LLC
Chambersburg PA
CBHW050344190726
48284CB00007BB/2141